Beautiful Beast

2 Fairy Tales Reimagined by Blue

BLUE SAFFIRE

Perceptive Illusions Publishing, Inc.
Bay Shore, New York

Blue Saffire/Perceptive Illusions Publishing, Inc.
PO BOX 5253
Bay Shore, New York 11706
www.BlueSaffire.com

Publisher's Note: This is a work of fiction. Names, characters, places, and incidents are a product of the author's imagination. Locales and public names are sometimes used for atmospheric purposes. Any resemblance to actual people, living or dead, or to businesses, companies, events, institutions, or locales is completely coincidental.

Ordering Information:
Quantity sales. Special discounts are available on quantity purchases by corporations, associations, and others. For details, contact the "Special Sales Department" at the address above.

Beautiful Beast/ Blue Saffire. – 2nd ed.
ISBN 978-1-941924-20-4

Let no one devalue the gift God has made you.

—BLUE SAFFIRE

Getting Ready

Blaise

Beauty, it surrounds me always. Sometimes, I don't know what's greater. The power I've been born into or the beauty I possess. Even my servants are beautiful.

I look around at them and smile. I've enjoyed the finest in life for as long as I can remember. Like now, I sit in a bath of milk and honey infused with twenty-four-carat gold.

Luxury I have an abundance of. The ivory claw-foot bathtub I'm in was made with some of the most powerful magic there is. It cools and warms with my mood.

Tonight's ball is in honor of me. Only proving how adored I am. It will be a night of beauty and glamour. I never thought I'd find joy again after my father's untimely death, but our people have continued to show me how beauty and refinement are the cure for all.

There's no need for broken or ugly things when you can surround yourself with beauty and power. I learned that from Father and it's what has gotten me through his loss.

With a smile on my lips, I lift a hand from the water and watch as I cause the cascading droplets to swirl around my wrist like a light rainstorm turning into a spinning waterfall. Such a small measure of my power but so beautiful.

"Your magic is always so stunning, princess," Soila says as she brushes my damp, curly locks. The scent of rose water and peach blossoms surrounds me. It's comforting and calming.

"Thank you. The beauty is in the simplicity. Never forced and always effortless," I reply with a smile on my face.

"Princess, if we don't get you out of that bath now, you will be late for your own affair," Ms. Posh warns.

I glance over at her lazily. Her full cheeks are flushed. Concern covers her face. She's always so worried about me.

I sigh. "Ms. Posh, it will take me all but a second to ready myself," I say and stand from the bath.

With a single thought, my hair lifts and wrings itself out before dropping to hang down my back. I step out of the tub and flick my wrist. A bath towel wraps itself around my body.

"I know you can dress yourself quickly, my dear, but the artist is here to do your face for the celebration. He will need time."

"Has my dress arrived?" I ask, ignoring her worry.

My subjects will wait for me. It's my celebration. They have come to see me. The ball begins whenever I arrive. They should all know perfection requires a hand of patience.

"Yes, the dress is awaiting you along with the artist."

"Very well."

I lazily stroll into my bedchamber and take time to smooth on scented body cream. It leaves a delicious scent on my skin and a gorgeous shimmering glow. When done, I stand and snap my fingers.

The towel disappears and in its place are my undergarments. The gold lace cups my breasts while another tiny scrap of fabric covers my most intimate parts. I move to the gown for tonight and allow it to drape itself on my body.

Ms. Posh and Soila work together to tighten the strings of my corset. I could use my magic to do it myself, but as their princess, it is an honor for them to dress me.

"You look stunning, princess."

"As always," Ms. Posh says with motherly pride in her voice.

My mother died when I was young. Ms. Posh has been the closest thing I've ever known to a mother.

I clap for a mirror to appear to examine my appearance for myself. A smile comes to my lips. The gold-and-cream dress is stunning, if I do say so myself.

The crystals and diamonds only add to the perfection of the delicate fabric. My amber eyes sparkle in my reflection. With a snap, my curls form into an intricate crown of curls in the front, the back cascading to the center of my back in a curly mass.

"I am ready for the artist. Bring him in."

I go to sit at my vanity. Looking in the mirror, I turn my head from side to side, admiring my reflection. Tonight will not be a sad night. Although the first time this ball will be held without Father, it will be a joyous affair. I demand it.

"Good evening, Your Highness," the man says as he places his filthy bag on my vanity.

"Ugh, what is this?" I say, turning to fully take him in.

I drop my gaze to his hands. His nails are dirty and paint stains them as if he's never heard of a bar of soap. My nostrils flare.

"This man will not touch my face with those hands. What is the meaning of this?" I snarl.

"I'm sorry, princess. The original artist fell ill. We had to find a replacement," Ms. Posh says cautiously.

"I assure you, princess. I am a clean man. I was painting when I was sent for. I wasn't given much time to clean up before I rushed here to the palace."

I frown and look his clothing over. He looks as filthy as his hands. The clock tower tolls in the distance. The party has begun.

"Enough of this, I will do my face myself. You can go."

I turn back to my mirror, the artist dismissed as far as I'm concerned. He takes his bag and bows as he backs away. His presence forgotten, I flick my wrist.

My makeup is already flawless. However, now gold and bronze paint slashes from my temple across my nose to my left cheek. Another flick and the same paint appear beneath my bottom lip, down my chin.

"See. As elegant and exquisite as any artist's work."

"Well done, princess," Soila sings.

Finishing the look with my diamond-encrusted crown, I stand ready for the ball. "This will be a night to remember," I breathe to myself.

CHAPTER ONE

Ball & Downfall

Blaise

Looking around the ballroom, I take in a deep breath. Everything is stunning. From the crystal serving trays the stemware rests on as the servers walk around with flutes of champagne to the magical champagne in the glassware that's bubbling and sparkling with flakes of gold.

Sparks of gold fly through the room, looking like little fairies flying about. I look to the stage and a smile comes to my lips. Dinesh, my music instructor and the kingdom's minister of music, couldn't find the perfect musicians to play for me, so he's using his magic to orchestrate a phantom orchestra.

The gold instruments are adorned with diamonds, making them simply breathtaking as they float in the air. I home in on the violins and smile. Light dances off the diamond-covered bows as they move back and forth across the strings.

The only thing more beautiful is the music coming from them. Father would have loved this. So much magic, so much elegance, all in honor of me.

The guests tonight will not want for anything. I've enchanted the walls with my magic, so when someone looks as if they need a drink or something to fill their stomachs, servers will come from the walls to offer refreshments.

I've thought of everything for tonight. Exquisite gold fabrics drape the ceilings, walls, and doorways. The room sparkles and shines with diamonds and crystals. No detail has been left unattended.

"Happy birthday, princess." I turn to find Princess Mona Lisa.

"Why, thank you."

"I think this is one of the best things to come from the earth realm," she says.

"Isn't it? Father was indeed wise to bring this concept to us."

My father made many trips to the earth realm. He returned with tons of things and ideas. Birthdays are one of the things he brought to us. He loved the idea of getting to spoil me for a day. Gifts and attention all focused on me. Although for us, it does take longer for a birthday to return.

These are the days he longed for. Times to celebrate me. This ball was the greatest way to honor his memory.

"Shall we dance?" I say to Princess Mona Lisa as I look over her teal-and-purple gown.

She looks lovely, perfect for the occasion. Giving a glance around the room, she then turns back to me. I give a little grin, already knowing what's on her mind.

"I guess we shall. Although, the selection of suitors could be better."

I give a laugh and tap her wrist with my fan. "You're just wicked. They're not all that bad. I've heard representatives from a few of the finer kingdoms will make an appearance. I'm quite looking forward to seeing what each prince has to offer and if any live up to the hype."

"My love, I'm sure none of them will."

We both burst into laughter. The sound fanning out through the ballroom like its own music. My heart lightens. This is why I decided to go through with this, this is what Father would have wanted.

"We shall see. Come, I do love this song."

***

Hours pass and I'm having such a good time. I stand with a group of my friends, talking and laughing while drinking champagne. Suddenly, I'm called.

"Princess."

I turn to find Helenier, she's the adviser my father brought on right before his death. I believe she was trying to help with the communications between the Kunglig Kingdom and ours. Perhaps another prince has arrived.

"Yes," I reply.

"There's someone here with a gift for you. Would you mind coming with me?"

I wave a dismissive hand. "Put it with the others. Thank you."

I turn back to my friends and go to continue our conversation. Gasps fill the air around the ballroom. I look up and smile. I timed a gold glitter shower with my magic. It's as if it's snowing golden snowflakes.

My musing, however, is interrupted. "Oh, but, princess. This one is special. It was commissioned by your father."

This gets my attention. My father always made sure the gifts given on this day were special. It's no surprise he'd have something in the works that would transcend his death.

"Very well then," I say and turn to follow her.

I notice Bach not too far away as he watches me follow after Helenier. He lifts a brow. I shrug. In the blink of an eye, he flashes to my side.

"What's this about, princess?" he leans into my ear to murmur.

"A gift from Father," I say happily.

"Hmm," he murmurs and continues to follow along.

Once we enter the foyer, we are greeted by the filthy artist from earlier. He's standing with what looks like a gift-wrapped canvas. I frown at the tattered wrapping and paint stains all over it.

"What is the meaning of this?" I say angrily.

"I'm so sorry, princess. In my rush to get here, the wrapping was damaged. However, I do believe the painting was unharmed," the artist says.

"Place it with the other gifts. I do not desire to open this now."

"Princess, there's one more thing Andres would like me to ask of you, if I may?" Helenier says.

"Andres? Who is Andres?"

"I am," the artist says and smiles.

"Oh, what is it?"

"Unfortunately, Andres's carriage was damaged in the stalls. He has no way home. Would it be okay to allow him to use one of your carriages?"

I look this filthy man over and frown. I can only imagine how he'd leave my carriage after. This woman has lost her mind.

"Absolutely not," I scoff.

"Oh," Helenier says with a little smile at the corners of her lips. I'm too annoyed to pay much attention to the expression. "Well, princess, maybe he could stay in one of your rooms. I mean, the castle has so many vacant chambers. It's the least that could be offered."

"No, I will not allow this strange man to sleep under my roof. This is a waste of my time."

"I understand, princess. I only wanted to deliver this painting and see the smile on your face," Andres says.

"Ugh," I growl and wave a hand to use my magic to tear the wrapping away.

I scowl as the painting comes into view. It's hideous. Grays and browns cover the canvas to make... "What is it?"

"It's a rose."

"It's ugly. Take it with you as you go. My father would never commission such an atrocious thing."

"Look more closely, princess. It's the beauty within that captures all."

"This painting captures nothing. Especially not beauty. Go now and take that thing with you."

"Oh, but it does capture something. Your father's beloved roses. The very roses he grew a garden full of just for you."

"How dare you? Those roses are beautiful. They captured the love my father had for me. A love I will always remember. This is just blasphemy. Get out."

"As you wish," Andres says.

However, something is off. His voice has changed from a masculine one to an eerie female voice. A slight wind picks up in the foyer and surrounds him. The next thing I know, I'm looking at a woman.

I can tell she has power and she's beautiful. I'm thoroughly confused. Bach steps in front of me to shield me.

"What is the meaning of this, enchantress?" he demands. "You have no business here."

"Oh, but I do. All the princess had to do was show me one single act of kindness. She could have offered me shelter in the stables and it would have stayed my punishment."

"Punishment?" I snarl. "Who are you to punish me?" My hand sparks with magic. "Step aside, Bach."

"Princess, no," he warns. "You don't understand."

"What is there to understand? This...this... woman enters my home and speaks of punishing me?"

I've begun to levitate. My magic increases and surrounds me. The woman's eyes widen. Ah, she sees the error in her actions.

Her lips begin to move, no sound to be heard. All at once, I feel as if my magic is bound. A gold-like rope captures me and I float back down to the ground.

I'm helpless to react. My arms are trapped against my sides. I growl and try to wiggle free.

"You didn't tell me she was this strong," the woman says to Helenier.

"Can you complete the spell?"

"I can, but I have to do it quickly, and her magic will not be snuffed out with it. I can only bind it to this castle and find a way to ground it within something here that she loves."

"You will not do this to me," I hiss.

"But it is already done."

"No," I cry out as I feel something within changing.

I'm unable to stop it. The ties on my power aren't the strongest, but I've waited too long to fight against them, thinking they were no match for me. That mistake has given them time to root themselves within the core of my magic.

"Stop this," I say, but it comes out like the roar of a beast.

"Because you are drunk off power and beauty, you will remain in this form. All those who serve you and live within these walls will be nothing more than pixies, like the magic you have floating around this night.

"Your power will be bonded to the roses you so love, but a rose will be your undoing."

A single rose appears before me, suspended in the air. Its closed red petals turn from a lush red to burning flames. "This rose will bloom when you turn twenty and five. If you can't love and find love by the time the last fiery petal falls, you will remain in this state forever. Your powers lost, and all of you forgotten forever."

"No," I roar.

Looking at Bach as he has turned into a tiny fairy, I begin to fight the spell. My magic fights back from deep within. I will not allow this.

"You and the others who do not reside here must leave now," the woman says to Helenier.

"Is it done?"

"It is. I will banish this castle to a far way realm. That will hold her power and the spell. Leave, all of you, leave now or be trapped here forever."

"And no one will remember this night?"

"No, you are the only one who will remember what has happened here. She and this castle will be all but forgotten by all of this realm." She looks Helenier over. "I warn you. If I die, this enchantment dies with me."

Helenier's face fills with anger as she purses her lips, but she takes off without a word. I continue to fight, but nothing is working. I roar loudly and begin to sob.

"Why?" I sob.

"Power such as yours needs balance. You weren't given this lesson. Your heart is cruel and knows not real love. You, my child, are spoiled."

Her words echo as she disappears. I can feel the castle in motion. My stomach tightens and my thoughts race. How could this be happening?

Suddenly, it's like the castle has been dropped. The loud sound of its landing fills the air. The binds around me fall away.

I stand and stumble over to the nearest mirror. Tears well as I look at my reflection. The enchantress's words come back to me.

This rose will bloom when you turn twenty and five. If you can't love and find love by the time the last fiery petal falls, you will remain in this state forever. Your powers lost, and all of you forgotten.

"Who will ever love this?" I cry and drop to my knees, using my magic to crack the mirror reflecting the beast I've become.

This can't be real. This isn't my fate. What am I to do?

CHAPTER TWO

Mismatched

Argon

One Hundred and fifty years later...

Heavy rain falls from the sky like the weeping tears of widows in the night, with no end to their sorrow in sight. I haven't seen rain like this in years. It speaks to my heart and its wariness.

With my magic, I stop the rain above and cause my cloak to vanish. Each step feels weighted as I move forward—much like my thoughts.

Sorrow fills the air. This memorial site always has the feeling of sadness. It's as if our world understands how great the loss of our queen was.

I glance around at the glowing flowers my father enchanted in memory of Mother. Magic dew drips from them. Giving the illusion that even the flowers weep for the loss of our great queen.

"Hello, Mother," I say as I sit on my knees before the statue. I can't bear to look up at its face. Father used the best sculptures to capture her likeness and they nailed it.

I still remember the day she fell ill. We sat in the library together. Me reading, and her looking through some holograms. I can still hear the gasp that fell from her lips before she collapsed to the ground.

Unfortunately, nothing could heal her, and she released this life only a few short months after. My father was devastated, as was our kingdom.

Although my pain was great, I don't think anything could come close to the pain my father felt. He has repeatedly said it didn't feel natural; it wasn't real. His response to her death was as great as his pain, and now... now my fate has been sealed, and as a result of it, I'm lost in sorrow of my own.

I stare down at my hand as I allow my magic to run through it. The blue light that surrounds my fingers is only a fraction of my true power. I close my hand and bare my teeth, finally looking up at the statue.

"How could a woman who can't use this small measure of power without harming herself be my soul match? Mother, nothing makes sense around here anymore. I wish you were here."

My thoughts go back to the ceremony. Nothing happened as my father said it should've. There was no burning sensation in my chest, revealing that my spirit link was open. I felt no pull.

I could barely feel enough magic coming from Coralo to believe she possessed any at all, let alone be my soul match. I am the prince of the Kunglig Kingdom. Our family has power that surpasses most kingdoms on our plane.

"And yet the oracles say Coralo is the one. How, Mother, how?"

I look up at the purple sky and sigh. My father and I need to talk when he returns. He's gone to another realm. I expected him back by now.

However, some realms have different timing. What is a day to us could be weeks to years where he has traveled. I can only have patience. He wouldn't tell me where he was going.

"Prince Argon, Prince Argon. You must hurry. It's the king."

I turn to find one of the castle guards rushing toward me.

"What has happened to my father?"

"Helenier has warned that he's in danger. You must come now. We need you to approve the warriors to go to him."

"I will give no such order," I say and stand.

"But Prince Argon, they cannot go without a royal sanction. Not unless we have concrete proof of—"

"I will go," I say firmly, cutting him off.

CHAPTER THREE

Take His Place

Argon

I step through to the realm my father's essence has led me to. His presence reaches out to me the moment my feet land on solid ground. I can also sense the enchantment of my surroundings.

Looking up at the old castle, I narrow my eyes. I take a step forward and a wall of flames rises to block my path. I lift my arm to shield my face, the heat pulsing against me. The scent of the scorching flames singes my nostrils.

I frown and lift my other palm to extinguish the fire. I continue forward through the smoke that begins to rise from the doused flames.

Stepping over the scorched ground, I make my way up the front steps to the large castle-like structure. The castles in my home are vaster and more ornate. This looks more like one of the old structures my people left behind as they fled lands like these so long ago.

I've only seen holograms from those times. Most warn those are days to be forgotten. As a boy, I'd always wondered why.

I lift a hand to knock at the large wooden entryway but unclench my fist and wave my palm instead. The doors burst open before me, slamming against the wall from the force of my strength—albeit just a small measure. The sound reverberates through the open empty space of the foyer I move into.

I come to a halt the moment I cross over the threshold. There's power here. Power, unlike the simple enchantment I encountered outside.

Within these walls, there is a presence that could match my own or, dare I say, a power that may rival mine. It's almost oppressive as it seeps from the walls.

A chill runs through me. My muscles coil for battle as an unseen threat lurks somewhere within this place. I can feel it in my bones.

"What have you gotten yourself into, Father?" I mutter the words to myself.

A rumble fills the air, causing me to look around the large foyer. A voice sounds, echoing through the halls, but the words it speaks aren't clear. It's like the voice resonates through the castle.

"Reveal yourself," I command.

A laugh fills the air. Not a masculine one, but that of a woman. Something about the sound raises the hairs on the back of my neck. Not in fear, it's... I'm not sure what to name the feeling that fills me.

"You dare enter my home and make demands?"

A figure appears at the top of the balcony, overlooking the double staircase. A hood shrouds their face as a long robe covers their body. Even from here, I can tell this being is smaller than I am. Although the men from my world would be considered giants to some.

"Hand over my father and we will be gone."

"Your father?" From the movement, I assume their head tilts to the side beneath the hood. "You mean the thief?"

"My father has no reason to steal."

"And yet he has. Your kind has no respect for other people's personal space or property. Your father will pay the price for his intrusion."

"Where is he?" My voice booms off the walls. My own power pulsing along with my temper.

The being reaches out a hand and an orb of light appears. I turn my attention to the ball of illumination and an image of my father behind bars appears. He looks weak and sickly. A version of my father I've never seen before.

I bare my teeth and growl. "Release him."

"He will pay for his transgression. He remains here. It's the price he will pay for trying to take that which isn't his," her voice vibrates with a shrewdness.

"I will pay his debt. Tell me the price," I reply.

"Some prices are greater than one is willing to pay. This, I am sure, will be the case for you. Leave and don't return."

"There is no price too great. Name your bounty. It will be given," I say, my voice rumbling through the foyer.

The orb disappears as quickly as it appeared. The being moves swiftly and leaps over the balcony railing, landing on its feet in a crouch.

The ground cracks with the force of her landing and debris rise in the air around her as her dark-blue-and-black robe billow out. The sound of her landing is deafening. However, as if not cracked and crumbled only seconds ago, the floor seals up and smooths out.

As she lifts to her full height, it's confirmed that I tower over this robed figure. However, the power that's coming forth from her presence is staggering. I proceed with caution.

She lifts a hand to point at me, revealing a slender finger from beneath the long sleeve of her heavy garment. The flesh revealed is a deep brown. The same color as the oracles and noble women of my plane and their families.

"You're willing to pay the price of that which he stole. Is this what you're saying?"

"Yes," I bite out in frustration. My fingers tingle as magic builds within, resting just on the surface, ready for me to attack.

"You will take his place—here, with me? This is your promise?"

"Yes, I will take his place."

"Argon, no." My father appears, falling into my arms.

"Father. What have you done?"

"I wanted to bring you a rose of fire to give to your betrothed."

"A rose that didn't belong to you. A rose that has a price greater than your life," the cloaked being says coldly.

"Allow me to get him home. He is weak. I will return to you as soon as I have him safe and mended."

"No," she says firmly. "You will stay in his place. My chariot will get him to your world safely."

The figure moves past us to the front doors that are still wide open from my entrance. Her power brushes my skin in passing, like a familiar caress. It's unnerving, but I don't cower to it.

I wrap my father's arm around my neck to support him. Turning, I guide him out, following our captor. He's moving slowly. So unlike the man I know. I bite back my worry. This shouldn't be possible.

A chariot with two horses—each with flaming manes—sits before us at the foot of the entryway steps. They both lift onto their hind legs, flames curling around their heads and smoke pouring from their nostrils.

The chariot is made of gold and studded with clear gems. Diamonds are what they call them on many planes. It's fit for royalty where I'm from, making me question who this being is.

"Say your goodbyes and get him inside. His passage will be made safely. You have my word."

I can't help but wonder what hides beneath that robe. My instincts tell me not to engage it before getting my father back to our world safely. I will be able to feel him in his travels and once he has arrived home.

"You go. I will stay here. Our people need you. Your bride will be waiting for you," my father says.

"Our people will want you to return well. I will get you home and return as soon as I can."

"Argon. You cannot do this," my father pleads.

"Father, I must. You are weak."

"You're young. Don't do this. She's a beast. You haven't seen her," he whispers and shivers.

"Enough," the robed woman says. I believe I detect hurt in her voice. "It's time. I will not hold the portal open long. I don't want any more of your kind entering. Once you leave, you cannot return."

"You can't take my son," my father says in protest.

"I have taken nothing. He has offered to take your place. Go before I change my mind."

Without waiting, she turns and heads back into the castle. I help my father toward the waiting vessel. Getting him inside and settling him. I'm torn.

"Come with me. While she has turned the other way, we must go quickly," Father urges.

"I have given my word. I will not go back on that. You know I can't go back on that."

"You owe her nothing. This isn't our world."

"But it is our way to honor everything we say. I will stay in your place. It will be fine," I reassure him.

"Don't do this to get out of your marriage, Argon. This is a sacrifice you don't have to make. I know you have been displeased with having to marry. This is my fault… I should never have made that blood decree, but we can make this right. Perhaps another year before the wedding will be enough," he says.

I look into the eyes of my father. They're so much like mine. A blue-and-gray color that looks like the storm clouds in the earth realm. At the moment, his gaze is troubled.

I am his only son. I will be taking over the throne when he steps down. He's been grooming me to take power soon.

The oracles have advised this should be so. Once I'm married, it's only a matter of time before the throne becomes mine. I've dreaded the day for so long.

Because of a broken heart, my father has unwittingly cursed me. To marry is to seal my fate. I will be bound to the life of my wife. When she dies, so will I.

It was the blood decree my father set forth after losing my mother. The nobles assured him it was the right thing to do. I wouldn't mind this if my betrothed were... stronger.

"Another year will not change who I'm to marry."

"The nobles have picked wisely. If I could have just gotten that rose..." His eyes become distant. He shakes his head. "The nobles seek the truth from the oracles. They have chosen from the best."

"But they have not chosen the best. Why her? I still believe...." I clamp my mouth shut.

This isn't the time for me to get into this with my father. I've had my suspicions, but I will let that go for now. For now, I need to get him home to safety.

I will deal with my engagement and impending wedding when I return home. I kiss my father's forehead and pat his shoulder. Standing back, I watch as the horses begin to move forward.

"Argon, Argon." He turns in the seat to look back at me as he calls my name. "We will come for you. When I am well, we will come for you. I'm so sorry, my son."

A Man

Blaise

"It's a man, Blaise," Hiasha squeals. "He could be the one."

I unfurl my tail from around my waist and start to pace. Yes, it's a man. A gorgeous man at that. Tall with blond locks in the front that spill into his face and dark-brown locks that hang down his back.

His corded muscles caused my belly to ache. His scent almost buckled my knees and caused my tail to tighten protectively around my waist as if my womb were in danger.

His face is a work of art. Too gorgeous for words, with his thick but neat brows and blue-gray eyes that rest beneath them. His lips—even parted in anger—called for my attention with their fullness and pink color.

Yes, a man indeed.

"Finally, I'll be able to get some life-sized pussy," Dinesh grumbles. Hiasha and I glare at him. "What? My tiny balls are blue. I need this curse to end. My hands aren't even big enough to rub one out."

"You could always get some fairy ass," Soila purrs.

Dinesh glares at her. Then raises a thoughtful brow. "Is that an offer, woman? I may consider it if this curse isn't broken and I'm doomed to be a tiny fae for the rest of my life."

Hiasha groans. "Don't talk like this. He is the one. I can feel it. He will break the curse."

"He's the one?" Dinesh snorts. "He better be. He's the only one who has come along in a hundred and fifty years who hasn't shit his pants and run. Oh, gods. Has it been that long?" His face crumples and he reaches for his crotch.

"Enough." My voice comes out in a roar that echoes around the space, giving the room a bit of a shake with it.

A room I once savored standing in. That, I can remember in all of its mundaneness. The size of two chambers fit for a king, my walk-in closet used to be a place I would spend hours in. Trying on the latest fashions that were sent to me, having custom garments made.

Walking along the walls of shoes, handbags, gowns, and pretty things. I nearly held parties right here in this closet. These walls have been friends.

I would stand before these mirrors and bask in my own beauty. I was spoiled rotten from the day I was born. Nothing was too great for me to have. My father pampered me with material things out of guilt.

"Your mother would have wanted you to have this," he would say. "Nothing is too good for you, my princess."

I grew up thinking the world belonged to me. Now, two of the floor-length mirrors in this closet sit smashed and the other. The other, I avoid as often as I can.

I look at the people in my life who have been forced to fly around with tiny wings and little bodies because of me. Full-grown adults, now little pixies—all with the exception of Hiasha, she's but a child in comparison or at least she was when we were cursed.

One hundred and fifty years have passed on this plane. I've been this monster for one hundred and fifty years. I walk over to the mirror and push my hood back. I turn away from my reflection.

"Not even I can stand the sight of me. How is he to fall in love with this?" I say brokenly.

The flutter of wings buzzes next to my ear. A tiny, plump body flies beneath my chin to turn my head back to the mirror. "You are gorgeous, love. We just need to show him."

I look at Ms. Posh in our reflection. She gives me a warm smile. Her motherly love causes a pang in my heart. She's the only mother figure I've truly known. Yet my father used to yell at her for cuddling me.

"Do your job and manage the estate, Ms. Posh. My daughter's happiness is none of your concern," he would say when she tried to get him to let me play with others and behave more like a normal child.

Anger fills me and the flames around my face ignite. Ms. Posh flies out of the way just in time. The fact that her little wing is smoking from getting singed makes my fury grow more.

"I'm a beast. How can he see anything past all of this?" I snarl and slap my tail against the floor to punctuate how hideous I am.

"No, Blaise. You are not a beast. You have a temper. A temper which has gotten you in a bit of a pickle," Ms. Posh says.

"A pickle? A pickle? Being turned into this"—I wave my hands over my face and body—"being banished here, having my power bound to this castle and that garden, and having everyone who was close to me turned into fairies is not just some little pickle.

"We all could remain this way forever. The petals are falling, turning to ashes with every decade, year, day, and hour that passes. We're running out of time. We'll all be damned to remain like this...." My words trail off, smoke coming out of my nostrils.

"Mom is right, you know? You can't give up," Hiasha says as she waves the smoke from her mother's wing.

I sigh. "Come, let me heal you."

Ms. Posh smiles and flies closer. I hold a hand over her little wing and begin to repair it. Magic flows from my fingertips and the wing begins to re-form. She stares up at me lovingly.

"Listen to me, Blaise. He has magic. He's not a human. He has to be the one. The curse sent you here to this realm to make this harder. He has found you *here*," she says.

I snort and smoke puffs from my lips. "His thieving father found me."

"He wanted a rose for the big guy's betrothed. Should we be worried about that?" Dinesh speaks up. Soila elbows him. "Ow."

"He didn't sound too enamored with whoever she is to me."

"Okay, fine, but why did the father want the rose? Do you think he knows its power? If so..."

"We're not going to concern ourselves with that," Ms. Posh says to Bach, who, up until now, has been sitting in the corner of a shoe cubby in contemplative silence.

"Do you think they are from our world? The chariots returned brighter. Could they have gone home to return his father?" Hiasha says in almost a whisper.

"We don't know, love. None of us can remember home. Just as they wouldn't remember us if they were from home."

I scoff. "I can remember frivolous things, but with each day, who I am and where I'm from fades. I'm even starting to forget Father."

Dinesh flies closer. His eyes soften as he looks at me. "It's happening to us all. If I didn't sing daily, I would've forgotten that I know how or that I was once your music instructor."

"What if I forget how to play?" I say as I stumble over to the chaise in the center of the fitting area of the closet.

"Oh, Blaise, that would never happen. You play for the ears of the gods. They would never allow your music to be silenced."

"Yet, they've allowed this," I bite out, flopping down onto the lounger.

Dinesh puffs out his chest. "I do remember this much. Our gods like to test the strong. It is their way."

"Their way for what?"

"To reveal to you who you are."

"Yes, he's right. This will make you stronger, Blaise. That wicked one will not prevail. You will see. Now, come, let's go meet our guest."

CHAPTER FIVE

Be Our Guest

Argon

"Hey, big guy." A gruff male voice echoes through my cell. I look around, not seeing anyone.

Suddenly, a small light appears at the lock and the door swings open. The light fades slightly, revealing two male pixies. Both with brown skin, one younger with a lighter tone and silky jet-black hair combed away from his face.

The other is noticeably older, with dark-brown skin and salt-and-pepper hair cut close to his scalp. Again, I'm reminded of the coloring of the oracles and elders back home.

The two fly inside and stop before me. I tilt my head at the men. There's something oddly familiar about their presence. I shake the feeling away as the older, plumper one flies closer to my face.

"You will do. At least you're not weaker than she is," he says.

"You sure about that? I'm getting something else from him. Not sure if it's an equal match, if y'know what I mean," the other guy says.

"Dinesh," the older one snaps.

"I'm only calling it like I see it. He could be holding back, but he's no Blaise," Dinesh grumbles and folds his arms across his chest. "As long as I can get my hands on a fat ass and warm pussy before I forget what it feels like, I honestly don't care at this point."

"Excuse me?" I say, interrupting them.

"Don't mind this hothead. Artists, they have no brains, just talent," the chubby one says.

"Bite me," Dinesh mutters before flying over to perch on my shoulder.

"Forgive him. This is Dinesh and I am Bach. We serve Prin... Lady Blaise."

"Lady Blaise?" I furrow my brows.

"Yeah, the badass chick in the robe. The one who was about to flatten your ass a few hours ago. Bach, maybe you can turn back time and show him," Dinesh says smugly.

"If. You. Don't. *Hush,*" Bach hisses through tight lips. "I'll turn back time to the day you were born and erase your mother from existence."

"I'll torch your ass first. You're not moving as fast as you did in your glory days. I'll turn you into a roast."

"Enough," I bark in irritation. "Is there a reason you have come here?"

"Well, excuse me," Dinesh says and lifts from my shoulder. "You almost sound like her. I might be wrong about you."

"I do apologize. This can't be easy for you. I assure you, your father will be well...." Bach trails off when I glare at him. "Well, yes, we came to escort you to your chambers."

"What, do you have a smaller cell?" My words drip with sarcasm.

I can barely stand up straight in here. I don't know how my father did it. I get angry every time I think of him in these confines.

"Oh, this guy thinks he's funny. I say we leave him here," Dinesh says.

"He will be better off in the upper castle," Bach grits out. "You will be more comfortable there. Prin... Lady Blaise truly is fair. Her roses just mean a lot to her."

"Enough to imprison a man. No, she has imprisoned two men," I seethe, heat rising up my face. "A rose can be regrown. A man's life cannot."

Bach's eyes grow sad. He shakes his head. "I'm afraid you are wrong. Some gardens are more fragile than meets the eye. What your father tried to take has greater value than you know."

"Leave."

"But you will be so much more comfortable upstairs."

I stare unyieldingly at the older flying annoyance. His eyes plead back with me. I have no sympathy for these beings.

"Leave."

"Don't have to tell me twice," Dinesh says, turning his back.

"If he doesn't want the comfort I offer, leave him. We owe him nothing."

I snap my head in the direction of the cell door that still sits ajar. The robed figure stands before it. Up close, now that I'm calmer, I can see the outline of a feminine figure beneath the cloak.

Curvaceous breasts and ample hips. Once again, I take note that she's not tall in stature. I stand to assert my dominance.

However, she doesn't shrink back. She moves forward, entering the cell. Her steps click as she moves. Once standing before me, she places a hand on my chest.

A burning sensation fills my inner cavity. Warmth surrounds my heart and only becomes increasingly consuming. However, I don't buckle to my knees as I'm sure she wants.

"Told you he wasn't a match," Dinesh mutters under his breath.

I cut my eyes to where he and Bach float. Two more have joined them. A plump woman with honey-brown skin flies at Bach's side, staring on with her hands clasped in what seems like worry. A younger, smaller girl fairy peeks from behind her back with wide eyes.

Sweat starts to gather on my face. I clench my teeth. My powers try to push back, but something has bound its way around them. Although I don't believe it's her.

Deciding to use brute force, I grab her wrist and tighten my hold to pry her palm away from me. The moment I touch her, something shifts inside me. An awakening that shouldn't be. I blink the feeling away and grind my teeth.

"Who are you?" I strain to say.

She pulls her hand away from my chest, granting me a reprieve. "To you, I am just a captor. Is this not what happens to prisoners? If this is the only way you wish to see me, I will deliver."

"Answer my question," I bite out, still holding her wrist.

"I have."

With my free hand, I yank her hood back. Gasps leave our lips simultaneously. I release her and take a step back.

This isn't what I was expecting. Her face... it's bisected ... by a slash that runs from her right temple across her nose to her left cheek, it's like an open wound with molten lava flowing beneath the skin. Another slash flows from beneath her bottom lip, down her chin, the same fiery lava moving between the seemly open flesh.

Wild reddish-brown curls cascade around her head and shoulders, with horns protruding from them. Her lips purse and smoke pours from her nose. Her eyes, which were an amber hue of brown just seconds ago, turn black.

"You have not," I breathe. "Who are you?"

"You will call me Blaise." With that, she turns and storms out. Her long tail swinging behind her. "Feed him nothing. He wants to behave as a prisoner, let him be so."

"You will starve him," Bach calls after her.

"If he dies, he dies." Her voice echoes back to me.

I drop back to my seat. Rubbing my eyes, I try to reconcile my thoughts with what I've just seen. I've seen many otherworldly things, but that was something else.

How did I miss the tail? It wasn't exposed the first time I saw her. What... in the gods is she?

Father, what have you gotten us into?

Blaise

"Blaise," Ms. Posh calls after me. "Blaise. Princess," she snaps, causing me to halt.

"What?"

She flies around my head to come face-to-face with me. Right away, I can tell she's winded from rushing after me. I sag my shoulders. I shouldn't have made her chase me.

"You have to be more patient. The last time he saw his father, he was unwell. He is now your prisoner in his father's stead. Be gentle, child. Give him time to adjust."

"I don't care for him."

"You will have to learn to if he is the one. You have to at least try."

"He doesn't want to be here." I pout like a little child.

"He will learn to love it here," Ms. Posh says with a smile.

She flies closer and strokes my unmarred cheek. The fire burning within begins to settle. Although, it's not just burning from anger. When I touched him, something strange happened inside of me.

"Did you see the way he looked at me?" I say sadly.

"He was a little startled. But, dear, he's still here."

I blow out a breath and let my tail swing behind me as I contemplate her words. I chew on my lip. As long as he's here, I have a chance at least.

"Fine. Tell the others not to lock his cell. He can roam free. Just keep him away from my quarters. When he's ready for his room, Bach can lead him there."

With that, I take off again. I need my cello. I have to play off some of this frustration.

My fingers tingle with flames. I ball my fists and snuff them out as I mutter to myself. "He will challenge me. I know it."

CHAPTER SIX

Roaming Prince

Argon

The tiny flying fairies left the door to my cell open. I've been eyeing it warily as if it's a trap. I'm not sure what will find me beyond these walls.

I look at my hands and access my power. It seems to be dimming. I wasn't expecting this. It is understandable how Father became so weak here.

Is that... creature the cause of it, or is it this place? The power pulsing in the walls leaves me cautious. My stomach rumbles and I make the decision to leave this cell in search of food.

"We'll see if she truly plans to serve me," I murmur as I stand.

I move out of the cell and stand tall as I make it into the corridor. I look left and right. Wind blows through the deserted space. I turn in the direction I saw all the rest of them go.

Bach said I could go anywhere in the castle except for the West wing. My curiosity burns to know what's there. Could it be an answer to how I shorten my time here?

I turn to look at the wall as the surface ripples. I stop and a mirror appears before me. My reflection gives way to the image of a hooded figure playing a cello. I tilt my head to the side as I study the image.

There isn't sound, but the movements reflect passion. The player seems to be lost in the music. Suddenly, beautiful music fills the corridor I stand in. It's soul stirring. I've heard this melody before.

However, this player brings a new sorrow to the sound. It's breathtaking and heartbreaking at once. It tells a story with each note.

It's her. A tail peeks from the cloak she wears, swinging in time to the music. She's an accomplished player. As if a gift granted to her by the gods.

Lost in the music, something catches my eye in the image before me. A rose of fire encased in a glass dome. As I turn my attention to the rose, it comes into clearer view. It burns bright and strong. A petal falls and the player stops its motion.

I turn back to the cellist. Her shoulders sag. I reach to touch the mirror with my fingertips and the surface ripples.

Before I grasp what's happening, I'm sucked into the mirror and standing in the room I had been watching. It's much larger in person.

I realize it's a bedchamber. A bed is on one side of the room. In a sitting area before a balcony is where she sits with her cello, and then there's the side of the room I'm on, farthest from her and the bed.

I'm before the table the rose rests on. It calls to me. I reach to touch the dome that covers it.

"No." The word is roared by my captor as she appears before me.

I take a step back. She covers the table with her back to the rose. Her breasts are exposed as they heave in the confines of a corset. Her hood has fallen back from her face.

Fear and anger cover her features. Anger wins out as she moves toward me. The blaze in her eyes turns to flames. Smoke comes from her nose.

"Who let you in here? What are you doing here? Do you know what you could have done?" she growls.

"A mirror brought me here," I reply.

"A mirror?" she furrows her brows. "What? Don't lie. You could have ruined us all."

"I never lie," I growl. "The mirror appeared and brought me through to this room. It showed me the image of you and the rose."

"Enough," she roars, her voice sounding through the room.

The force of her single spoken word pushes me back. I cross my forearms before my face and dig my heels into the floor to stop my backward motion. When I'm no longer being pushed back, I stand straight once again and glare at her.

I tilt my head. "Why are you so hostile toward me? Am I not your prisoner? First, you imprisoned my father, and now me for something as simple as that rose you're protecting now.

"Are you so barbaric that you have no regard for the life of others over plants that die and regrow?"

She vibrates with anger, taking a step away from the table and the rose. Her eyes turn the color of white-hot fire. She flips her cloak out to her sides.

"You know nothing of what you speak. It is life that I preserve with this rose." Her words come out with so much pain. "You look at something that's more precious than gold and know not its value.

"Stand there and judge me, but you will never understand how much I value life, whether man, creature, plant or beast. *Now go*," she exclaims the last words.

I clench my fists at my sides. An ache within keeps me rooted to my spot. Not the same pain as when she placed her hand on my chest. Something else I can't explain.

If I didn't know better, I'd say it's the pain of a spirit link. However, my betrothed back home has not begun to bond with me. It's one of the reasons I've questioned the elders.

This feeling is too strong to be her. If I didn't feel her when I was in my realm, I wouldn't feel her here. Blaise groans and clenches her chest.

I narrow my gaze. The amber color of her eyes returns, her face contorting with pain.

"What...what are you doing to me?" she says tightly.

"I have done nothing."

She lifts her gaze to me. I go to step closer, but she takes a step back. Her face softens as if she's a frightened bird.

I continue to move forward. She holds out a hand and roars at me, pushing me back again. I take the same stance to shield my face and slow my backward motion.

"Get away from me. *Get out.* You're a thief and a liar. Get out."

Anger rises within, overriding the pang in my chest. I turn and storm from the room without further thought. It's a great disgrace to call a Kunglig a liar. I will not stand here for this.

It's clear I've given my word to a madwoman. There seems to be no reasoning with her. I would never go back on my word with a sane person. However, this Blaise isn't sane.

I keep moving until I reach the front doors of the castle. I release my powers and fling my arm out, causing the doors to burst open.

I grind my teeth as the action takes more energy than it should. I don't stop moving. I step out into the dark night.

A howl sounds in the distance, but I keep moving. I fear not what lives in the woods of this place. I need to find a location with enough energy to tear through to the next realm.

My instincts lead me farther into the brush. Agitation rises as my power seems to remain bound somehow. I bare my teeth and focus.

The howling continues as I get deeper into the woods. I'm getting closer to the source of great energy. My powers start to pulse in response to it.

I'm so focused on it I don't pick up on the wolf that attacks me until it's right on me. It lunges through the air, clawing my shoulder as I turn out of its way. I bite back the grunt from the searing pain.

I find myself surrounded by big gray-and-white wolves. I crouch, ready to defend myself to the death. Two of the beasts jump into the air, flying at me. I grab them both by the throat and smash their heads together.

A third wolf charges me before I can drop the first two to the ground. I have just enough time to wrap my arms around its body. I squeeze, releasing a loud roar of my own and crush it in my hold.

When I drop it, I take note of the fact that I'm still surrounded, and it seems the numbers have doubled. Five of the larger ones all attack at once. I go to release my power right as they're airborne, but flames suddenly surround me.

The barrier acts as protection, sealing me in. A tailed figure lands before the flames encasing me and the ground shakes beneath my feet.

It's her.

My eyes widen at the sheer force of the power I feel coming from her. The five wolves remain suspended in midair. Frozen.

Blaise releases a roar, and they turn to ashes at her feet. The other wolves turn and retreat. I'm in awe of what I've seen.

Suddenly, the flames turn to smoke and Blaise tumbles to the ground. I rush forward and catch her before she hits it. I lift her into my arms, shifting her body a bit to accommodate her tail.

"Too far from castle... magic weak... must hurry back before they return," she murmurs before she passes out.

I look at her face. Her features are softer when she's not snarling at me. I war for a moment. She has less power out here. I could leave her and get to the portal I feel tugging at me.

I sigh. She has saved my life. I'm indebted to her. I would not leave her here to die after she risked her life to save me.

"I am a man of my word," I mutter and start back the way I came.

CHAPTER SEVEN

Let Me See

Argon

I stroke her cheek and find that her skin isn't hard as I thought it would be. I search her face with my gaze. I want to touch the lavalike skin, but I don't think she would like that.

As I crouch beside the chaise I placed her on inside the great room, I brush a lock of hair from her face. I can't say that there isn't something pretty about this creature.

"She's waking," Ms. Posh says nervously.

"Blaise," I call her name.

She moans and opens her eyes. I startle at how they suck me in once focused on me. In the moment, her gaze is far from that of a beast. I'd swear I could see a woman from my home.

I shake it off when she starts to sit up. I back away to give her room. Her little friends have been flying about her with worry. It's clear they all care for their master.

"You scared the shit out of us," Dinesh says. "Next time, let his ass get eaten. He shouldn't have gone out in those woods."

"Dinesh," Bach growls.

"What? Screw him. She could have been hurt."

"I'm fine," Blaise says. She looks to me and her eyes widen. "You're bleeding."

She reaches out for my shoulder but halts and pulls her hands back. I nod for her to continue. The wound burns, but I've been more concerned with her.

She touches the flesh gently with her long clawlike nails. Her face pinches and she sucks her bottom lip into her mouth. Something about the gesture makes her less beastly.

"There is poison, but I can heal it," she says. "You will have to take my venom as a counter. I can't seal the wound until we get the poison out."

"Your venom?"

"Yes, it's not poisonous like this. It won't kill you. You may hallucinate after. For how long, I can't say. Everyone reacts differently," she warns.

"I guess that's better than death. Go on." I nod.

She lowers her lashes. Her brown cheeks seem to glow with heat as if flames rest beneath the skin. I'm curious when I realize it's her way of blushing.

"What? What is it?"

She releases a heavy breath. "I'm sorry."

Before I can ask her for what, she grasps my jaw in her palm and tugs my face to hers. Her lips crash to mine, her tongue brushing them. I open my mouth in surprise.

She sticks her tongue inside and flicks it against mine. Instantly my face warms and a unique flavor bursts into my mouth. Saliva and something else fill my open cavern.

Blaise strokes my neck, causing me to swallow. My shoulder begins to warm and tingle. At the same time, that ache in my chest turns into a fierce stirring.

I groan, reaching for her waist. I feel like I'm floating as I take over the kiss and devour her mouth. Blaise whimpers as she buries her fingers in my hair.

It's as if I leave the room we're in as I keep her clenched to my body and continue to kiss her surprisingly soft lips. I'm at a loss for understanding.

"Daddy, Daddy," a little girl calls.

I turn to find a small child with eyes like mine, brown skin, and reddish-brown-and-blonde ringlets bouncing as she runs toward me. Her arms are open wide as her little legs carry her forward. She launches in the air and my heart races.

The distance is too great, she will fall if I don't catch her. However, I'm thrown when she floats as a pink translucent orb encases her.

"Thank you, Mama." She giggles. "Daddy," she squeals happily as I open my arms to catch her when the bubble pops and she falls toward me.

"Damn, that was hot as fuck." Dinesh's voice brings me back to the here and now.

Blaise steps away from me quickly and pulls her hood up over her head. "You will be fine by morning. You should eat something. My venom can be hard on the stomach when it's empty."

With that, she rushes from the room. I fall back on my heels and stare after her. Lifting a hand to my lips, I find them seared.

"Don't worry," Ms. Posh says. "They will heal in a moment, as will the open wound. It will seal right up."

I nod and swallow thickly. I don't know what just happened, but something has changed within me. I have no doubt that my spirit link has opened.

"This can't be," I whisper.

"I get the feeling shit's about to get real around here," Dinesh says.

"Hush," Bach chides. "Come, we will feed you. Her warning is very real. You don't want to suffer that stomachache."

I nod and lift to my full height. "Lead the way."

Blaise

I pace my bedroom as my body buzzes. I can still feel his hands on my waist. Such big hands.

My lips are still tingling from that kiss. I was so angry when I felt him leave the castle. I had a mind to let him find out what those woods had waiting for him.

I never should've let him get that far. Any further and we both would have been in trouble. My powers don't work at their max strength that far. It's a part of the curse.

"Are you okay?" Soila asks.

"Yes, I'm fine."

"He's the one. He has to be. I could feel the connection from you both. It pulsed off of you."

"It was the use of my powers, nothing more," I mumble.

Soila flies to float in front of my face. Her lips are pursed at me. "You know that's not true. Don't keep fighting him. It's not going to help us."

I close my eyes and shove a hand into my hair. I have no idea what happened back there. That wasn't normal. Every time he's around me, I get this ache in my chest. It has only gotten stronger. It's a burning sensation that makes me uneasy.

When we kissed, I felt like my heart would explode. It wasn't until he started to hallucinate that it eased a little. Now I feel this pull. I want to go in search of him.

"Don't you think I understand this?"

"I'm sorry, princess. I have overstepped."

"No, no, you haven't. I'm just frustrated. I don't know what to do. Look at me. He wouldn't have kissed me if he had a choice." I frown.

"Oh, Blaise. You were not the only one enjoying that kiss. He was right there with you." She giggles.

"Ugh, this is stupid."

I turn and throw myself across my bed. I should go to sleep. Maybe when I wake, this will all be over. I bite my lip and groan.

"Can I offer a suggestion?"

"Go on."

"You should put on something pretty and go down to dinner with him. I'll fix your hair. Come on. It's worth a try," Soila says.

I lift my head to look at her. The pleading in her eyes makes me reconsider throwing this day away and starting over tomorrow. I sigh.

"Okay. I'll try."

An hour later, I feel like a fool. Soila and Hiasha worked together to straighten my hair and recurl it to cascade around my shoulders and down my back in deep body waves. Heavy feathered bangs fall across my eyes and distract from my scars a little.

The tight blue corset and leather pants are what I normally wear under my cloak. However, they insisted that I not wear the cloak. I feel so exposed.

My hooves are revealed, as is my tail. I drew the line when Hiasha tried to paste rhinestones on my hooves. It already looks as if I'm trying too hard.

"Stop fidgeting. You look great," Soila says.

I nod and wipe my hands on my thighs. I blow out a breath and push the doors of the dining room open to enter. A gasp leaves my lips when I see him.

There he sits at the head of my table. His head is bent, and his long locks hide his face as he stuffs bread into the broth before him and then into his mouth.

That sensual mouth that felt so nice against mine. I lift my hand to touch my gloss-painted lips. They still tingle from his warmth.

Slowly, he lifts his head slightly and pushes his hair from his face to look at me through his lashes. He looks both dangerous and sexy as he does so. I have no doubt this man is a warrior where he's from.

He drops the remaining piece of bread back onto the plate at his side. His mouth opens as his eyes roll over me from head to toe.

He lifts to stand. Again, I marvel at his height and strong body. His sleeveless shirt fit against his muscled chest. The leather pants he wears are loose enough for battle but fit snug enough to showcase his strong thighs. His gaze is intense when he lifts his eyes back to mine.

"Come sit with me," he says as he moves to pull out the chair beside him.

My cheeks warm. I stumble forward a few steps but stop and wrap my tail around my middle. I bite my lip.

"I didn't come to disturb you. You can eat alone if that's what you wish for," I say.

"There is plenty of food here. I'm sure you need to eat. You used a lot of energy to save me."

I continue to chew my lip as I move closer. I wince as my hooves make noise against the wood floors. I wish I could hide them somehow.

"Thank you," I murmur when I reach the chair and release my tail to take the offered seat.

"You're welcome."

He returns to his seat. However, he doesn't start to eat again. Instead, he watches me. His eyes fall to my breasts, but he quickly shakes his head and lifts his gaze back to my face.

"How is your shoulder?" I blurt out to fill the silence.

"I don't feel a thing." He looks down at his shoulder. "It has healed. Thank you."

"You're welcome. Thank you for not leaving me in the forest to escape."

"It isn't my way," he says, setting those intense eyes on mine.

I look away from his penetrating gaze and reach for the bread as Bach and Dinesh place a bowl of soup in front of me. My cheeks heat as Dinesh gapes at me with an open mouth. I know he's going to say something with his smart mouth.

"Holy shit," he breathes.

"What he means to say is you look lovely tonight," Bach says.

I shift in my seat uncomfortably. I don't like having all this attention on me. I reach for my hood but realize it's not there.

"You do look lovely."

"Thank you, Argon? I heard your father call you that."

"Yes, that's my name."

I frown. "It's nice to meet you?"

He gives a small chuckle. "Yes, Blaise. I think it is nice to meet you. Interesting, at the very least."

I turn to my bread and soup, and he returns to his. Silence falls once again. That is until I lift my bowl and slurp down the rest of my soup. Ms. Posh clears her throat in the distance and I blanch.

Quickly, I place the bowl down and peek at Argon to find him watching me with a smile at the corners of his lips. Without taking his eyes off me, he lifts his bowl and slurps down the rest of his broth.

"That was delicious," he says once he places the bowl down. "Can I carve some of the meat for you?"

I stare at him as if I've lost my voice. I've been nothing but terrible to this man. I've imprisoned him and his father. Yet he's kind to me.

"Why are you so gentle with me?"

"You're a lady. Ladies should always be treated with respect," he replies.

I want to laugh in his face. I'm a beast. Not a lady. I haven't been a lady in… I don't remember how long at the moment.

I lower my head. "Yes, thank you. I would like it if you would carve the meat."

He proceeds to fill both our plates with meat and vegetables. I'm starving from the altercation in the woods and healing him. When I realize I'm eating like a slob, I look up to find a smile on his lips. He nods for me to continue as he tears into a drumstick. I smile back and return to my food.

"I saw your copy of *Frankenstein*. I used to read that as a boy," he says after a while.

I blink at him. *Frankenstein* is one of my favorites. I remember I'd been reading it before his father tried to steal the rose.

"Yes, I love that book. Do you still like to read?"

"I love to read," he says and his eyes light up. "I will read anything I can get my hands on. These days, I've been reading up on the history of my people."

"Where are you from?"

"The land of Kunglig."

That sounds so familiar. My brain tickles from its mention. Still, I can't make the connection. I shake my head.

"You are a warrior there?"

He searches my face before he nods. "Yes, and more."

I tilt my head as I notice his lids getting heavy. My venom mostly likely has begun to make him drowsy. He will want to lie down soon.

"I think I should show you to your room. You won't be able to hold your head up much longer. Another side effect," I warn.

"I believe that would be best. This meal was very hearty and delicious. Thank you."

"You're welcome."

Argon

I think her venom has caused me to lose my mind. I shouldn't find this creature attractive. Nor should I want to treat her with kindness.

However, after watching her at dinner, I can see she's soft beneath the hard shell she puts up. She's quite adorable. As I sway at her side, I tell myself my thoughts are an effect of her healing.

"Here, this one will be yours," she says as we stop outside of one of the many doors. "If you need anything, Bach or Dinesh will be of service to you."

I turn to her and lean my shoulder against the wall beside the door. I reach to cup the side of her face and brush my finger across her cheek. She looks up at me.

"And you? Will you be back?"

Her lips part as she looks up at me through innocent eyes. She's so small, but her body is full of lush curves. She takes a step back and her hooves click, reminding me this isn't a woman like the ones in my realm.

"What do you need me for?"

"I don't know. Maybe the poison isn't all gone," I say before I think better.

She shakes her head. "It's gone. I made sure of it. You should turn in. You're a large man. If you pass out, I don't think my magic is ready to carry you."

I give her a crooked smile. "Good night, Blaise. Thank you again."

"You're welcome," she says quickly and turns to rush off.

I stand watching her full hips sway. She looks over her shoulder to find my eyes on her. A gasp leaves her lips, and she wraps that tail around herself.

I tip my head back and laugh. The booming sound fills the hall, causing me to laugh more. Um, maybe this won't be so bad after all.

CHAPTER EIGHT

A Gift of Thanks

Blaise

"Rise and shine, princess," Ms. Posh sings.

I groan and turn in my bed, burying my face into my pillow. I haven't gotten any sleep. I spent the night dreaming of a certain sexy giant.

I'm frustrated and exhausted. I want to sleep for the rest of the day and only come up for food. I intend to do just that.

"Come, child. The man has been up for hours now. He has asked after you several times already."

"Why?" I groan into the pillow. "What does he want?"

Ms. Posh flies over my head and sits on my pillow. "He wants to make sure you're okay. I believe he's concerned about you. He knows you used a lot of your power to save him."

"Tell him I'm fine."

"Oh no, dear. You must do that yourself. Come on, princess. It's time you enchant this man and cause him to fall in love with you."

"Love or lust? You didn't see the way he looked at me last night. I don't want to go out there."

"I've been telling you for years that you're still gorgeous. A real man will see that."

"I don't even know what to say to him," I murmur.

"You will figure that out as you go."

I roll onto my back and look at the ceiling, allowing my tail to lift in the air and sway back and forth as I think. I don't want to go out there and embarrass myself. I feel like that's all I did last night.

"Should I give him something? You know, to thank him for bringing me back to the castle," I say nervously.

"Yes, *yes*. That's a great idea," she says excitedly.

I sit up on my elbows. "But what? What should I give him?"

"I say you give him some pussy and save us all," Dinesh says as he flies into view.

"Don't you have some work to do?" Ms. Posh chides.

"Nope, fed the giant and made sure his room had new towels. I'm here to see if I can be of assistance. I used to pull the ladies in all the time, if y'know what I mean," he replies, wiggling his brows.

"She doesn't need to get him into her bed. She needs him to fall in love." Ms. Posh folds her arms over her chest.

"They all fell in love with me if I remember right. I can tell you a thing or two."

"Dinesh, please." I palm my face.

"Okay, okay. You want to give him a gift. It should be something that piques his interest. What did you learn about him last night?"

"Nothing."

"Think, dear. You had to learn something. He tried to be engaging. It was very sweet of him," Ms. Posh coaches.

I think back to last night. She's right. He was very sweet to me. I'm still surprised by that.

I gasp. "Books."

"Dear gods, I'm never going to get laid again," Dinesh groans and drops down onto the bed.

"Shut it, you," I snap. "He said he loves to read. His eyes lit up when he said it. I'll give him books."

Dinesh lifts his head. "Oh, that sounds promising, but I have a better idea."

"Oh goodness," Ms. Posh murmurs.

"Trust me."

Argon

She has her cloak on again. I'm a little disappointed to see that. I've been warring with that fact since she found me roaming the halls.

"Are you taking me back to my cell?"

She tilts her head back to look up at me. I give her a smile to ease the tension. She blinks at me.

"No, would you like to return there?"

"Not particularly."

She turns back to focus on the hall before us. My curiosity grows as we move down the long corridor. We stop in front of double doors and she hands me a key.

I take the key and lift a brow at her. She reaches up to pass a hand over her waves. Seeing that she's nervous, I don't press her.

Turning to the doors, I stick the key into the lock. When I push the doors open, I wave for her to walk in before me. She shakes her head.

"You first, please."

I shrug and walk in. A smile comes to my lips as I cross the threshold. It's a library. A vast one at that. I turn in a circle as I take it all in.

"This is a very nice library. I could get lost in here," I say.

"Good, it's yours. I hope it makes your time here easier. Again, I thank you for not leaving me to the wolves."

I saunter over to where she stands watching me. She's very small compared to me. She cranes her neck to look at my face.

I pull her into my embrace. "Thank you. This is kind of you."

She tugs away, her cheeks on fire again. I think it's so cute. She looks everywhere but at me.

"Yes, well, you're welcome. It's the least I can do."

"Would you like to read with me?"

She begins to wring her hands. "I… you… Would you not rather be here alone?"

"No, I've been alone all day. Sit with me. We can pick books to read and keep each other company. That's if you don't have anything else to do," I reply.

"Yes, I'd like that. I will stay."

I close the distance between us and wrap an arm around her shoulders. The pulsing in my chest settles to a dull hum. It's the first time all day that it's settled.

"Come, I'm in the mood to get lost in some pages."

Blaise

I peek up from my book to watch him. He's sitting in the window seat with his head bent over a book. He's gorgeous. Half of his hair is up in a tie. The other half rests around his shoulders. A few strands have come loose to play around his face and temple.

His lashes are so long I can see them from where I sit in the overstuffed chair. The sunlight coming in through the window highlights his face. He's breathtaking.

"Have you picked a book that doesn't hold your interest?" he murmurs but keeps his eyes on his book.

I drop my eyes to my own and turn the page with my tail. "I've enjoyed this book many times," I reply.

"Then it must be that you have never seen a man before," he says. This time he does turn to me and lifts a brow.

I shift in my seat. "I've seen a man before."

He closes his book with a loud popping sound. It causes me to flinch. I frown at myself and close my book to place it on my lap.

"What do you do for enjoyment other than read?"

I chew on my lip. I have to think over his question. I don't do much outside of playing my cello and reading books. I can't remember the last time I could say that I enjoyed myself.

"I—I don't do much."

"Fine, then we will improvise. How are you feeling? Are you up for a stroll? I'd like to see these roses I'm serving time for," he says.

I bow my head at the mention of his imprisonment and the roses. Argon stands and moves closer to me. He squats and places a hand beneath my chin.

Lifting my head, he stares into my eyes. I search his, not understanding this change. He tried to leave. He was angry when he had to take his father's place.

"I want to understand. You say the roses have a greater value than I know. I'm trying to understand why I'm here and why you're here alone."

"I'm not alone," I whisper.

He tilts his head. "Maybe not, but you're not happy."

I shut down and turn away from him. I don't like this. He's too close and that feeling in my chest pulses with his nearness.

"Come for a walk with me. We don't have to talk. I need to stretch my bones." He stands and holds his hand out.

I hesitate for only a moment before I take it and stand. His touch sends a spark of electricity up my arm. We lock eyes and I know he feels it too.

This could prove to be dangerous. I think I like this man.

CHAPTER NINE

Just A Peek

Argon

"The weather is beautiful here," I say into the silence as it's taken over once again.

We've been strolling around the castle for a while now. I was able to get my first glance at the roses as well. Oddly enough, I find comfort in Blaise's presence.

"Yes, that it is."

"Come on, Blaise. There has to be something to do around here. You can't mean to tell me you only read and play music."

"But it is all I do. The others are busy with chores most of the time. I don't force them to entertain me. Reading and my music are all I have."

"Now you have me," I say, my voice seeming to drop deeper than usual. She shivers beside me, bringing a smile to my lips. "I'm determined for us to find things to do."

"Why?"

"Because I'll go crazy sitting around this big palace with nothing to occupy my mind."

"Okay, fair enough. I guess I'm used to it. However, I wouldn't want you to lose your sanity. I'll assist you in your quest. We will find things for you to do."

"Good. You seem like you could use a little fun in your life, Blaise."

I look down to find her making this adorable face. Her cheeks are blushing again. I'm starting to find I enjoy that.

"You seem shy. Do I make you nervous?"

"I…um…you make me curious. It's been so long since… I don't know. I might be shy. You are the first visitor who hasn't run from me."

"Have you had many visitors?"

"No, not really. None who have gotten far. Most don't make it past the fire wall."

"Ah, I see. That makes sense."

"What did you do for fun in your home?" she asks, seeming to want to change subjects.

I get the sense I've made her uncomfortable. She's wringing her hands in front of her and she's slowed her pace. I don't mean to make her uncomfortable. I'm just trying to get to know more about this creature.

"Training took up a lot of my time, but I've always enjoyed it," I reply.

"Training? As in, to be a warrior?"

"Yes. Speaking of which, you don't have warriors here. Am I to believe you are the only defense you have?"

She gives a dangerous snort. "I'm all the defense I need. I will train with you one of these days and show you."

"I look forward to it."

"Good, are you hungry? We should head back, I'm sure dinner will be ready."

"I could stand to eat a bit. This was a nice walk. Thank you for the company."

She ducks her head and nods. I reach to give her hand a little squeeze. She lifts her eyes to mine.

"I mean it. Thank you."

"You're welcome," she says with a smile.

Blaise

I don't know if he loves to talk or if he's just trying to be nice to me. I still don't understand his kindness. However, he has kept our conversation going all day.

I enjoyed our walk. I find I like the sound of his voice. It caused a shiver to run through me a few times throughout our walk and tonight during dinner.

I look up at him as we stand in the foyer. He looks back at me with what seems like a genuine smile on his lips.

"I had fun today. I think I've forgotten what it's like to hang out with someone," I say quietly.

"I enjoyed myself as well. I'm sure we can find more to do in the coming days. I look forward to it."

"As do I. Sleep well, Argon."

"Yes, Blaise. Do sleep well. I'll see you in the morning, right?"

"See you in the morning."

I turn and rush off before I say something stupid. Looking back over my shoulder, I find him watching me like last night. I wave quickly before I turn and focus on making it to my room.

Once in my room, I close the door and place my back to it. My chest heaves as I close my eyes and try to calm my nerves.

"You like him." I startle as Dinesh's words sound in my ear.

I open my eyes. He flies from the side of my face to the front to look me in the eyes. I wave a hand in front of my face as if to shoo him off.

Instead of flying away, he opens his palm and the flame within the center of it lights the space between us. I frown and start farther into the room.

"Ah, yes, now I see it in the light. You do like him."

"What difference does it make? He'll never fall for me."

"It makes all the difference in the world. You will see. The fat woman hasn't sung when it comes to you. There is still hope for us all."

"Dinesh, why are you here?"

"I'm here to help. I think you should spy on him. Come on, make one of your orbs. Let's take a peek."

"A peek of what?" I huff.

"For one, you can check out his body. See if he has what it takes to please a real princess."

"Oh gods. Why have I been stuck with you?"

"You love me, princess. Without me, this all would have been a bore."

"What makes you like this?" I groan.

"You know… I don't remember."

"Ugh, get out."

"Not until I know you're going to peek in on him."

"Fine," I breathe and create an orb.

Argon comes into view shirtless and barefoot. With little to no warning, his pants vanish. I quickly burst the orb. Little particles of light float before me as it shatters and I sit in stunned silence.

"Magic," I murmur to myself.

He's still able to use it in this castle. I figured his magic would be a lot weaker by now. I shake my head, feeling like a perv for violating his privacy.

"It might be, but does he know how to use it?" Dinesh says, reminding me he's still here.

"Does it matter? He won't get to use it in this castle."

"I don't see why not. That was pretty impressive."

"Why do I know you're not talking about the same thing as me?"

"Because I'm probably not," he says with a cheeky grin.

I roll my eyes at him. "Whatever. I've taken a peek. Happy?"

He grins. "I'll just leave you to finish taking a look. You have a good night, princess."

I growl and shake my head. "Total mess," I mutter under my breath.

I could just take one more peek. No, no, you need to respect his privacy. Go to bed, princess.

CHAPTER TEN

Magical Books

Argon

I can't sleep. I've been thinking about Blaise since I bid her good night. I've learned that she's shy and much like a young girl looking for friendship.

I'm intrigued by her. Once I coaxed her into that walk, I learned a lot about her. I was even able to coax a smile to her lips.

"Fuck."

I fling the covers off and throw my legs over the side of the bed, then wrap the sheet around my waist and grab the key to the library. Maybe a book will help me distract myself enough to rest.

I pad through the hallway barefoot, remembering my way back to the massive library. When I find the doors I'm looking for, I stick the key into the lock and push my way in.

I inhale the scent of leather bindings and old pages. This would be a place of peace for me back home. I head for the shelves on the left, not searching in any particular order.

When I stop before the shelves, I find old books from the earth realm. I enjoy these. I run my fingertips across the spines. I stop short when I find a section with romance books based on alchemy.

My interest is piqued. I beckon the first book in the series from the shelf and into my palm. Then begin to skim through. I chuckle as I fall upon a love scene.

I probably shouldn't read this. My head is already muddled with thoughts of a being I know nothing about. Yes, she's a woman, but she's also half beast. I've never seen a woman like her before.

"For the love of the gods," I murmur and tuck the book under my arm.

I return to my chambers and climb back into bed with the book I've chosen. Thankfully, the words pull me in and I'm able to focus. Not like earlier when in the library with Blaise.

While she studied me, I felt her eyes on me. I grew more curious as she stared. The words on the page had become a blur as questions about her continued to circle in my head.

I'm well into the book when I get to the heated imitate scene. I shift beneath the sheets as I read, my cock growing hard. I decide to put the book down to see if I can get some rest.

However, I start to feel strange as I did during that kiss. My eyes become unfocused and the room around me is a haze. I rub my eyes and that's when they become clear again.

I draw my brows in confusion as the room comes back into focus and it's evident I'm no longer in my bedchamber. The darkly decorated room is no more. I now sit in a cream-and-teal room.

I look down at the bed and it's not the soft large four-poster one I've been lying in. It's been replaced with a low mattress surrounded by soft pillows. It dawns on me this is the exact setting of the room in the book I'd been reading.

Feeling a presence at my other side, I turn to find a curvy form beneath the sheets beside me. The reddish-brown waves make me think of Blaise. Although I can already tell this woman has no tail.

She moans and rolls onto her back. My lips part and my mouth waters as her full breasts are exposed to me. I reach for the sheet and tug it back.

Smooth brown skin is revealed, but that's not what grabs my attention. There are no hooves or furry legs. Her smooth, sexy shapely legs lead to cute little feet.

I allow my gaze to travel back up her body, stopping at the apex of her full thighs. Soft, inviting curls rest over her plush mound. I lick my lips and my nostrils flare.

I focus my gaze higher. Again, her breasts grab my attention and appreciation. Her dark nipples are more than an arousing sight.

Finally, I lift my eyes to her face. Her eyes are open and she's observing me as I take her in. Frustration rises when I can only see her eyes. Her head and face are covered in teal fabric.

It reminds me that the heroine in the book I was reading wore a head-and-face covering. However, Blaise's eyes are something I've grown to find interest in. They are so expressive.

She lifts a hand to cup my jaw. "This isn't real," she whispers.

I shake my head. "No, this must be the hallucinations you warned me of."

She snorts. "Right, because I would be hallucinating as well," she mutters more to herself.

I don't give her words much attention. Her enticing body has all my focus. I brush my fingers along her thigh, and she gasps.

It's such an arresting sound. I want to hear more. I return my gaze to hers as if asking for permission to touch her more.

Her eyes are pleading, causing me to trail my fingers to the soft curls between her legs and then lower. When I find her slick with arousal, I groan. My cock is painfully hard.

Not able to restrain myself, I dip my head to suck one of her nipples into my mouth. Her cry is husky and arousing. Her skin tastes of sweetness.

I'm stunned by that fact at first. It's common for the women in my realm to have flavored skin. However, that's not something other realms are known for.

At least not according to my studies and encounters on other planes. I want to see if she carries all the traits of my people. I shift to settle between her legs.

She opens her thighs to me so easily it brings me great pride. It is considered a gift to have a woman open herself to you in my realm. I take this gift with gratitude as I release her nipple and move down her body.

I glide a hand up her side to reach her other nipple and pinch it as I kiss my way down her smooth stomach. The sounds coming from her mouth are so sexy.

When I get to her soaked entrance, I can already smell the scent of vanilla and apples. I look up at her with curiosity. I really look into her eyes.

Perhaps it's the hallucination making her more like the women from my home. That would explain it. Just as her legs and feet have been altered.

"Lie back, I'm going to taste you," I command as she rests on her elbows, watching me.

She nods her head and obeys. I lower my head for my first taste. My mouth waters as her flavor bursts against my tongue. I eat at her essence, parting her folds with my hands to get better access to her delicious center.

"Yes," she cries. "Please. That feels so good."

I continue to feast on her as her thick thighs shake. I cup one in my palm and turn to kiss and lick it, giving her a short break. Her back arches off the mattress as she grabs for the pillows at her sides.

I return to her center and continue to bring her pleasure until my mouth fills with her sweet nectar. It's like drinking a warm glass of cider. I kiss my way back up her body.

I want to see her face and kiss those soft lips once again. My loins still burn with desire when I think of that kiss. I reach for the fabric covering her face.

Right as I touch it, I feel that pull again. My vision blurs. I blink rapidly, trying to bring her back into view.

I'm by myself once again, back in my bedchamber, alone. I reach for my stiff cock and groan. Biting out a curse, I flip onto my back.

My head is too heavy for me to keep my eyes open long enough to think about what just happened. I close them with a smile on my face and a hard cock in my hand.

CHAPTER ELEVEN

Good Morning

Blaise

I stumble into the dining room. I've been fighting with myself all morning. I hadn't planned to show my face after that dream.

It was so real. I had to convince myself that Argon wouldn't know I dreamed about him in such vivid color and in such a way. I felt every kiss, every touch. I wanted that kiss from his lips so badly.

"Stop it," I chide myself as my thoughts travel back to the dream.

I can't help wondering if it was all a result of peeking in on him. I shouldn't have done that and now I'm paying for it. Dream Argon was as perfect as the image I saw through the orb.

"Good morning."

I lift my head to find Argon standing behind the chair he has pulled out for me. He has an odd look on his face. I stare at him for a moment, trying to figure out what he's thinking.

Does he know?

His eyes fall to my breasts, then move farther down my body. His nostrils flare and he licks his lips. I bounce nervously from hoof to hoof and furrow my brows.

I don't know his powers, but I've felt them. I wonder if he can see my thoughts. He looks down at my hooves and his brows crease as his cheeks turn red.

"Good morning, Blaise," he says.

His voice comes out husky and deep. I clench my thighs, remembering how he commanded me to lie back in the dream. I've never experienced the touch of a man. At least, it's not something I can recall.

"Good morning," I reply, ducking my head away from his penetrating gaze.

I move to take the chair he pulled out for me. My cheeks are burning as I keep my eyes on the table before me. I'm relieved when Bach and Dinesh fly in with breakfast.

I tear into my oatmeal as soon as it's placed in front of me. I'm famished, as if I used real energy in that dream. Gods know, I woke soaked between the legs, my body still convulsing from the pleasure Dream Argon inflicted on me.

"Did you sleep well?"

I jump at the sound of his voice. I place a hand over my chest to still my heart. Looking out the corner of my eye, I question if he knows.

I lick my lips. "Yes and no."

He lifts a brow in question. I start to fidget in my seat. Remembering what it was like to be a lady, I reach for my napkin and place it in my lap.

Smoothing my hands across the fabric, I buy myself time to answer. When I look at him, I nearly whimper. His gaze is heated and fixed on me.

"I had a dream," I breathe. "It was very real and unsettling."

He licks his full lips. "Must be something in the food," he mutters.

It's almost too low for me to hear. Actually, if not for my enhanced hearing, I don't think I would've. I look at my bowl of oatmeal and wonder if Dinesh could be playing with the food again.

"Excuse me?"

"Nothing," he says, shaking his head. "Those hallucinations. Were they limited to the night you healed me?"

"No," I say cautiously. "My venom is still in your system. It will be some time before it leaves. You can have them as long as it's in your blood."

"Hmm." He purses his lips and nods.

"Ha… have you had one?"

He pulls a hand down his face. "I may have had more than one. Would you like to take a walk with me again today?"

I turn back to my food. I had an excellent time with him yesterday. Argon is funny and wise. I believe he's a great warrior in his world.

My heart aches. His people probably miss him. Losing him has most likely changed his world.

"Yes, I'd like that. I also believe I have an idea for something to do that you will enjoy."

His gaze heats even more. "Do you?"

"Um, y…yes. I believe you still have enough power for this."

"*Hmm.*"

Argon

I stand before the mirror in my bedchamber with a towel around my waist after a shower. I thought it would help me to clear my mind. It has only left me with more thoughts swirling in my brain.

I shouldn't be so nervous about going on a walk with this creature. Nothing can become of us. Even if I think that my spirit link has opened to her.

"Think, Argon," I growl at myself.

I need to know what all of this means. Once my link is open to my mate, it will not accept another. I have to figure out what has opened it and how I can close it back.

"You know. You should stop fighting what you feel and go with it."

I turn to find Dinesh and Bach watching me. Dinesh is the one who spoke. He watches me closely with his light-brown eyes.

"What do you know of what I feel?" I fold my arms over my chest.

"It's in your eyes. You look at Blaise with great interest," Bach says as if proud of something.

"I'm to wed someone else," I say with little conviction. "Besides, Blaise and I are from two different worlds."

"If you say so."

"What Dinesh is trying to say is that Blaise may be more like the women you are used to than you think," Bach says as he glares at Dinesh.

"I doubt that. None of the women where I'm from are half woman, half— what is she exactly?"

Bach frowns and shakes his head. "You continue to look at things with your eyes and not your heart. Things around here aren't to be seen but felt."

I mull over his words. Frustration grasps me as the spirit link pulses for its other half. I clench my jaw against the ache.

"Is it safe to say something is going on between you and Blaise? I mean, beyond your curiosity about her. These pains she is complaining about when you're not around.

"They're more severe for her than they are for you. You know what they are, don't you?"

I look into Bach's eyes and note the concern there. My own concern wins out. I'm in motion before I answer him.

I use my powers to dress as I walk. I will not allow her to be in pain because of me. I move faster as the link pulses.

"Well, I guess that means he does know," Dinesh says behind me.

"Yes, I do."

CHAPTER TWELVE

It's Okay

Argon

I rush into Blaise's bedchamber and find her curled in a ball on her side, whimpering in pain. I kick my boots from my feet and climb onto the bed beside her head.

"Shh, it's okay. Come here," I coo and move her head to rest in my lap.

I brush a hand over her hair as her body relaxes. She releases a sigh and snuggles her head deeper into my lap. I continue to stroke her hair, being mindful to watch out for her horns.

"Is that better?"

"Yes," she says softly. "Why does this keep happening?"

I furrow my brows in thought. "I haven't figured that out yet, but as long as I'm near, you should be fine."

"Would placing you in this wing help?" Bach asks in concern.

"It might. She would at least be able to come to me."

Blaise lifts her head and looks at me. "Come to you? Are you doing this to me?"

"Not so much doing it to you, but I do believe it's because of me. Somehow, we've triggered a link."

"I'll prepare your new chambers," Bach announces before he takes off.

"Why does it hurt so much?" Blaise says.

"That I don't understand. We should feel the link equally. However, I don't know much about you. Maybe it has something to do with the differences between us."

"We're missing our walk," she whispers tiredly.

"We have time. Rest, I'm not leaving your side. We'll walk later."

"Argon?"

"Yes, Blaise."

"Thank you."

"Anytime." I continue to brush a hand over her hair as we shift and settle more comfortably.

Blaise against my chest as I lie back on her pillow. Her scent surrounds me. It's more pleasant than I expected. The dream was accurate in its depiction.

"You're so warm and you smell nice," she says.

Before I can answer, she begins to snore. I chuckle at the sound. It's adorable.

As she sleeps, my mind circles what's happening. I don't know why or how, but somehow, she's opened my spirit link. I wish Father were here for me to ask.

Could it be this place? Will it close once again when I return home? Do I even want to return?

I've enjoyed my last few days with Blaise more than I've enjoyed anything in a very long time. I find I'm more confused than I was before I came to rescue Father.

Blaise

We step into the room, and I cause the lights to come on. I hardly ever come in here, but Ms. Posh and the others keep it clean and functional.

"What do we have here?" Argon asks as we enter the castle's fencing room.

"We had to change our plans a bit, but I still wanted you to get to spar. This is Father's old fencing room. We can train in here sometimes," I say hopefully.

He looks down at me with a smile. "Blaise, you're half my size."

"Are you afraid, Argon? I didn't take you for a coward," I taunt.

He lifts a brow. "Don't say I didn't warn you, my lady."

I wave a hand and a glowing sword appears in my palm. I circle my wrist with the blade in it and take a stance. He turns to look at the practice swords against the wall.

"Allow me," I say before conjuring a sword and shield to his hands.

I noticed his powers feel weaker today. I picked up on it when he came to my room. The more he uses them, the more they will fade.

I wish we could have gone out as I had planned. It would have allowed him to recharge for a bit. Oh, well. Next time.

"Focus, Blaise," he chides as I stumble a little.

Seeing he's a serious warrior, I focus and show him I'm no damsel in distress.

"Let's go," I say tightly as I call forth my own shield.

A smile curves his lips. I find myself with a smile of my own as well. We spend the next few hours taking each other to task. It's more fun than I could have imagined.

CHAPTER THIRTEEN

Snow

Blaise

"Is that... snow?" he says and looks out of the window.

"Have you never seen snow before?"

"I've only seen it through holograms in my world. I've never experienced it firsthand. I heard it used to snow all the time, but something happened many years ago," he says, still staring out the window with awe.

"Come, you have to go outside," I say and grab his hand to tug him out of the castle with me.

I've been waiting for him to meet me in the foyer after breakfast. He wanted to freshen up. I needed time to collect my thoughts, so it was a win for me.

I haven't been sleeping well. My thoughts are always filled with him. Knowing his new room is just down the hall messes with my head every night.

"This is more beautiful than in a hologram," he murmurs as we stand out in the little storm.

I look at his face as he looks up at the sky. Snowflakes fly onto his high cheekbones and against his full lips. I want to reach out and touch them, even as they melt against his skin.

He lowers his gaze to mine, and I quickly look away. He pinches my chin and brings my face back to face his. His finger brushes my scar beneath my lip and his eyes fall to where his skin meets mine.

"I thought it would feel different, hard or liquid-like. It's soft like the rest of your skin," he says in awe. I drop my eyes to the ground. "Blaise, look at me."

I look into his blue eyes. They seem to sparkle out here in the open light. I can see his breath as the cool air chills it. He moves closer to me.

"Your eyes are the color of the sky. Not only blue but blue and gray. They look like clouds," I say, not able to stop the words.

"Your eyes are expressive. I can see your thoughts through them."

This moment has become too intense. I pull away and move quickly to grab a handful of snow to throw at him. The look of surprise on his face causes me to laugh.

A slow smile comes to his lips. "I like it when you laugh. However, I'm going to make you pay for that one."

I yelp and run away as fast as my hooves will take me. Argon is faster. A snowball hits me in my shoulder and I stumble forward a little and trip over my own feet.

"Blaise," he calls in concern, rushing to catch me.

His arms are around my waist, tugging me into his chest before I know it. I look up into his eyes and blink. He's truly fast.

"I'm okay," I whisper.

"I shouldn't have thrown it so hard. I'm so sorry."

"I'm fine. I tend to trip over myself sometimes."

He searches my eyes. I don't realize I'm holding my breath until he reaches to brush a snowflake from my hair. I bite my lip.

"Come on, let's go back inside. It's cold out."

I shake my head. "Come with me. I want to show you something."

Argon

Blaise takes my hand, her eyes full of excitement. She leads me to the rose garden, where the fire roses are. I don't know how my father found his way to them.

They're encased within a maze. The walls shift, closing off passages we've moved through as we go. Blaise maneuvers the path easily as if knowing the way by heart. However, I get the feeling anyone else would be lost in these mazes forever.

Their magic alone threatens to suffocate. The leaves ripple with power as we pass by. They whisper warnings with every step.

Go back... Enter at your own risk... Do not touch what isn't yours. A price will be required.

I narrow my eyes. How could my father have been so foolish? Was that rose really worth it?

Argon, beware.

Blaise squeezes my hand gently. "They will not harm you as long as I am here."

"How does one make it through without you?" I question.

"You mean, how did your father make it into the garden?"

"Yes."

"I was curious. I allowed it. He seemed to know where he was going."

Her words imply I shouldn't pry further. I tighten my jaw and hold in all my inquiries. There's no need to frustrate us both over something we cannot change.

The snow continues to fall overhead. As we approach the opening of the rose garden, I grow worried about her beloved roses. This snow will surely put out their fire.

However, once we're closer, I can feel the heat of the roses. It's warmer than the last time she brought me here. When we step into the garden, I understand why.

As the snowflakes fall on the petals, the flames consume them. It's as if the snowflakes are fuel to the roses. The cold from when we were in front of the castle is no longer a concern.

"You're warm," I say as I note the beads of sweat on her upper lip. "Shouldn't you remove your cloak? I will hold it for you."

She chews on her lip for a few seconds. I reach for the button that closes the cloak at her throat. Releasing it, I push the fabric from her shoulders. I go to place it across my forearm, but it vanishes.

I grin at her as I cause my own coat that I summoned when we stepped out of the castle to vanish. Her lips twitch and her eyes sparkle. I note the end of her tail swaying behind her as the length is wrapped around her. Its heart-shaped tip rocks from side to side like a pendulum behind her.

"Do you know why your father wanted one of these roses?"

I tilt my head and think over her question. Stories of fire roses tickle my memory, but I can't for the life of me remember them in this moment.

"No."

"They are roses of eternal life. At least, that's one of their powers. When you give one to someone you truly care for, they will live forever. No weapon will be strong enough to take them from you," she says.

I watch as she reaches for one of the roses and hands it to me. I smile down at her as I hold the rose. Its flames dance as the snow falls onto it.

I run my finger over the flames and watch as they caress my skin without burning me. My smile broadens. Lifting my gaze to Blaise's amber eyes, I have an idea.

I reach to brush my fingertips along her temple, tracing the hairline of her thick hair. I push her hair behind her ear as I search her expressive eyes. With my other hand, I gently place the rose in the side of her full locks.

It settles into place and the flames calm. It's as if it belongs right where I placed it. Blaise places a hand over her chest, and I know she has felt the tug on our link.

I slip my hand into hers. "Come. Let's see what we can get into for the rest of the day."

CHAPTER FOURTEEN

Time for Fun

Argon

"Thank you," I say to Ms. Posh as she brings me a glass of wine while I sit in the library awaiting Blaise's arrival.

"You're welcome, my dear, can I get you anything else?"

"No, thank you. I'll wait for Blaise."

Dinesh and Bach have set the game table and brought in refreshments. I look around and the setting feels so normal, like an evening set up for some fun with my comrades back home. Blaise looked so excited when I suggested a game night.

My mind goes back to the pull of our link in the garden. I still don't know how it's possible, but I'm almost positive that's what's going on. As I have the thought, my link starts to pulse.

The door opens and in steps Blaise. She looks lovely. Her face is made up with glossy lips and her hair is styled in those big waves again. She's wearing a dress. I allow my gaze to travel lazily over her.

The dress is a tight-knit fabric that shows off all her curves. If not for the hooves and her tail, I'd take her for an ordinary woman. I shake my head clear. Ordinary, she is not.

I haven't found an ordinary thing about her yet. Even as she moves closer now, her hair bounces with each step and her magic pulses around her. It's like I can see the aura of her magic swirling.

The depth of her power brings me a bit of pride. This is what my soul match should feel like.

"Why are you smiling?" she asks as she takes the seat I've pulled out for her across from where I've been waiting.

I move to reclaim my own seat and stare at her for a moment as I gather my thoughts. I'm caught in her gaze. Blaise is truly gorgeous. Take away the tail and hooves and she's stunning, scars included.

She lifts a brow at me, then ducks her head and turns away. I clear my throat as I realize I've been staring and haven't said a word.

"I was smiling because you dressed up for our game night. I wasn't expecting that."

"I don't think that's why you were smiling, Argon, but I won't argue."

"The last thing I want is to argue. You look very nice, Blaise."

I feel for my magic. I have just enough still coursing through me to pull this off. I watch Blaise's face as I go from wearing my leathers and tunic to wearing a gray suit and white dress shirt with the top buttons sitting open.

The front of my hair pulls back away from my face and up into a man bun, the back half remaining down. I grin and lift a brow as her lips part and her eyes fill with lust. This time she's the one who can't stop staring.

"Now we are both ready for game night," I murmur as I reach across the table and brush her bangs out of her face.

Bach clears his throat. "Um, shall we choose a game?"

"Yes, I believe we should," I reply.

"Why in the heavens did you interrupt that moment?" Dinesh groans, drawing my attention.

I look to him and Bach. They're dressed in little outfits as if dealers in one of those casinos in the earth realm. Solia and Hiasha are dressed in the same manner as they look on and fly around the refreshments.

"It's fine. We should pick a game. Thank you," Blaise says.

A floating carousel of games appears, glowing with magic as it spins. I notice a few from my realm and a bunch from the earth realm. I've played many of these as a boy.

"You choose," I say.

Blaise's eyes light up. "There are so many I would like to try. Have you played any of these?"

"Most of them."

Her smile falls. "I can't remember which I've played before."

"You don't remember?"

"No, I've begun to forget things." She pauses and shifts in her seat. "Um, never mind that. I'm willing to learn something new. It could be fun."

"Pick, and we will figure out how to play it. If I know the game, I will show you."

Her smile returns and she cradles her hands to her chest as she looks the carousel over with wide eyes. I love the excitement coming from her. She reaches for a game but pulls her hand back and chews on her lip.

"How about this one?"

"Sorry." I shrug. I know the game well. It's from the earth realm. "I've played it."

She claps her hands in excitement. "Good, this should be fun. You can teach me."

"My pleasure, Lady Blaise," I say.

Blaise

I lift a hand to cover my glass as Dinesh tries to fill it with more wine. I've already had enough to drink. I've been giggling at everything Argon says. At least the pain in my chest isn't happening tonight.

However, I can barely focus on the game at this point. I look up through my lashes and Argon is staring at me again. I bite my lip and look him over.

"What?" I say as his gaze drops to my lips.

"I'm just watching you enjoy yourself. It's nice to see you have fun. Are you done with the wine?"

"I think I've had enough to drink. You don't seem to be fazed at all."

"It would take a lot more before I start to feel the effects. Most times my magic burns right through it."

"Oh," I reply and turn my focus back to the game.

"Would you like to stop and talk? You've counted the same spaces three times."

I blush and look at him in surprise. "Did I?"

"Yes, you have. We could call it a night. I've had fun, but your lids look like they're growing heavy."

I suck my lip into my mouth, not able to look away from him. He looks so sexy tonight. I love his hair and the suit he has on.

My fingers itch to reach into his shirt and touch the smooth-looking skin. If I were closer, I can't say I wouldn't make a move. I shake the thought away.

"I don't think I can play anymore, but I don't want to call it a night. Will you read to me? I love the sound of your voice."

I clamp my mouth shut as the words come out. I can't believe I just said that. He reaches for my face and runs his thumb across my bottom lip.

"Pick a book. We can move to the sofa. I'll be happy to read to you."

CHAPTER FIFTEEN

The Voice

Blaise

"She wraps the red scarf around her head and takes a look in the mirror," Argon reads while I lie against his chest, where he pulled me in before he started the book. I'm not sure why he's tugged me in so close, but the alcohol won't allow me to think too deeply.

I chose an action-and-suspense romance to try to stay awake and focused on his words. His voice is so deep and soothing. It's like I'm wrapped in a cocoon of his scent and the melody of his voice. He could read anything, and my attention would be riveted to every word.

As he reads, my lids get so heavy. I fight to keep my eyes open, but it's no use. The cadence of his voice is like a spell luring me in. Soon I have no choice but to give in.

I close my eyes and drift off. Suddenly, I'm no longer in the library, resting in Argon's embrace. I'm in a room. Through the mirror, I can see a bed behind me. I focus on my reflection and gasp.

Once again, as in my other dream, I have normal legs and my feet are in a pair of red stiletto heels. I'm almost giddy to see the silky-looking limbs. I take a turn and the skirts of the deep V-neck dress I'm wearing spin up.

Someone clears their throat and I stop and turn for the door. I inhale sharply as Argon comes into view. He isn't wearing the gray suit from our date, but a black one with a black shirt and tie like the bodyguard from the book he was reading to me.

He pushes off the doorjamb and saunters closer to me. My chest heaves as he gets closer. The way he looks at me makes me squeeze my thighs together.

He stops before me, reaching for my waist. He tugs me close while staring into my eyes. His gaze is so intense it almost feels like this is real.

He glides his hands down to my backside. I breathe in relief, knowing he won't find my tail. However, a gasp leaves my lips when he dips his head to kiss the tops of my exposed breasts while kneading my behind.

He moves to his knees and reaches beneath my dress to peel my panties down. He taps my ankle for me to lift my leg. I do as he asks and step from my panties one foot at a time.

"You're so beautiful," he murmurs as he runs his fingertips up the back of my leg.

He dips his head and starts a path of kisses up my inner thigh. I widen my stance, but he lifts one leg over his shoulder and steadies me as he continues his trip up to my core.

I chew on my lip. I can't believe this is happening again, but I'm not going to stop him. I want this more than anything in the world. When I feel him pause, I look down to find him staring back at me as if asking for permission.

"Yes, please," I breathe out.

He laces his fingers with mine and dives in as he holds my hand tight. Something about the gesture makes me feel safe and cared for. I tighten my hold on his hand and throw my head back.

"Argon," I whimper and rock my hips.

He hums as he continues to bob his head between my legs. My eyes roll into the back of my head. I never knew something like this could feel so good. No wonder the heroine in the book was in love.

I gasp as I have the thought at the same time as my release hits. Argon laps at my folds and my soaked thighs while groaning in contentment.

"So good," he croons.

Standing once again, he pulls a hand down his face. I look up at him shyly. Leaning forward, he runs his nose up the exposed bridge of mine before kissing my forehead.

Pulling back, he locks eyes with me once more. "Remove the scarf. I want to see your face. I want to kiss your lips," he demands.

"But Argon," I breathe.

"Do it. Now."

I reach for the scarf to tug it away and obey. I want to feel his lips on mine again as well. However, as I pull the silky fabric down, I'm pulled from the dream.

I want to scream and cry, but I only gasp and open my eyes. The room comes into focus and sure enough, I'm back in the library. I pout and look up to find Argon fast asleep.

Embarrassed and shocked by how vivid that dream was, I peel away from his chest and look at his face as my cheeks burn. He stirs in his sleep but doesn't wake.

"Blaise," he groans.

I jump to my feet, wave a hand for a blanket to appear and cover him, then rush from the library. That dream was too real. I have got to stop having those. Even now, as I rush to my room, I feel the slickness between my legs.

This is crazy.

Argon

I wake in the library to Dinesh buzzing over my head, looking concerned. I don't bother to ask him what's wrong. My link is pulsing so strongly my head hurts. I rushed to Blaise's room to find her thrashing in her sleep.

Images of the dream I had while sleeping in the library come back to me. Again, the dream was so real and palpable. I can still taste her on my tongue.

I'm tempted to strip down and climb into bed with her to hold her and ease the pain of our link. However, as she kicks out and the sheet falls away, I'm reminded the dreams aren't real.

This still isn't a woman I can bed. She's part beast. My heart sinks. I'm growing feelings for her, but we will only ever be friends. In my dreams is the only place where we can be more.

"Blaise," I whisper as my suit jacket and shoes vanish before I climb into the bed with the rest of my clothes still on. "I'm here."

She rolls into my warmth and snuggles into my embrace. My link stops pulsing and calms along with her. I tighten my arms around her and kiss her forehead.

"What are we doing to each other?" I murmur.

Turning to look out at the balcony of her room, I note the sky is starting to lighten. I get lost in thought as I watch the two suns come up. I fall back asleep after hours of thinking of a solution and coming up with nothing.

CHAPTER SIXTEEN

In My World

Blaise

When I wake in the morning, I almost believe I'm having another dream. Argon is lying beside me, with his arms around me. His warm breath on the back of my neck is what woke me.

For a while, I refuse to move because I don't want this to end. However, when he draws a hand down my side and gives my waist a gentle squeeze, I know I have to get up. Quickly, I use my magic to freshen my mouth.

I want to do more with my hair and clothes, but I don't want to be obvious. I sit up and look down at my legs and tail. This is definitely not a dream.

I groan and roll my eyes. Argon runs the back of his fingers down my tail, sending a shiver through me. I bite down on my lip and peek over at him.

"It's soft. Nothing about you is as I expect," he says.

I look him in his eyes. His brows are drawn in thought. I shrug.

"You're not what I expected either."

He lifts to place a hand under his head and rests on his elbow. He looks so comfortable in my bed. My mind goes back to those dreams and seeing him naked in the orb. I wouldn't mind finding him the same way now.

"What were you expecting, Blaise?"

"I don't know. I thought you'd still be angry with me. I didn't expect for you to become my friend."

He lifts and we come face-to-face. I don't know why I'm surprised to find him minty fresh. Clearly, he used his magic as I have.

"Am I your friend?" he breathes as he holds my gaze.

"I...I... um, I think we are friends. I want to be."

He searches my eyes for a moment. I don't realize I'm holding my breath until he falls back to resting against his elbows.

"So what's the plan for the day? More reading?"

"No," I say much too quickly.

My cheeks heat and I tighten my thighs. If only he knew about those dreams. I calm my racing heart and drop my eyes to the bed.

"Would you like to stay here... to talk? You can tell me about your world. I'd like to know more about you, if you'd tell me."

"Sounds good to me. Maybe you can tell me more about you."

I get ready to tell him I don't know much about me, but I clamp my lips shut and keep the words to myself. As long as I keep him talking, I won't have to reveal much about myself.

"Who are you, Argon?"

"In my world, I'm Prince Argon. Next in line to the throne of the kingdom of Kunglig."

I gasp. "You're a prince?"

He smiles. "Yes, my father is the king, but he will be turning the throne over to me soon. Well, that was the plan. Things seemed to have changed."

"Oh," I say and look into my lap.

"Don't look so sad. I had questions about my future before I came here for my father."

"Questions? What questions could you have? You seem like an honorable man. I think you'd make a great king."

"I think I will lead well. However, there are other things that come with the throne that I have questions about."

"Things like?"

He frowns and looks away. I get the feeling I'm prying. He doesn't sound happy, yet I know he will honor his word and duties. That's something I've come to know about him. I like that trait.

"We should eat," he says instead of answering the question.

"We can have breakfast in bed," I suggest, my cheeks heating.

"Sounds good. Do you mind if I change first?"

"No, I'd like to change as well."

He stands from the bed and stretches his long arms over his head. As he stretches his long body, his suit pants change to black silky pants and the dress shirt becomes an open black matching shirt. I turn away as the bulge in the front of the pants shows.

He climbs back onto the bed and stops to kiss my cheek. "Your turn."

"Good morning," Dinesh sings as he and Bach appear with trays of breakfast. "We thought the two of you might be famished."

"Oh, I was just about to summon breakfast," I say, ignoring his words.

I change my clothes quickly and take the floating tray of food. I look anywhere but at Argon. I can't help but wonder if he's being kind to me so he can return home to his people. That has to be it.

"We have ripe fruit like this back home. The best of the best. I've never known better."

"Ms. Posh grows the fruit with her magic. It's delicious."

"Where are you from, Blaise? I get that this is not your original home."

I stare down at my food. My emotions begin to swirl all over the place. I'm angry because I can't remember where I'm from and frustrated because I want to so badly.

"I think you should go. I have things to do today."

"What happened to breakfast in bed? What's wrong?"

"Go," I roar, turning over the trays in front of us.

Argon scowls as he stands and starts out of the room. I immediately feel bad. Using my magic, I clean up.

Looking after Argon, I bow my head. "I'm sorry," I whisper after him.

Argon

I storm into my room. Rage consumes me. We were taking so many steps forward. I don't know what happened. I feel more rage with myself than anything.

I know something is wrong. Blaise can't be my mate. It's this place. If we were a match, our spirits would have linked. My link has opened, but so much more hasn't happened.

"If I'm doomed to be in this place, I need to close this link," I growl to myself.

"Excuse me."

I turn to find Hiasha flying by the door. She peers back at me shyly. I calm my anger as I clench my fists at my sides.

"Hello, Hiasha. How can I help you?"

"I'm the youngest here. The others… they want me to stay out of things, but I think you should know. Lady Blaise has a temper, but she means well. She's trying."

"I guess I'm asking for you to try with her. There's a lot on her shoulders. We mean the world to her and…"

"And?"

"I'm sorry, I've said too much. If you need anything… have a good day, sir."

I clench my fists tighter as she takes off. There's something going on here, something more that no one will talk about.

"Something that's probably none of my business."

CHAPTER SEVENTEEN

Magic Movies

Argon

It's been days since I've spent time with Blaise. She hasn't left her room. I can hear her playing her cello. The music is so melancholy.

I feel her sorrow deep down in my soul. I've thought of going to her, but my pride won't allow it. As long as I don't feel her in pain, I'm choosing to keep my distance.

However, I'll admit there is a part of me that misses the time we used to spend together. I've spent most of my time meditating to keep my magic from fading completely.

Like now, I sit on the floor in the middle of my room with my legs crossed. As I'm in deep meditation, my magic swirls around me with a blue light. It's not its strongest, but it still glows brightly.

"Impressive. I was sure you'd be powerless by now. Perhaps I've underestimated you."

"Hello, Dinesh. Can I help you with something?"

"Yes, you can. Stop being a dick and spend some time with Blaise before I set your pants on fire. I can still wield my flames I'll have you know."

I sigh and allow my magic to return to its resting state. The blue light falls away like ropes dropping to the floor. I turn to glare at Dinesh.

"She's the one who doesn't want to spend time with me," I bite out.

"That's not true. Gods, are you blind? She's playing the way she is because she misses your company. So she got a little testy. Don't punish her for it."

"I'm not punishing her for anything. I'm trying to give her space."

"Newsflash, she doesn't want space. She doesn't have time for space. Come on. Bach and I have set up a little rendezvous," he says and wiggles his brows.

I roll my eyes. I'm sure these little guys are up to something. However, my link pulses, causing me to miss Blaise. What could it hurt?

I stand and roll my neck. "Lead the way."

"Oh, no. You will not go dressed like that. Change your clothes, I'll wait," he says and folds his arms over his chest.

I look down at the loose-fitting pants and T-shirt I have on. It's not my usual attire, but there's nothing wrong with it. I wave Dinesh off and start out of the room, allowing my clothes to change to my leathers and tunic as I go.

"Ah, now that's much better. I believe Blaise likes you like this."

I snort and keep moving. He flies up ahead of me, causing me to follow after him. We move through the castle in silence, although I sense Dinesh has more he wants to say.

I think his words over. If Blaise hasn't wanted space, why hasn't she come to me? Her music has been filled with such sorrow, but could it be sorrow because she misses our time together?

I can't allow myself to let my guard down as I have in the past. My priority has to be getting back to my plane one way or the other. There will be nothing between Blaise and me.

I have that thought as we step into a large room. Blaise comes into view as I step through the door and my thoughts become muddled. She stands before a roaring fireplace that highlights her beauty. It's like she's one with the fixture.

The flames dance in time to the power that pulses from her. Almost as if her magic has a heartbeat. She's standing in a red dress. Her hair is pinned up, with sweeping bangs in the front.

"Beautiful, isn't she?" Dinesh says.

My link pulses as if to reach out for her. "Yes, she is," I reply.

"Looks like my job is done," he croons.

However, I'm already in motion toward Blaise. She looks down at the floor as I move closer. When I stop before her, she slowly lifts her head.

I cup the side of her face and run my thumb across her unscarred cheek. All thoughts of nothing being between us go out of the window.

"I'm sorry," she says softly.

"I'm not your enemy, Blaise. I want to be your friend, but I can't do that when you shut me out."

She draws her brows in and looks away. "Friends. Yes, friends, we should be friends." I don't miss the disappointment in her words. "I'm sorry about my behavior. I just... I—"

"Let's start over. It looks like this place has been set up for something fun. What did you have in mind?"

"We have these things. I can't remember what Father called them. They're moving, talking pictures. I forgot all about them. Father brought them back from the earth realm.

"Bach found them. I can make them work. I would like it if you would join me to watch them. It's been lonely without your company."

"Movies, you mean movies. I love those," I say with a smile.

"Movies," she whispers to herself. "Yes, I think that's it."

I take her hand and lead her over to the plush seating awaiting us. The moment I wrap her hand in mine, I can feel the magic pulsing through her. We take a seat, and she gives me a shy smile.

Blaise

He came, he really came. I didn't think he would. Not after... I'm so sorry for the way I behaved. I've missed him so much.

His smile, his laugh, the way his voice rumbles, I've even missed him in my dreams. He hasn't been in one since our fight.

Our fight, was it a fight? Either way, I'm so sorry. I've never been more lonely or sad. He has been so near and still so far.

He looks absolutely handsome as he sits beside me. I search the side of his face for a hint of anger but can't find any. I'm ashamed as he turns to look at me and smiles.

Why does he continue to be kind to me? I tell myself this is his strategy. He will befriend me to make his escape. These growing feelings I have are one-sided.

Be that as it may, when I'm with him, I'm happy. I've learned that I missed out on having friends in the past. As I think back, I'm not sure if I ever had real ones.

People were kind to me because they had to be. My real friends are the ones here with me—Ms. Posh, Dinesh, Bach, Soila and Hiasha. I think I took that for granted. Always looking for beauty and power and never true connections.

Yes, Argon is beautiful, but his heart is more gorgeous than anything. He's shown me more kindness and care than anyone ever has without being forced to.

"Tell me what's on your mind. I've missed your voice," he says.

"I don't understand why you're still nice to me."

"We both had things we didn't want to talk about that morning. Whatever it was that you didn't want to share with me made you upset. I was angry, but I think I understand," he replies.

"Thank you for understanding."

"You're welcome. What shall we watch?"

"The...movies?"

"Yes, movies."

"They come in themes like books. Pick a theme and I'll play one."

"Let's laugh. If you have anything with humor and action, I'm sold."

Using my magic, I produce a binder with humor and action movies. Bach said Father had them categorized. This makes it easier to find one to watch.

"This sounds good," Argon says, pointing to one.

I touch the title and bring the image up before us on a white backdrop. I smile, feeling quite pleased with myself. Ms. Posh and Bach float in with popcorn and drinks.

"Movie night," Argon says beside me. I turn to find him staring at the side of my face. "That's what they would call this."

"Oh."

I turn back to the movie and focus on it so I don't fall into his eyes. We sit quietly and watch. I like this. It's simple but fun.

The movie comes to an end, and I sigh. "I love their clothes," I whisper. "I still have glossy picture books of their clothes. I... sometimes I dress like them and put on shows for Soila and Hiasha."

"Fashion shows and magazines. The glossy picture books are magazines."

"You know a lot about their realm. I love their music too. It's just been so long since I've heard any."

"Have you never been to the earth realm?"

"No, father promised to take me, but he died before he got the chance."

"Sorry to hear that."

"I've never heard you speak of your mother. Is it okay if I ask about the queen?"

"It's fine. Mother passed on. It devastated everyone. It's just me and Father now."

"I'm sorry. I never knew my mother. She died when I was still a baby."

He nods and works his jaw. I feel bad for bringing up his mother. I think quickly before he asks to end the night. I don't want him to go.

"Shall we watch another?" we say at the same time.

We both laugh; I nod and use my magic to place the binder in his lap again. He lifts it and puts it in mine.

"No, you pick this time."

"Oh, in that case."

I wave a hand and switch the binder out for the romantic comedies. Dinesh suggested I start out with one of these. However, Argon is my guest, so I gave the choice to him.

I find one that pulls my interest and start it. I find myself smiling halfway through. This night is perfect.

CHAPTER EIGHTEEN

Recharge

Blaise

I had so much fun during our movie night I decided to do something fun for Argon today. Something to allow us to spend more time together. I know from looking into my orbs that he has been meditating to hold on to his magic.

I want to give him a chance to recharge. I didn't trust him enough before to share this with him, but I don't think he'll try to escape like before. The last thing I want is for him to lose his magic.

That is my greatest fear. To lose my powers and never be able to use magic again. I wouldn't wish that on anyone.

"Blaise," Argon calls as he walks up behind me. I turn to him and smile. Dinesh and Bach are flying on each side of him.

"These guys told me I'd find you out here. Is it okay for you to be this far out from the castle?"

"Yes, it's fine," I say and grab his hand. "I want to show you something."

I take him past where the fire wall enchantment is. Here my power is still strong. However, this is also where his will begin to reawaken and recharge.

"Do you feel that?"

He looks down at me with wide eyes. I watch as he lifts his hand and his magic sparks to life. His eyes glow a bright blue like the magic circling his hand.

"But how?" he breathes.

"Your magic will always begin to recharge once you get to this point. I thought you would like to stretch it and use it for a bit."

"Why would you tell me this? Aren't you afraid I will try to take advantage?"

"No, you are my friend. Friends trust friends. Now, would you like to train with real magic, or should we go back inside where I need to loan you mine?"

A slow grin comes to his face. He holds a hand up and a bow appears. He lifts a brow. "Feeling like some archery?"

"I thought you'd never ask."

I flick my wrist and targets appear before us in the distance. Argon allows a blue ray of light to form in his empty hand. Pulling the bow tight, he releases the bolt of light.

It hits the target smack in the center. The sound of impact is deafening. So much so, I cover my ears.

"See, your strength has returned," I say with a smile.

"Not quite, my friend, not quite," he says with a wide smile of his own.

"That's not your full strength?"

He winks. "No, give me a bit. I will show you my full power."

I smile and conjure my own bow. My hand lights with purple-and-gold light as my arrow forms. As I load the arrow, the tip lights with a flame.

I release and the colors change while the arrow of magic flies through the air. My shot, too, has a thunderous sound as it splits through the center of Argon's and impales the target.

"I expected nothing less," he says and chuckles.

Without a word, he takes another shot. This time it goes through the center of my arrow, but that's not all. The force of it vibrates back to us and thunder fills the sky above.

"Now I'm starting to feel more like myself," he croons.

"Did you just…"

"I owe the man an apology," Dinesh says out of nowhere. "I don't know what's sexier. The fact that he has that kind of power or that he's actually getting close to matching hers."

I want to say both, but I'm stunned into silence. I felt he was powerful when he first arrived, but this is much more than what I felt.

Suddenly, pillar-like beams of light slam into the ground, one by one, surrounding us all. I go on guard; surely Argon hasn't decided to betray me. I'm so angry with myself.

However, as I focus, he stands before me protectively. His back is to me as a sword rests within his palm. I give a quick scan for danger.

"Stay back," Argon demands as I go to step around him.

It's then I see them. While shooting arrows, I hadn't been paying attention. Two wolves creep from the woods, snarling as their focus is locked on us.

They must have sensed us using magic. It's unusual for them to come this close. I release a roar and they fly back, flipping through the air before landing on their paws and turning to run back the way they came.

"Lady Blaise, are you all right?" Bach asks.

"Yes, I'm fine. Thank you, Argon."

He turns to me and brushes a finger over my cheek. "No, thank you. I think I've stretched my powers enough for one day. Let's go back inside where you are safe."

I scoff. "I'm safe anywhere I am."

"Yes, but I like knowing you don't need to have your guard up. Let's have a game night or watch a movie."

I look up at him through my lashes. "I'd like that."

Argon

It felt good to use my magic. I'm grateful to Blaise for her trust. However, something didn't feel right about those wolves or the woods they came from. They were surrounded by dark magic, no matter how faint.

I've been analyzing what I felt for hours now. If it wouldn't risk Blaise's trust in me, I'd go out there to investigate for myself.

"I'm sure she would have felt someone else enter her realm. Stop overthinking," I bite out to myself.

I pace my room, deep in thought, not able to shake this feeling. My power is still heightened. I reach out to feel for Blaise, just to check on her.

The moment I find her, a sharp pain runs through my chest. It's my link. It opens wider as if reaching for Blaise itself.

Earlier, when I felt she was in danger, I was almost certain my spirit reflection would fully manifest. In this moment, I'm not sure it won't.

Not wanting my spirit reflection to surface or fully open without knowing what this means for Blaise and me, I stumble over to my bed.

"For now, I need to rest this off. There has to be an explanation."

CHAPTER NINETEEN

Perfect

Argon

I look in the mirror at the black suit and blue ascot I have on. My eyes look brighter than they had. A smile comes to my lips. Blaise sent a magazine to me and asked that I dress up like this for tonight.

I still don't know what we're doing this evening. However, I did feel the excitement coming off of Blaise throughout the day. I use my magic to braid back the front of my hair on each side and leave the rest in long waves down my back and around my shoulders.

"This is good," Dinesh says.

"Very good," Bach adds.

"Hmm," I grunt and nod. "Is she ready?"

"Yes, we will lead you to her," Dinesh offers.

We all start out of the room. I pull at my cuffs to straighten them. I wave my fingers before me, then place my hand behind my back as we reach the double doors.

They open and I step through to the large ballroom. The first things to grab my attention are the gold music notes floating through the air like bubbles. They are floating in time to the music.

"Come, come, we must get you in place," Bach says as I stand frozen, taking the ballroom in.

I follow him to the ornate illuminated crest in the center of the floor, right below a winding double staircase. As I step into the center of the crest, Dinesh gasps while looking up toward the top of the stairs.

I turn to follow his gaze. There she is. Blaise stands at the top of the stairs in a blue-and-gold gown. The corseted top lifts and displays her supple breasts. Her hair is in huge, cascading curls around her face and bare shoulders.

My breath is taken away. I can't pull my gaze from her as she walks down the stairs. It's like she's floating to me. I stand with my hands behind my back, clasping the magical rose I created between my fingertips.

"You look handsome," she breathes once she stops before me and looks up into my eyes.

"You're beautiful."

"I look a mess. This was a dumb idea."

"You're perfect," I murmur under my breath before I can stop myself. I bring my hand from behind my back and hand her the glowing blue rose.

Her eyes soften as she takes it from me and brings it to her nose. "It smells of you," she says in surprise.

I wink at her and smile. My mind goes back to when she said she loves the music from the earth realm. I once heard a song from there that describes this very moment. I know I'll probably use up most of the power I've restored, but this is worth it.

I take over the music and play the song I'm thinking of. If I remember right, it's called "Perfect," the version I remember had a male and female vocalist. The male was pale like me, and the woman was brown. Not a deep brown like Blaise, but brown still.

"Will you dance with me?" I say, holding out my hand.

"Yes."

I take her hand and wrap my other arm around her waist. We begin to spin around the room as I turn the floor beneath us into a grassy plane. The gold music notes continue to float around us.

However, I add my magic to hers and create blue notes for the parts when the male singer sings as hers follows the female vocalist's words. Our magic is in perfect sync.

My link tugs, but I don't fight it this time. It sets in that I haven't been fighting it because of my betrothed back home. I've been fighting more out of uncertainty.

I let go and stare down into Blaise's eyes as I spin her around the room. Placing her hand against my chest, I cover it with mine. She leans her head against my chest carefully.

It's a subtle reminder of her horns. A reminder that they don't matter at all in this moment. Blaise is sweet and caring.

She's beautiful on the inside and out. I look up and watch our magic dance together. It's all perfect. The perfect match.

Blaise

Tears burn the backs of my eyes. It's happened. I've fallen in love.

I try not to get lost in the words of the song, telling myself this isn't him speaking to me. I'm filled with emotions and confusion.

Pulling away from him, I look up into his eyes. He looks back at me, searching my face. I have so much I want to say, but none of it is right.

He leans in, pressing his nose and forehead to mine. My chest starts to ache. It's not the type of pain he has to save me from. It's more like a caressing ache. A stir to bring something to life.

"I want to show you something," I say to save myself from the moment.

I take his hand and lead him up the stairs I came down. He laughs as I rush up the stairs, holding my gown in one hand and his palm in the other.

I squeeze my tail around my waist beneath my dress in anticipation. I've been excited about this all day. Hiasha gave me this idea. I lead Argon over to the large window.

As we stand before it, the fireworks show begins. I can't stop smiling. It's so beautiful. I look at Argon and he has a smile on his face as well. He moves to stand behind me and wraps his arms around my waist.

I blush and my heart races. He gives me a gentle squeeze and I relax into his hold. This is perfect. I close my eyes and wish this could be more.

"Thank you, Blaise. This has been most enjoyable. You've taken my mind off so much. Thank you."

"That's what friends are for, right?"

"You have become one of my best friends," he breathes.

I close my eyes as the pain sears through me. While I've fallen in love, I'm only a friend to him. I knew it would be this way, but a part of me had held on to hope.

That hope bursts along with the fireworks outside. To love and not be loved—is it not better to not love at all? I don't know if I can say it is.

CHAPTER TWENTY

Music Notes

Argon

It's been another long day. They seem to be longer here. I've lost track of how many days it has been since I've been here.

Days and nights, like the other night, make them all seem like one amazing day. However, I believe a few weeks, maybe even months, have passed. I've grown more restless with each night. My mind wars with my feelings and my spirit link.

I've avoided reading before bed since my last encounter after reading to Blaise, but tonight my mind has too much going on to sleep. I decide to try reading again. However, I steer clear of the romance novels.

I don't know how the humans used to read those. The vivid imagery and drawing of emotions can be taxing. I shake my head as I think of the draw it had on me.

I decide on a book about mystical musical theories. Thinking of our ballroom date, the topic brings a smile to my face. It should be safe enough to help me fall asleep.

Although, I do think about a certain cellist a few times as I turn the pages. Blaise has something about her that draws you in. I'm more intrigued with her the more time I spend with her.

It's something beyond the blushing flames of her cheeks and her watchful glances. She has a playful personality. I've found her heart to be kind, which has surprised me. Her musical laugh is something I enjoy pulling from her.

"Argh," I groan as I start to think about her again. I force myself to focus on the pages before me.

The passage I'm reading talks about music rooms and how artists can draw from their surroundings to perform. Everything from the acoustics to the vibe of the room affects the artist.

Suddenly, my vision blurs. "Oh no," I breathe.

It happens so quickly this time. I stand in the middle of Blaise's bedroom, where she plays her cello. I have no clothes on, it's the way I'd gone to bed tonight.

Blaise sits in the chair in a silky black robe. Her hair is pulled up on top of her head, exposing her neck. I focus on her and note a few things.

Her form is that of a woman again. Her small feet are planted on the floor, encased in red heels as she plays. Her long black nails are not as long or sharp looking.

Candles are lit around the room, providing a romantic ambience. The music she's playing isn't the sorrowful song she's played before. It's majestic and romantic, much like the setting around her.

She's playing with such passion. Each note caresses my skin and ears. I've never heard a musician play the way she does. She breathes life into the song.

Moving closer, I want to see her face. I have to see if it's covered again. This time, I want to be able to kiss her lips.

I stop behind the chair she sits in and place a hand on her shoulder once she stops playing. Cupping beneath her chin with my other hand, I tip her head back. A smile comes to my lips when the face I've become accustomed to comes into view.

Wordlessly, I slide my hand from her shoulder down into the opening of her robe to cup her breast. Her lips part and a moan leave them as I pinch her tightened peak.

"Argon." My name falls from her lips.

I think of her essence on my tongue in the other hallucinations. I want to taste her again. As I have the thought, the cello vanishes. She then stands and turns to me.

I push the chair out of the way and place a hand on her waist to bring her closer to me. Reaching for the tie of her robe, I tug it free. Slipping my hands into the silky fabric, I watch her eyes for a sign of protest.

She looks back at me shyly but offers a nod. I push the fabric from her shoulders, and it floats to the floor. Her gorgeous skin is revealed to me, causing me to salivate for a taste.

Blaise reaches to touch my chest. "You're a beautiful man."

I place my fingers under her chin and tip her head back. I brush her lower lip with my thumb. My gaze drops to the scar beneath her lip. I draw my finger across it and her lips part.

"You're a beautiful creature, Blaise." I lift my eyes to hers. "Inside and out. You're very beautiful."

Her cheeks heat and those flames under her skin show. I lean in and kiss one cheek, feeling its warmth on my lips. I smile. So many things about her intrigue me.

I place more gentle kisses across her skin until I reach her lips. Taking the plush pillows in a passionate kiss, I savor the flavor of her mouth. Blaise wraps her arms around my neck. I bring her into my body.

Her full breasts mold against my chest. She fits me perfectly. She releases a cross between a sigh and a moan. I groan in return and deepen the connection.

I allow my palms to glide down her smooth skin and grasp the globes of her round ass. Blaise whimpers. The sound drives me wild for her.

"Tell me you're mine. Mine to take," I breathe against her lips.

I want her so badly, but it's my realm's custom to have consent before claiming a woman. She has to offer herself to me. I search her eyes, waiting and needing her to give herself over as my cock throbs in pain.

"I am yours."

Her words are spoken forth softly, but they carry a power that blows around us like a forceful wind. The room shakes with it and my hair lifts in the gust of wind. My spirit link bursts open completely. My eyes widen as my spirit reflection reveals itself.

Blaise turns to see what I'm staring at, then yelps and jumps into my arms. I chuckle and hold her close. Dipping my head into the crook of her neck, I nuzzle her soft skin.

"Have you never seen a dragon before?"

Granted, my spirit dragon is huge. Half of his body is outside on the balcony, while the rest of his massive body spans the space in the room. His black iridescent scales reflect the blue glow that surrounds him.

She turns back to me slowly. Her eyes are wide and her lips are parted. I give another chuckle.

"Where'd that come from? What... we don't have dragons here."

"It is my spirit reflection. You have unlocked it." I look deeply into her eyes. Her reflection should have come forward as well.

I shake the thought away. This is just a hallucination. However, I see my match in her eyes. Perhaps it's the illusion that prevents her reflection from joining mine.

"Spirit reflection?" She repeats. "I've never done this before. I had no idea a dragon was involved." She knits her brows and looks away shyly. "I've said too much."

My spirit dragon snorts and licks its lips in anticipation. He tilts his head and studies Blaise. He, too, can sense our soul match on the inside of her.

"Dragons aren't always involved," I explain, trying to keep the humor out of my voice. "Where I'm from, our spirit reflection forms according to our power. It's like our spirit animal. Mine happens to be a dragon."

"Oh."

"Come, he would never hurt you."

I take her hand in mine and lead her over to my dragon. He lowers his head as if bowing. I smile as Blaise turns to me and then looks back at him.

The awe on her face makes her so much more beautiful. Again, I note the innocence I've sensed from her. When she reaches out to rub the dragon, she pauses and looks over her shoulder at me.

I brush my fingertips against her cheek as I grin. She gives a little smile. I cover her hand with mine and press our joined hands to my spirit dragon's scales.

She giggles as he snorts and licks her shoulder. I frown at him. His mate is on the inside of Blaise; this part of her is all mine.

He looks me in the eyes, knowing my thoughts. He huffs and turns away. A tingle rises in my spine. It's my spirit dragon urging me to take her.

"Take her. Free my mate." My frown deepens. While I want to release her spirit reflection, I'm not entirely sure claiming her will release it. *"I don't care. Try."*

The need to try consumes me. I press my front to her back, allowing my cock to throb against her plump backside. Reaching around her with my free hand, I palm her pussy. She links the fingers of our hands against my spirit dragon.

"I will show you pleasure, Blaise. Pleasure like you've never known," I say and kiss her shoulder.

She moans, pulling our joined hands from my dragon, then parts her legs for me. I swiftly take the invitation. Sliding my fingers over her folds, I find them slick.

"Argon," she cries. It's a plea I won't deny.

I push my fingers into her and work to bring her to climax. With our hands still laced together, I wrap my arm across her breasts. Her palm covers her heavy mound and I cause her to knead her own flesh.

Her temperature heats as I bring her closer to her peak. Her cries get louder by the second. I lick her shoulder and savor her sweet flavor on my tongue.

She comes so hard; she collapses within my embrace. I smile and lift her into my arms. My dragon dips his head for me to step onto his snout. With Blaise in my arms, I stand firm as he backs out of the room onto the balcony.

Once outside, he places us both on his back. I settle Blaise gently as I take her lips to kiss her. My spirit dragon takes off and bursts into the air.

Blaise gasps into my mouth. I break the kiss and smile down at her. Brushing a lock of windblown hair from her face, I peck her nose.

As powerful as I know her to be, it warms my heart to see her give over so much trust and control to me. Blaise could probably slay us both and land on her feet. However, the trust in her gaze says a million words.

"He's a part of me. We are safe on his back. We are bound to each other. We won't fall off unless he allows it," I explain.

"What if he decides to allow it?"

"Then he has a reason, and he will catch us. You're precious to him. He won't let harm come to you."

With that, I kiss her again. This time she holds me close and wraps her legs around me, allowing her heels to dig into my ass as her heat burns into me.

"Do it," my spirit dragon commands.

I bite down on Blaise's lip as I enter her. For the first time in I don't know how long, I feel the absolute full force of my powers coursing through me. Blaise cries out and locks her legs tighter around me.

Her plush body receives me as if we're old friends. Her tight pussy sucks me in deep. I groan and roll my eyes in my head.

"Argon, oh gods, Argon," she pants.

I haven't even started. She feels so good. I have to find my sanity to please us both before I pound into her and lose myself inside her warmth.

I lift to my knees and grasp her calves. Pushing her legs into her body and spreading them wide, I drive in and out of her warm, wet pussy. I lock eyes with her and find the fire that burns within hers.

"Come for me."

She licks her lips and nods. It only takes a second before her juices gush around me. I pull out and lower to my belly for a taste. Her screams are more than satisfying.

Yet my dragon is getting pissed. Her spirit reflection hasn't been released. I can sense his determination as he shifts in the air and starts to fly upward.

I ignore him and continue to devour her sweet pussy. I drink her up and shove two fingers inside her to bring her to another climax. In awe, I place a hand over her pounding heart and grin.

"Let go, sweetheart. Come for me, my Blaise."

Blaise

I don't know if it's his words, the feel of him eating my pussy, or flying up through the sky that has my body obeying his command, but I come and I come hard. He grunts into my core and lifts to thrust back into me.

His large, thick length stretches me until I want to cross my eyes and scream. My heart is beating so fast. There's a pulling on the inside of me, but I hold on to it, not sure I should release whatever it is clawing at me.

"Blaise, give it to me," Argon demands.

It's as if he knows I'm holding back something from him. He lifts a leg, planting his heel on his dragon's back. Again, he pins my legs back by my calves. His fingers flex against my skin as he dives into my heat.

It feels so good. I cry out as I lose my grip on my restraint. It's like he's splitting me in two. I grab his wrists and double down on the hold I have on controlling myself.

I look down at the connection between us and it's so sexy. His pale flesh continues to move in and out of me while my brown skin invites him in. He's thrusting down into my body with strokes of possession. The more he thrusts, the more I want him.

I lift my gaze to his and find those blue-gray eyes fixed on my face. I blush, but I don't turn away. There's something in his eyes that arrests me.

"Oh gods, please," I beg.

"Let go for me. Stop holding back."

I can't let go. It feels too strange. However, I do come again.

The dragon releases a loud roar. It vibrates through his body and shakes us. Without warning, he dives for the ground below, spiraling as he goes.

Argon is unfazed. He cups my throat and squeezes as his eyes stay on mine. My body won't stop convulsing. I'm coming rapidly and repeatedly as he continues to plow into me.

I can't hold on anymore. Between the rapid plummet to the ground, the choke hold on my neck, and the feel of Argon's massive shaft inside me, I lose the hold I have on whatever is pulling from me.

As I feel like I'm leaving my body, I climax one long, hard final time. Argon leans over my body and kisses me hard. His dragon roars again as if in triumph.

Argon releases inside me as I wrap around his body and hold him close. It's not until he begins to swell inside me again that I realize we're floating through the air.

We're no longer on his dragon's back. We're just free-falling as he kisses me with so much passion my toes curl. I claw at his back as a mix of ecstasy and panic takes hold of me.

He breaks the kiss. I look at him wildly. "Trust him."

Argon

I see the alarm in her eyes, but there's no need for it. I groan as her nails dig into my flesh. Grabbing two handfuls of her ass, I slowly guide her up and down my shaft.

I know my spirit reflection won't allow us to hit the ground. He's just greeting his soul match. Blaise still doesn't understand what she has just released.

My heart aches as I begin to think of the illusion this all is. Wanting to feel this forever, I turn our bodies, so our feet face the land coming up beneath us. I bring her down harder onto my shaft.

She throws her head back and releases a loud cry into the air. We come together this time. As our bodies are overcome with our release, my spirit dragon swoops in and catches us.

I kiss Blaise's forehead. "See. I told you. Trust," I say before I pass out along with the beauty in my arms.

CHAPTER TWENTY-ONE

Awe and Lust

Argon

I look at the scratches on my back in the mirror. That wasn't a dream or hallucination last night. It was very real.

I don't know how to feel about that. I don't understand how this is happening. I shake my head to clear it.

The passion between us was enough to set its own fire. I can still feel the tingling in my spine and the fire in my chest. I've never experienced anything like it. But it was with a woman that's not a woman in my waking hours.

I smile as I think of Blaise during our walks and dates. She does tend to trip over her hooves as if her feet would turn in if they weren't hooves. Pigeon toed, that's what I've read humans once called it.

It's odd because she's so graceful in battle. We've sparred together a few times. She's a fierce warrior. No, she's not always clumsy at all. It's more like she trips herself up when she's nervous or excited. It can be quite adorable and endearing.

"Well, damn. What happened to you?"

"Hello, Dinesh," I say without turning.

I'm becoming used to him and his antics. It's quite amusing at times. I cover myself and pull my hair back in a tie.

"Blaise has requested to see you. Wait, what happened to your back?"

I turn to face him. "It's nothing. Is she all right?"

He eyes me warily for a moment. I get that he's very protective of Blaise. All of her little friends are.

Still, I grow impatient waiting for his reply. "The princess means the world to me. Don't you hurt her," he says tightly.

Princess? I don't point out his slip. Although it brings to mind the near slips my first day here. Lady Blaise is a princess.

I get the feeling there are so many other secrets I want to find out about her. I itch to gain all the knowledge I can. My spirit roars to know what I'm missing about my soul match.

"I would never hurt her. I could never."

"Um, sure." He rolls his eyes at me. "Let's go. I think this is important."

He doesn't have to say another word. The thought of something being wrong with Blaise has my feet in motion. I try to will my way to her, but my power is nowhere near as strong as it was last night.

Frustrated, I pick up the pace. Our spirit link requires I be near her as soon as possible. Although, I still question everything—including my feelings for a half woman, half beast. I have no doubt that she has become my soul match.

Father and the elders are not going to like this.

Blaise

I stare at the rose beneath the glass and let another tear roll down my cheek. Two more petals fall and turn to ashes before they can even hit the surface beneath them. Time is running out.

These dreams are confusing me. They are full of passion and lust, but those are not love. Not to mention, they're dreams.

I need Argon to fall in love with me in real life. Not in my fantasies. I need him as more than a friend. And now, I will never have that chance.

"Blaise," he says as he moves to stand behind me. I close my eyes as he places a hand on my waist. My skin heats and tingles run up my side. "What is it?"

I'm too choked up to say a word. I conjure a sphere to appear beside us. When the image in the orb appears, I feel him stiffen.

His hand falls away from my waist and he steps toward the orb. I turn to watch him as he watches the image. His father lies in a bed, looking ill.

His skin is pale, and his body is thin. He looks worse than when he was here. I have so much sorrow as I take in the image for myself.

"Argon," his father says weakly. "You must find my son."

Argon turns his head away from the orb. His head is bowed and his body is full of tension. I lift a hand to reach out to him but drop it.

"I had only wanted to surprise you with a view of your home. When I summoned the image for myself, I found this. I swear to you, this isn't my doing. He should have been well upon returning to your home."

Argon vibrates with silent rage. His hands spark with magic at his fingertips. Not as bright as the day he arrived or when I allowed him to recharge.

His magic has become too dormant for that. I drop my head in shame. I know this wasn't from my magic or the castles, but if I didn't keep Argon here, he would be home to protect his father, to care for him.

"I'm releasing you," I murmur. "You can go and help him. Your blood still holds my venom. I can sense it. It's enough to heal him. He just needs a few drops from you."

Argon spins to face me. I'm thrown by the indecision I see in his eyes. A war plays across his face.

"I—He's unwell. I must go."

"I know. That's why I'm releasing you. Your powers will restore themselves once you're away from here. It will strengthen my venom in your blood. That will help."

"Blaise…" He pauses and looks away from me.

I give him a wobbly smile. "It's fine. I just ask that you leave at nightfall. It's the safest time for me to send you through. I will open the portal for you. My chariot will get you there safely."

He nods and swallows. "I will go to see to my father's health and then I will return to serve my time."

"No, you don't have to. Don't make promises you won't keep. You have people who count on you. You will be king someday, just as you told me."

"Blaise—"

"I've enjoyed your company. You will never know what your friendship has meant."

"Blaise, I'm a man of my word. I will return."

"It will be too late, Argon. I don't want you to return. I won't be here. Not like this." I choke off a sob. "The one you've grown to know will no longer exist."

"What does that mean?"

"Nothing, nothing at all," I reply and turn to leave.

"Blaise, Blaise," his voice thunders after me, but I can't stand to look at him a second longer.

That dream last night changed something for me. I'm in love with Argon and I will ache to the depths of my soul when he leaves me. I have learned to love, but I have failed to gain his love in return.

When the sound of his heavy footfalls begins to follow after me, I phase to the roof of the castle. I sit perched on top of my home as he bellows through the halls in search of me. It's better this way.

CHAPTER TWENTY-TWO

Don't Forget Me

Argon

I've been trying to will myself into one of those hallucinations. I haven't seen Blaise since she ran from me or, should I say, vanished on me. I need to see her.

I pick up a book from my side table. If I can't will the vision to happen on my own, I'll try the way it's been happening. My anger grows as I go through several chapters, and nothing happens.

I get ready to snap the book shut and set it on fire when my vision finally begins to blur. In the blink of an eye, I'm standing before Blaise. She has her back to me as she looks over the balcony into the dark night.

"You can leave. The chariot awaits you at the front of the castle," she says softly.

"Why have you hidden from me?"

"It's better this way."

I wrap my arms around her waist and my spirit reflection roars for her. I calm him by burying my face into her hair. It has been returned to its wild curls from the first time I saw her.

"Better for who? I didn't want to leave without saying goodbye."

"You have said it. Now you should go."

I brush her hair from her neck and dip to kiss her soft skin. "I have yet to say goodbye," I murmur against her flesh and palm her breasts.

"Argon," she says breathlessly.

"I love the way you say my name." She shivers. "I shall return, Blaise. I will keep my word."

I turn her face to me to cover her lips before she can protest. Deepening the kiss, I knead her full breasts. I ache to have her once more and my spirit link demands I do so.

She combs her hands into my hair as I savor her sweet mouth. I growl when she bites at my lip. A smile comes to her lips, but I can feel that it's a small, cautious one.

"I will remember this always," she says softly.

"Then I will make it a memory never to be forgotten."

I tear the back of her corset open and fling it over the balcony. Her pants are the next thing I tear free and discard. The little panties on her full ass cause my cock to swell.

I lift her into my arms and carry her to the large bed inside. I gently place her in the center of the bed and begin to descend her body. I don't want to rush this.

Lifting her foot to my mouth, I kiss her cute toes. Her cheeks glow and she looks away. Stroking my fingertips lightly up her calf brings her attention back to me.

"You are beautiful, Blaise. In this world and in the one we wake in. Don't be ashamed to allow me to worship that beauty," I murmur against the pad of her foot.

"Would you so easily kiss a hoof?"

"If it belongs to you. I think I would," I admit to my own surprise.

"Again, promises you would never keep."

I move quickly to take her lips and kiss her deeply. She gasps into my mouth. I reach for her panties and tear them from her body.

She shoves her hands in my hair and tugs hard. I groan as I make love to her mouth. I show her that I'm a man of my word as I reach for her folds and begin to make this a night she'll never forget.

"Relax, Blaise. I'm here to pleasure you," I whisper in her ear.

I plant kisses from her chin down her neck. I latch on to her silky skin and suck it into my mouth. My spirit link demands I mark her as mine.

I smile when I pull away and her skin bares my mark. I move to her shoulder and flick my tongue out against her flesh. I drag it down across her delicious skin to her breast.

"You taste so fucking good. Like you were made for me."

Blaise wiggles beneath me. Her pussy is so wet it soaks my fingertips. I can smell her arousal. It makes my mouth water.

"My Blaise," I murmur against her nipple, then draw it into my mouth.

She bows her back off the bed. I look up into her eyes through my lashes. The questions I see in her eyes tear at my spirit link. I don't like her doubting me.

"You're mine, Blaise."

Blaise

There are no words to explain how much I want this dream to be real. When he looks at me, I feel cared for and cherished. The way he makes my body feel makes something inside me swell.

No matter what I look like inside these dreams, he speaks to me as if it doesn't matter. Beauty or beast, he cares for me. In these dreams he makes me feel like anything is possible.

"Argon," I whisper as he calls me his.

I want to be his. I want to give all of myself to him. His nails bite into my skin as he drags them down my side.

"Do you feel that, Blaise? That's our bond. I'll forever be with you," he murmurs against my belly.

Dream Argon has all the right things to say. I allow myself to latch on to his words in this world. It's better than listening to the part of me that says I'm about to lose him.

I cry out when he settles between my legs and starts to feast on me the way only he can. I grab the sheets and rock my hips against his face. This time, something is different.

The possessiveness is still there, but there's something more. I don't dig too deeply. I'm already emotionally overwhelmed.

Which is evident in my lack of control over my powers. The bed is surrounded by flames. Still, Argon continues to push deeper and sip at my essence more. When I gush all over his face, he laps it up then turns onto his back.

"Come to me," he commands.

I sit up and crawl over to him. He guides me to straddle his hips and lowers me onto his length. With his gaze, he gives me a silent command to ride him.

I start to lift up and down on him, finding a comfortable rhythm. He's stretching me so much more this way. I circle my hips to relieve the ache within and moan loudly.

The movement brings more pleasure than I expected. I repeat the motion again and again while I bounce more vigorously in between. He lifts and latches on to my breast, sucking at my flesh and overloading my senses.

Argon's nostrils flare as he releases my skin from his mouth and licks his lips. When he starts to thrust into me from beneath me, I lose my mind and toss my head back. He begins to pull me down to meet his thrusts.

"Argon, yes, oh yes."

With lightning speed, he flips me onto my back and kisses me hard. When he breaks the kiss, he goes down on me again. Stars burst behind my lids as I come.

He climbs back up my body, dropping kisses on his way. I cup his face as he kisses me. The taste of vanilla and apples is on his lips. I moan as the flavor bursts on my tongue.

"Blaise," he breathes as he lifts my right leg over his arm and slides into me. "You feel what you do to me?"

I brush his hair behind his ear and look into his eyes. He's so perfect. I wish this was another life. A life where I could remember who I am and where I'm from.

However, his eyes tell me none of that matters to him. I push my head back into the pillows and have to look away from the intensity of his gaze. I watch the flames that surround us.

They burn hot, but not as hot as his passion for me. Sweat drips down his back as I run my hands along his skin. His hard muscles flex as he moves in and out of me.

I can feel my own sweat gathering as the heat increases. Argon dips his head and licks a path across my scar, causing me to turn back to him. Tears build in my eyes.

"I want you the way you are," he says softly. "I want you any way I can have you."

I gasp and cling to his back tighter. Tears roll back into my ears. The flames roar around us and Argon smiles down at me.

Seconds later, the sound of crackling ice fills the room. I turn to find he has iced over my flames. The bed is encased by walls of ice. His hot body keeps me warm in spite of it. I look back at him. He kisses me senseless.

"You're my other half. The yin to my yang. The fire to my ice. The noise to my silence. You are mine, Blaise."

"I belong to you," I whimper.

A loud roar fills the room and the ice scatters around us. It falls around us in tiny sparks of blue light, kind of like snowflakes. Argon's blue-gray eyes glow as he stares down at me, but his lips haven't moved. My gaze darts around for the dragon from last time.

I chide myself for thinking that this dream would be the same. Argon dips his head to latch on to my breast as he picks up the pace. I bite my lip and my eyes roll.

My entire body quivers as I come for him. It's so intense my head spins. He spills inside me and I smile in sated bliss.

Argon

"I love these dreams," she whispers before she blacks out.

I smile and shake my head. She believes these are dreams. If only she understood what my real feelings are for her. I resolve this isn't the time to wake her and tell her.

I have to tear myself away from watching her sleep. I brush my lips across hers and she stirs. I would love nothing more than to bury myself in my soul match once more, but I have to return home to help my father.

My spirit link pulls as I climb from the bed and dress myself with the wave of my hand. Not able to help myself, I lean over the bed and peck her forehead and then her lips one last time.

"I'll be back," I whisper the promise.

CHAPTER TWENTY-THREE

Healing Father

Argon

I step out of the chariot and stand before the portal that Blaise has opened for me. I hesitate to walk through as our link tugs at me. Closing my eyes, I inhale deeply.

"It won't remain open for long," Dinesh says as he flies to my side. "It will close with the rising of the suns."

"I will return."

I don't know if I'm saying the words for him or for myself. I clench my fist at my side. I need to tend to my father. However, I get the feeling as if I'm leaving something unfinished here.

"I know. The problem is. You may be too late."

I turn to him and narrow my eyes. "Too late. She has said this same thing. What aren't you both telling me?"

Dinesh shakes his head. His eyes close as a look of sorrow covers his face. My stomach sinks.

"It isn't my story to tell." He opens his eyes and reaches into his little pocket. "I have a gift for you. No one comes through to this realm more than once without a key. Blaise will have my ass if she finds out I gave you this.

"Be quick to handle your business and return. This will guide you back," he says and holds out a timepiece. It's a clock pendant hanging from a chain. "Bach said to use it wisely."

I take the watch and nod. When I place it around my neck, it levitates away from my chest as it increases in size. It glows with a yellow beam of light before settling and dimming until the light is no more.

"I will see you soon, my friend."

"Don't fail her," Dinesh says harshly.

"I don't intend to."

His features soften. "See you soon, my friend."

Knowing my father needs my help, I force myself through the portal. I step through, right into my father's bedchamber. I find him in his bed, just as the image in the orb revealed.

"Argon," my betrothed cries from my father's bedside.

She stands and rushes to me. The moment she wraps her arms around my waist, I notice how much weaker she is than I am, than my true soul match. How could the oracles get it so wrong?

"Coralo." I free myself of her hold and take a step back. My link pulses angrily from her touch. I, too, don't feel right with her arms around me.

"Are you okay?"

"I'm fine. It's my father who I'm concerned with." I begin to move toward his bed.

Coralo rushes to stand before me, blocking my path. I look at her and narrow my eyes. She licks her lips nervously before pushing a smile onto her face.

"It's been so long. I was so worried. I didn't know if you would return. We were worried that you had fallen to the same fate as your father.

"Now that you're back, you can prepare to take the throne. We should move the wedding up. It will put the people at ease during this difficult time," she says.

I push her aside. I have no concerns about a wedding or taking the throne. My father is still alive and I plan to keep it that way.

"You speak as if my father isn't alive."

"He has been very ill. We've tried everything. This monster he speaks of. We must punish her for her crimes."

I spin on my heels and storm back toward Coralo. She takes a few steps back from me. My fists are clenched, and I can feel the rage coursing through me. No one will touch my Blaise.

"You know nothing of what you speak. I will care for my father. You can go," I seethe.

"Your father said she imprisoned him, and you offered to take his place. He said she was awful. A disgusting beast. How can you not want to get justice for him?"

"Leave," I say through clenched teeth.

She jumps as my voice vibrates the room. My powers have gained much strength already. Coralo looks at me in surprise. After blinking a few times, she nods and scurries off.

I turn to my father once again and rush to his side. He looks so pale and fragile. Brushing a hand over his head, I take note of the dark magic coming from his essence.

Blaise was many things, but dark she was not. I never once felt darkness in her or in the venom she passed to me. If that were the case, I'd feel the same source within.

"Son, Argon. Is that you?" my father says weakly.

"Yes, it's me, Father."

"Thank the gods you got away. Did she hurt you?"

I work my jaw. I hate that he sees Blaise as some monster. I ignore his question, not wanting to get into all of that.

"I thought you would be well by now, Father. What has happened?"

"It was that castle. It drained my power. I felt it as she placed me in that cell."

"Yes, the castle does bind our powers, but you should have been restored once you returned. You weren't there nearly as long as I was. My powers are already nearing their full strength."

"I don't know. I returned and tried to send you help, but no one would listen. I've grown weaker with each day. None of the healers or the potions have worked to heal me," he says hoarsely and in such a small voice.

"We will fix this and I will get to the bottom of this treachery."

I summon a blade to my right hand and prick my finger with it. Causing the blade to vanish, a cup appears in its place. Placing a few drops of my blood into some wine, I watch as my blood turns the liquid clear.

"Here, drink this," I say as I take the chair beside his bed and reach for his head to hold it up.

As he drinks from the cup, the color comes back to his cheeks. His face starts to look fuller and his hair gains some shine. I smile and say a silent thanks to Blaise.

If she were truly evil, she wouldn't have released me or given me the key to help my father. My smile falls as I realize she wouldn't have had to help me if someone hadn't tried to poison the king.

"What was this?" my father inquires after draining the cup.

His voice is steady and strong. He sits up and tosses the covers aside. He throws his legs over the side of the bed and stands to his feet.

"Blaise's venom is in my blood from an injury she healed. It allowed me to heal you."

"That beast saved you and then me?"

"She isn't a beast. Never mind that. Someone has been poisoning you. You should have healed upon arriving home. Who has been caring for you?"

"Coralo and her handmaiden. Her mother has been working the potions," he replies.

"With dark magic?" I lift a brow.

He folds his arms over his chest. A dark look comes over his face. I can see the wheels turning.

"Now that you speak of it. My powers were very low, but something did feel off. As if my spirit was fighting against something whenever it tried to build up," he muses.

I stand and mirror his stance. It's time we talk about what's been bothering me all along. There's no way Coralo should have been named as my match.

"Father, do you honestly believe she was chosen for me?"

He narrows his eyes. Again, he falls into deep thought. I know he has to see what I do.

"I've questioned it. However, it came from the oracles. If what you're implying is true, that means someone has tainted the system. An oracle can't lie," he says.

"They can't lie, but they can reveal things that have been altered."

My thoughts start to race. Blaise was able to alter my blood, allowing me to save my father. Saving him from something that had altered his blood. That's the same kind of shift it would take to alter an oracle's vision.

"If someone tampered with Coralo's essence during the soul match ceremony, she would've had the spirit to be named my soul match."

"Many are called, few are chosen. Of all the women called to the ceremony, she would've had to have some powerful blood and power to pull that off," my father replies.

"Her mother is an elder. It's not a secret how much Helenier has resented her husband for *diluting* her blood. She has looked at Coralo with disapproval since she was a child," I point out.

"We have no proof and this would cause great trouble if we make accusations. Even if they were able to fool one oracle with a tainted essence, it's the job of the second seat to confirm the connection.

"Someone should have spoken up. We bring this to light; it'll damn more than Helenier and Coralo."

"Which is how they think they will get away with this. We can't challenge them without proof," I snarl.

We both freeze as footsteps outside of my father's room grab our attention. We whip our heads in the direction of the door. I narrow my eyes as Helenier and Coralo enter.

They both stumble to a stop when they find my father standing strong. The blood drains from Coralo's face and Helenier's expression hardens. I glare at the two but hold my tongue.

I don't want them to know we're onto them. We have to find out a way to get proof. My mind goes to Blaise. I need to get back to her as soon as I can. This is going to keep me from doing that.

"My king," they say in unison and bow.

"It's wonderful to see you well," Helenier says.

Coralo comes to my side and places a hand on my chest. I cringe but stay still. If I want information, I'll have to play nice for now.

"This is amazing. Everything has worked itself out. We can still move the wedding up to lift the spirits of the people. They have been so distraught over your absence and your father's illness."

"I don't believe moving the wedding up will serve to do much but distract from the king's improved health."

"Argon is right. There's no need to rush things. There is much else to be addressed."

"Yes, like that beast. She needs to be dealt with," Helenier says.

I grind my teeth to suppress the growl that rises in my belly. It doesn't sit well with me that they keep bringing her up. There's a nagging in the back of my mind that tells me to be guarded.

"That reminds me. Father, how did you know about that realm? What took you there?"

My father furrows his brows. A blank expression covers his features. My hackles rise. Something is very off.

"I can't remember. I know I was on a quest for something. After... it was after..."

"You should rest, my king. You've been through a great ordeal. I'll have the kitchen bring you some broth and that brew you like," Helenier rushes to say.

"No, thank you," my father and I say in unison.

"Well, I say we send our best warriors there to avenge our king," Coralo pushes.

"We will do no such thing. That portal has been sealed. I made sure of it when I stepped back through."

Once Dinesh gave me the watch to make my way back, I thought it best to seal the portal. No one else needs to find their way from the land of Kunglig to Blaise's world. I will be the only one with access.

"You what?" Helenier shrills.

"I sealed the portal. We have no use for that world."

"You would allow that beast to harm your father with no consequences? You must unseal it."

"Are you telling *me* what I must do, Helenier?" My words come out just as dark as I mean them to.

"No, no, my prince. Not at all." She pauses as her gaze falls to my chest. "Coralo and I will go. I'm sure you both want to catch up. I'm so happy for your return, my prince, and your healing, my king. Coralo, come."

Coralo looks at me longingly before she reluctantly retreats with her mother. Helenier grabs her wrist and drags her from the room. I don't like the feeling I get as they go.

"You feel that too?"

"Yes. What do you think this means?"

"She's tapping into dark magic and has become unstable. Argon, I truly don't remember what led me to that plane. I have no recollection of anything before I left," my father says.

I turn to him and search his eyes that are so much like mine. "You said you wanted to retrieve a fire rose for my betrothed."

"A fire rose? The roses in the garden. Yes, I remember those." He rubs his forehead. "Vaguely, but I remember them."

I move closer and place a hand on his shoulder. "Rest. We will get to the bottom of this."

Blaise

I toss the sphere across the room and smash it. I had only wanted to make sure Argon made it to his father and healed him. I did not expect to find him with the arms of another around him.

Sinking to my knees, I cover my face and start to sob. I've fallen in love like a fool. I never thought about his betrothed back home. I'd forgotten about her.

Why wouldn't he go back to her? I allowed those dreams to fool me into thinking I had something with him. Our time together was only a ruse for him to escape. It doesn't matter now.

"Oh, honey. Please stop crying," Ms. Posh says, causing me to lift my head to look at her.

"What are we going to do?"

She flies closer and palms my face with her tiny hand. With the flick of her wrist, a steaming cup of tea appears. I hold the warm cup in my hands.

"We're going to do what we always do. We're going to survive. It's all going to work out, it always does."

"Have you seen the rose? The petals are almost gone. We'll remain like this forever," I cry.

"You, my dear, haven't seen the way that man looked at you. He will return. I don't believe you're the only one who fell in love."

I turn away from her so she can't look into my eyes. I'm ashamed of myself for falling for him. I'm even more embarrassed by the dreams.

"He has someone. He didn't fall in love with me, and I can't be sure if I fell in love with him or a dream," I murmur.

"Dream?"

I blush. "I've been dreaming of him. He comes to me and… things happen."

Ms. Posh chortles. "Blaise, let me show you something."

I lift to my feet and follow her into my closet. She leads me to the full-length mirror. I look at her in confusion.

"Remove your cloak, princess." I do as she says. "I didn't want to point it out when I helped you bathe. You're a grown woman."

She flies closer and points to my neck, then flies down to my breast. I gasp when I see the marks she points out for me. Moving closer to the mirror, I finger the blemish on my neck.

I release a gasp. "No."

"Yes, my dear. Those are marks of passion. You haven't been dreaming of Argon. You've been with him."

I stumble toward the chaise in my closet. Palming my forehead, I think of all the times I've been with him. They were all real?

"But in the dreams, everything was so different. My body"— I shake my head—"I had normal legs and feet."

"Princess. I don't know if you have been in denial or if the castle hid his power from you, but he was special. I think something in your venom or something about his magic, or a mix of it all, caused you two to come together.

"Call it an answering of your hearts' desire. You both got what you wanted," she says with a smile.

"Did we really?"

"Yes, dear, you did. He will return. Give it a little time."

"But he can never come through again on his own. You know this."

"I also know a fairy with a gift of time. You didn't think we were going to let him leave here without a way back, did you?"

I give a small smile. "No, I guess not."

CHAPTER TWENTY-FOUR

A New Plan

Coralo

"What are we going to do?"

Mother paces before me in our home with a scowl on her face. The king was on his deathbed this morning. Her plan was almost complete.

I don't know what Argon did, but he restored the king seemingly effortlessly. He shouldn't have been able to undo Mother's spell so easily, or so we thought.

"How did he do it?" she mumbles to herself, still pacing.

"Argon is very powerful."

"Yes, but he did it so quickly. He didn't have time to figure out that spell to create a counter. His power has boundaries," she says, waving me off.

"But the power of a Kunglig is still more powerful than any dark sorcery."

I jump as she causes a wooden chair to fly across the room and shatter against the wall in a million pieces. Her anger is palpable. She's been growing angrier each day as the king has resisted her magic.

It's just like Mother to underestimate those around her because she's so overconfident in her own power. My father wasn't nearly as useless as she made him seem. His greatest weakness was loving her.

"He's back and that old fart looks healthier than ever. This changes everything," Mother seethes.

"He sealed the portal and from the sound of it, he didn't slay the beast like you thought he would. You were so sure he would kill her for harming his father."

Mother spins on me. Gold-and-black sparks of light begin to circle her hands. I take a step back. Her power has become unstable with the black magic she's been using to try to poison the king.

I bite my tongue. I always say too much. It's clear in her eyes that I've gained her ire.

"Thank you for stating the obvious, genius. The wolves I enchanted failed as well. There, we have all my failures out in the open.

"Now we can get to solutions. She will be a beast forever soon. She's the least of my worries. I need the king to drink another dose of the poison."

"Mother, respectfully, that ship has sailed. Did you not see the king? He looks way too strong for the poison to work. Didn't you say you needed him to go to that castle to weaken so the poison could take root?"

I hold my breath as her nostrils flare and she narrows her gaze on me. The magic circling her hands fades. She runs a hand over her hair.

"You're right," she mutters. I release a breath and sag my shoulders in relief. "I need to deal with them and that beast."

"Argon doesn't seem like he plans to go back to destroy her. Besides, he can't return on his own."

Mother scoffs and flips her long braids. Her brown eyes light up as she thinks her plan through. I note the moment her plan begins to take hold.

"Her time is coming. Once she has become a full beast, her powers will weaken once and for all and I'll take care of her myself.

"That curse has always been problematic. The castle was meant to bind her, not her visitors. Yet, she's gotten stronger within those walls," she murmurs more to herself.

"I know I altered the original curse properly. It had to be that silly enchantress. Perhaps I should've disposed of her after I fiddled with it."

I shake my head at Mother. Of course, *she* didn't do anything wrong. I roll my eyes. We have to fix this mess before we get caught.

"How do we unseal the portal? Argon has no reason to unseal it. Again, he doesn't seem to want revenge," I say.

The bitterness in my voice is clear even to my own ears. His anger when I mentioned that beast is still unsettling, as if he meant to protect her. It's no secret that the prince has never wanted me as his soul match. He thinks I'm weak, just like Mother does.

"He wears the answer to that. The pendant watch around his neck. I've seen one like it before. Once I get my hands on it, we can open the portal and he won't be able to follow," she says with renewed joy.

"I can get it."

"No, it's our only chance. I'll handle this myself. Go do something with yourself. You look pale and frumpy. Bring some color to your cheeks and change your clothes. You're still his fiancée."

"Yes, Mother."

CHAPTER TWENTY-FIVE

Forbidden Pages

Argon

I've tossed and turned all night. My spirit link has pulsed greater for my soul match with every passing hour. Something is wrong, I just haven't put my finger on it yet.

Agitated and restless, I toss the covers and get out of bed. It's as if the soul link guides my steps as I grab a robe and exit my room. I find myself in the royal library.

When I stop before the hologram machine, my spirit roars. I knit my brows. Without thinking, I type in the coding that comes to me.

I stare intently as an image begins to appear. A grand party appears before me. People dance around happily as beauty and elegance surround them. As I look closer, I realize I know the room. However, I can't think for the life of me from where.

The hologram zeroes in on a group of laughing women. The ones facing me have their faces painted. Some gold, others silver. The one with wild reddish-brown curls falling down her back catches my attention. My spirit roars loud and deep, I have to grit my teeth to keep from separating.

"Princess," a woman calls.

As if in slow motion, the one with the full springy curls turns. I inhale sharply as Blaise's face comes into view. However, where her scars would be are bronze and gold paint.

No scars. She's breathtaking as she smiles. The paint on her face causes me to long to see her the way I know her, with her lavalike scars.

I pause the player and print the data file on this reel and all related files. I collect the pages and search for the reference numbers in the bound books section.

I get lost in the information until the sun rises. When the light starts to creep into the library, I'm fuming and determine to destroy the web of lies and magic that has been spun. I don't know how, but we have all forgotten Blaise.

The daughter of King Basil of the kingdom of Puissance. A kingdom that has all but vanished from our history. It's time I bring the princess home.

CHAPTER TWENTY-SIX

Remember This?

Argon

"Good morning, Father. I'm glad to see you looking so well," I say as I walk into the dining room.

"Argon, my son. Just who I wanted to see. Come, sit."

I move to his side and take the seat next to him. He looks me over and a smile comes to his face. I'm happy to see him like this. It seems his strength has fully returned.

"Something is different about you. There is a light in your eyes that hasn't been there in a very long time."

"I can say my time with Blaise has changed me for the better."

He furrows his brows. "The beast?"

"Father, Blaise is more than a beast. To be honest. I don't think she's a beast at all. Do you remember King Basil or his kingdom?"

"King Basil. Sounds familiar, but I can't say I remember the name."

"Then you have no memory of Princess Blaise either?"

"No, I can't say I do. What is this about?"

"Father, there is so much going on. Coralo was never my match. In fact, I believe I know who is. We need to find out what happened."

"Yes, I agree. We need evidence of the foul play."

"I say we have another ceremony. That's the only way to prove what I already know."

"I know just where to begin. I don't like this deception within the walls of my kingdom. Our ways have been trusted since the beginning of time as we know it."

"Then I say we restore the truth and build that trust back before it's too late."

"Yes, this is true. We must act quickly. Fill your stomach then we will settle this matter."

CHAPTER TWENTY-SEVEN

True Match

Blaise

"Princess... Blaise."

Peeking out from under my pillow, I groan when I find Hiasha, Soila, Ms. Posh, Dinesh, and Bach floating above me. I roll onto my stomach and cover my head.

"We only want to check on you, dear," Ms. Posh says.

I know that's why they're here. I haven't moved from this bed in hours. I can't. It feels like my heart has truly broken into pieces. I also feel like I'm going to split in two or something.

That's the biggest reason I refuse to move. It's as if my soul is searching for something outside my body and I'm afraid if I move, I will lose myself forever. I'm going out of my mind with this ache in my chest.

"Princess, princess, princess," Dinesh says as he lands on my shoulder. He sits, swinging his feet until I turn my head to face him.

"What?"

"First, you reek," he mumbles and falls onto his back as if he has fainted. I think hard about plucking him right off my shoulder. "Like really. This is unhealthy. Do you guys smell this room?"

"Dinesh, if you don't shut your mouth," Bach growls.

"I'm staying in bed. You all can go find something to do."

"You're not the only one about to lose everything," Dinesh says.

"Ugh, we all know you will miss sex," I huff.

"Yeah, right," Hiasha coughs into her hand.

Dinesh sits up and turns to look at her. I roll my eyes and hide my head under the pillow. I'm not in the mood for this.

"What's that supposed to mean, you little brat?"

I swear I can hear Hiasha roll her eyes. "You think we never hear you and Soila when you two hide in the closet?"

"Oh my gods, oh my gods, oh my gods," Soila says. "I told you."

"What? We're grown and this isn't about me. It's about the princess. Thank you very much. I still think he's coming back," Dinesh says.

"Please tell me we'll forget this day if he doesn't return," Soila groans.

"If I bathe, will you all go away?" I grumble as I turn over and sit up.

"Hey," Dinesh complains as he lands on the bed, falling off my shoulder with my quick motion.

"Maybe you're getting slow in your old age," Bach teases.

"Screw you and that little tight-ass suit you're wearing," Dinesh tosses back.

"Everyone out."

"But, princess, your hair is a tangled mess. You will need us," Ms. Posh says.

I reach to touch my hair and pout. It is a mess. I could use my magic to fix it, but I don't want to be alone. The look in Ms. Posh's eyes says she knows as much.

"Goodbye, Dinesh. Thanks for checking on me, Bach," I say.

"Soila," Dinesh purrs. "Since our secret is out. How about a trip to our favorite closet?"

"Get out," Soila hisses.

"It was worth the try." I shake my head as Bach pushes Dinesh from the room.

Without the distraction, the ache in my chest returns. I look down into my lap and wonder what Argon is up to. I miss him and his voice. I wish he were here to make me laugh.

"This place was happier with him here," Hiasha says.

"Yes, it was, but he will be back," Ms. Posh says. "Come, child. Let's get you cleaned up. You don't want to be a mess when he comes for you."

I look over to the rose on the table and another petal falls. There are only three left. I close my eyes against the sight of the petal turning to ash.

"I don't know if he should bother at all."

"He'll be here. Don't give up. It's not like you," Hiasha says.

"I agree," Soila adds.

I blow out a breath and fall back onto the bed. I don't know who I am anymore. All I know is I ache for someone I don't think I'll ever see again.

"I want bubbles," I say like a spoiled brat.

"You got it, princess."

Argon

I find it odd that no one remembers anything about the princess or the information I found about her and her kingdom. No one. Not even my father.

It's as if she never existed at all. If I didn't find the information for myself, I wouldn't believe it either. I refuse to forget it now that I do know.

All I need is the thread that links Helenier to Blaise's disappearance and the mismatch for my soul match. However, I've yet to find that link, and I have this feeling like I'm running out of time.

"King Arkyn, you're in favor of this request?" Elder Samson asks with furrowed brows.

He's the oldest elder and an old friend of my father's. He's the one my father trusts most. I hope that trust will lead us to answers.

"Yes, I support it," my father replies. "I believe my son is on to something."

"You want to challenge the oracles? This is... I don't know what to say. I trust that you have good reason. It's just... it's never been done before."

"It must be done and it has to be without warning. We can't give time for more treachery," I say firmly.

Samson looks between us. "My king, is it safe to say you believe Helenier has made a play for the throne?"

"Yes, it is. We all heard the murmurs at the ceremony. Everyone was shocked to hear Coralo's name called. She isn't my son's match. I want to know what foul play is taking place here."

"I see. And yes, I was very surprised to hear Coralo's name called. I figured her mother's strength may be within her after all, but foul play seems more likely.

"That would take great use of black magic, but Helenier would be the one to have enough power to wield such a thing and hide it. This is quite the development. Noel and Sefira were the only oracles who weren't at the ceremony," he muses.

"Exactly, Helenier pushed to have the ceremony in their absence. Why have it with the two most powerful oracles not in attendance?" I say.

"I questioned this as well. However, the others were in agreement with her." Samson shakes his head. "I will call for Noel and Sefira. We will perform a new ceremony. It will be private; only a few we can trust as we need others as witnesses. We shall see what comes of this."

"We shall do this immediately," I say.

"It will be more difficult without the young ladies present, but if anyone can do it without them, it's Sefira. Go, prepare. I will take care of everything else."

"I will find you in a moment. I have more to speak with Samson about," my father says.

I nod as he claps a hand against my shoulder. It's good to feel his strength and to see him well. However, my heart calls to Blaise and my spirit link makes me wish I'd never left her.

I go to leave the room as my thoughts turn to her. I need to get back. I feel in my bones that I need to return soon.

"Oh, Your Highness. I'm so sorry, my prince," Helenier says as we collide. I was so deep in thought I didn't see her.

"Excuse me. I'm sorry."

"No, it was I who should have been more focused. I've become clumsy in my old age," she chortles.

I narrow my eyes at her. I've been wary of any interaction with Helenier. She smiles at me sweetly.

"Is there a reason you are here?"

This hall leads to my father's office. She has no business here as far as I know. I tighten my fist as I think of the deceit she could be here to cause.

"I was told I would find you with your father. I wanted to talk to you. Coralo has been dying to spend time with you.

"If it pleases you, I can let her know to come to your chambers for a little alone time," she says.

"No, I have things to tend to. I will let her know when I want to see her. I've been catching up on my duties, I haven't had time for much else."

"Ah yes, well. I won't take any more of your time."

She begins to back away with her hands behind her back. I narrow my gaze further. This woman is up to something.

I get ready to stop her and demand to see her hands, but she pulls them from behind her back and waves to me with both. I grind my teeth. I still don't trust her.

A smile comes to my lips. We'll know for a fact that my soul match was tampered with. Soon enough, I'll make her pay for her crimes and I can return to my true match.

Soon, my love. I'm coming to you soon.

CHAPTER TWENTY-EIGHT

Out of Time

Coralo

The door to my bedroom bursts open and my mother storms in. The crazed look on her face has me lifting from my seat. I hastily try to push my artwork under the other papers on the desk behind me.

Like my father, I love art. Mother hates that I've followed in his footsteps. She loses it anytime she finds me sketching or painting.

"I have the pendant, but we have a new problem," she says.

I draw my brows as I watch her form begin to flicker before my eyes. I knew this was coming. She's becoming completely unstable.

It's best for me to proceed with caution. We need to get her one of those roses before she can't come back from all she has done.

"Mother. What did you just do? You're um... you're flickering."

"I'll be fine. I used a bit more magic than I thought it would take."

"What would take?"

She huffs and holds up the watch Argon wore around his neck. It glows with a white-and-yellow light. My gaze bounces between her and the watch.

"I had to split in two. One of me distracted him, while the other me stole the necklace. He's so untrusting of me. He was completely focused on the me standing right in front of him.

"It couldn't have worked any better. Now, the real problem is what I overheard while waiting in the hallway. They're going to redo the ceremony.

"I don't have enough time to give you my essence." She starts to murmur to herself. I become alarmed when she also starts to reply to herself. "I could try, but I've used so much power already.

"Yes, you have. There has to be another way. She has to be the chosen one or all this ends here.

"I know, I know," she says in frustration.

"I think we should go after the rose. You said that the beast is almost powerless. I can take your warriors and retrieve one of the roses for you. That will give you the power you need, won't it?"

Mother turns to me and her face lights up. She moves to me and cups my face. I lift my head and stand straighter.

"Ah, you are displaying my wisdom. That's exactly what I need. Those roses encompass the true depths of the princess's power.

"It couldn't be stripped from her with the curse. It could only be forced into the roses. For now, I just need one. Once I destroy her, I'll have control of that garden and her power," she says.

"I will leave now."

"No, *we* will go. You should remain here for the ceremony. Yes, *we* will take care of this."

"Mother," I say cautiously as she speaks of herself in plural. "If you don't return in time and they find out I'm not his soul match, they will kill me."

She lifts a brow and gives me an expressionless look. For a moment, I believe she means to sacrifice me. She rolls her eyes and waves a hand.

"I guess we don't want that. You will come along, however, you will not get in my way."

With that, she turns and storms out the way she came. The door slams shut behind her. I draw in a deep breath. I don't have a good feeling about this.

Argon

We are in the throne room as the ceremony begins. I look around at the small gathering Samson has pulled together. Noel and Sefira have begun to summon the heavens for an answer.

My father and I sit on the throne in wait. I don't realize I've been holding my breath until Sefira speaks. She has a frown on her face.

"My king, my prince, you have been wronged. I do not see a match for you with Coralo. In fact, she is very far from the one you have a true soul match with," she says.

"What does that mean?" My father demands.

"It means... my king, I've never seen anything like this before. It would seem Argon is already linked to his soul match. His link is sealed, he has claimed his mate already."

I can't hide the grin that comes to my lips. Blaise. She's my true match. My spirit roars at this truth.

Noel is the next one to speak. "My prince. Your mate is in danger. You must go to her. Those who wish to overthrow the crown have gone after her."

"You will right a wrong, but you must do so before the fire burns out. The past must meet the present to right the course of the future," Sefira says and collapses to the floor.

A collective gasp rings out. Noel rushes to her side. My father and I stand to our feet.

Noel looks up at us. "She will be fine. We have walked between worlds to find your soul match, but I get the feeling you know this, my prince. Go, she's waiting."

Without another thought, I reach for the necklace with the watch. However, my hand is greeted by its absence. I pat my chest and the rest of my clothes.

"No," I roar when I cannot find the pendant.

"You don't need help getting to her," Noel says. "Allow your bond to carry you forth."

"Go," my father says. "We'll handle things here."

I nod as I work my jaw. I close my eyes and, for the first time, allow my spirit link to take over fully. My power courses through me and my spirit link reaches out for its match.

"Blaise," I say her name.

I open my eyes as the sound of glass and light shattering fills my ears. Sparks of light shoot out before the throne room darkens and the floor starts to shake. Everyone around me begins to cry out, all except my father.

"My son," he says proudly.

My spirit pulls from my body. It forms a dragon once again. This time it seems larger as it sits in the center of the room. I move to it quickly and brush its side with my palm. The moment I make the connection, the throne room falls away.

CHAPTER TWENTY-NINE

Love's Battle

Blaise

The pain hasn't gotten any better. In fact, it's gotten worse. My heartache has physically manifested itself. I can't eat. I don't want to move. All I want to do is sleep.

I tried to play the cello, but it's as if I've forgotten the notes to songs I know by heart. It's too much to bear. I'm forgetting most of the things that have kept me from being nothing more than a beast. The others are forgetting things too.

Ms. Posh flew in circles, trying to remember her purpose a few hours ago. She became distracted by her own magic until Hiasha came to take her to her room. I hate watching this happen.

He's not coming back.

I've made my peace with that. If only it didn't hurt so much. Not even my magic will wipe this away.

"Blaise," Bach whispers.

"Yes."

"I thought I'd bring you something to eat. I can feed it to you if you like," he says.

"Leave it. I'll get to it."

He sighs and puts the bowl down on the nightstand. His wings buzz in my ear as he flies closer to sit on my pillow. I blow out a breath, too tired to turn away.

"I haven't given up, you know," he says.

"None of you have. I know better."

"Princess—" He cuts off. He jumps up and looks at me. "The portal. It's opening."

"What?"

Even as I ask the question, I feel the gate to this realm opening. My heart skips a beat as I note the magic of Bach's timepiece. It's him. He's come back.

"I told you he would return," Bach exclaims.

I throw off the covers and scoot until I can throw my legs over the edge of the bed. Lifting my palms, I create an orb to view the portal and watch Argon make his way through. My brows furrow when not Argon but two women and a group of warriors step through the portal into my world.

I narrow my eyes as I see who the woman in front is. I get this nagging feeling that I know her. My brain won't make the connection, causing my anger to rise.

"This isn't good," Bach whispers beside me.

"I know her," I say.

"Yes, I was thinking the same thing."

My lips part with a gasp as I realize who the other woman is. She's the one who had her arms around Argon's waist in the sphere's image of him returning home.

"I don't have a good feeling about this. You and the others guard the castle."

"What? Where will you be?"

"I'm going to protect us."

"Blaise—"

"Do as I say." My voice echoes through the room, shaking it.

"Yes, princess."

I stand and summon my cloak to wrap my body. I don't so much as think before I shift the atmosphere outside the castle. I darken the sky and create a storm of snow and lightning.

"If you want to enter my world, you will play by my rules," I mutter before phasing from my room to the courtyard, where I stand ready for battle.

Coralo

We step through the portal right at the edge of a thickly bushed forest. Right away, I can feel the power of this realm. I look up at the sky as it darkens.

"She knows we're here," I say.

"Yes, but she's weakened."

This is weakened? Oh, Mother. I think you're underestimating your enemy again.

I release a sigh. There's no use in telling her that. We need to do what we came here to do and get back. Hopefully, before we're exposed. Although, I don't think that's going to be likely.

"Surround the castle. Push her to me. We need to draw her into the woods. I have a greater chance there."

I nod and turn to our warriors to signal for them to split up. The group who remains with us, I wave forward as Mother moves toward the front of the castle. The closer we get, the more concerned I become.

"Argh," Mother shouts when a wall of fire rises before us, almost singeing our faces off.

We all jump back. Mother lifts her hands as she murmurs a few words. She flickers in and out, but nothing happens to the wall of flames.

I purse my lips. Maybe I should've stayed behind. This woman is about to get us all killed. She begins to chant a little louder, and this time, the fire douses.

She turns to me with a satisfied grin. "See, piece of cake."

"Sure," I murmur under my breath.

"What was that?" Mother says, lifting a brow.

I look away so she can't read my expression. A gasp leaves my lips. "Look, there she is."

Mother whips her head around to face the castle once again. Standing in the courtyard is a cloaked figure. I assume that's the beast Mother has been ranting about most of my life.

"Archers, attack," my mother commands.

The sound of multiple bowstrings tightening fills my ears, followed by arrows zipping through the air. The cloaked figure stands completely unbothered as the arrows head for them. I understand why when the arrows stop midair, inches away from the being.

"Oh shit," I breathe when the arrows turn to ashes and fall to the ground.

The cloaked figure flips back her hood, revealing a mass of curls. Even from this distance, I can see the glowing of her eyes. On instinct, I turn and put distance between myself and the warriors at our backs.

Mother leaps in the air just before our warriors go up in flames. Their cries of pain fill the air. I watch as the fire they're in is consumed. I jerk my head up to look at Mother. She's fading in and out again, but the warriors—though charred—are no longer on fire.

"You will fight," she commands and the warriors stand at attention. The glow that surrounds each of them tells me they're no longer living beings but creatures of my mother's creation.

"I didn't sign up for this."

I quickly look around for cover. This is about to get messy. My mother is in way over her head.

Or maybe not. The warriors we sent to surround the castle start to move forward behind the beast. She seems unaware of their approach.

Suddenly, the beast speaks and everyone behind her flies backward as if her words rippled through the air and punched them all in the chest. My mouth drops open. I can't believe my eyes.

"Welp, she's not playing with us. Fuck this."

I turn and hide in the shadows of the forest. Just far enough to hide but still see what's going on. My mother is going to get us flattened or burned to a crisp.

This beast has the power of the royals of the land of Kunglig. Now I see why Mother needed Argon to be the one to come destroy her. If this is her weak state, what the hell would have happened to Argon had he tried to fight her?

The battle before me continues as Mother begins to throw orbs of light at the beast. Each orb is countered by a ball of flame that eats them up. However, something distracts the beast and she turns her head for a split second.

Mother takes the opportunity to form the largest orb yet and throws it. I cover my mouth with my hands as it hits the beast in the center of her chest. Three things happen in that moment.

The beast falls to the ground, Mother transforms into a translucent force of energy, and a loud, piercing roar fills the air. I look up at the sky and have to blink to make sure I'm seeing right. Sure enough, it's him.

"Dear gods, I have to get out of here."

Blaise

I will defend my home. This woman and her dark magic will go back to where they came from. In the back of my mind, it burns me to think that Argon sent them.

He didn't come back because he hates me. This is my punishment for what I did to his father. I was such a fool to think he could fall in love with me.

Her warriors are closing in on me, but I don't show that I know they're there. I allow them to get closer as I keep my attention on the floating woman. It still nags me that I know her from somewhere.

"Get back," I roar right as I feel her warriors get too close.

I don't have to turn to know the command has thrown them back. I flip my cloak out at my sides and take a stance. I'm ready for the next attack.

The floating woman begins to throw energy orbs at me. However, her magic is no match for mine. I toss out fire orbs that consume her magic one by one.

Growing tired of her and this fight, I get ready to go on the offense. Only the sound of Ms. Posh's cry catches my attention. I turn toward the castle, setting aflame the warrior who's swatting at Ms. Posh and Hiasha as they work together to keep him from entering the front doors. I grin in satisfaction.

That's until I realize my mistake. It all happens so fast. One simple mistake and I'm tumbling to the ground.

Argon

I'm drawn through the portal on the back of my spirit dragon. Right as we come through, I see the orb that's heading for Blaise as she stands in the courtyard. She's distracted.

I don't have time to react to block it. I release a roar that comes from my toes and travels through my being up to my throat. When the sound releases from me, my dragon opens his mouth and flames fly out. The ground below singes as the unnatural warriors Helenier has at her back are burned to ashes.

We dive for the ground and land in front of Blaise's body. My spirit dragon cries out for her. I jump from his back with my attention on Helenier.

The dark magic has consumed her. She floats above the ground, but she's no longer herself. I can see through her.

She's in between the worlds she's pulled this magic from. It's eating her essence right from her. Rage fills me to the brim. This has been going on for a while for her to be in this state. How did we not know?

"You will pay for everything you have done," I bellow.

"I have only just begun. I've waited so long to come back here to finish that beast. My mistake was counting on others to do this for me."

"What?"

The thought of others being involved in her schemes makes my blood boil. I already plan to clean house upon my return to the land of Kunglig. If there are others I need to find, I will hunt them all down, one by one.

"Blaise was such a vain girl. A spoiled princess. I knew it wouldn't be hard for her to call the curse upon herself. I only guided the right enchantress to her.

"My mistake was allowing her to send the princess to this realm to be forgotten. Such a nuisance. No one has been able to return on their own after one visit. I've been trying to figure out a way around it and then you walk right through the portal with the answer around your neck," Helenier cackles.

"How did you get the oracles behind this?"

"The same way I got your father to do my bidding. A little spell here, a little dark magic there." She shrugs.

"All of this for what? Why forsake your kingdom? What has she done so wrong to you?"

She tilts her head at me. I narrow my eyes on her as she studies me. I may not have memories of Blaise, but so much is starting to fall into place.

"Oh, you are a fool. Have you come to care for that beast?" She looks behind me and her brows draw. She inhales a sharp breath. "That's your spirit reflection."

The sound of Blaise's groan draws my attention, but I don't turn to face her. I have to stay focused on the witch before me.

My people are never meant to play in dark magic. It taints our true spirit.

"I have always seen you as unworthy of your station. You look down on the other elders and the people. Everyone's beneath you.

"Now that I know what you've been plotting and scheming"—I shake my head—"did you really think you could overthrow two kingdoms?"

"Are you not paying attention? I've already taken one. Yours is next."

She tosses an orb at me, but I throw up a shield. Her magic bounces right off it. Lowering the shield, I prepare my next move.

I summon my blades. The weight of their carved metal handles in my palms brings bloodlust with them. Each double-edged blade glows with blue light as they charge with my power.

"You have played with the wrong one, Helenier. Now, you will die."

I toss one of the blades and it sails through the air. It slices into her arm—as she tries to dodge it—spinning back toward me like a boomerang. I lift my palm as the blade returns and settles in my grasp.

Yanking my hand downward, I watch in satisfaction as Helenier's body is thrown to the ground. One strike from my blade creates an invisible tether between my enemy and my blade. Helenier stumbles to her feet after rolling on the ground in pain.

She straightens and tosses a ball of energy at me. The force of it rips through the ground as it heads for me. Debris flies from the path it makes.

This time I release both of my blades. They make a singing sound as they tear through the air. They crisscross as they cut through the force heading for me. Crossing each other again, they slice the sides of Helenier's torso before they return to my waiting hands.

I tighten my grips on the handles and pull, dragging Helenier toward me. She tries to dig her feet into the ground, but she's no match for my power. However, the invisible tethers pop and she tumbles to the ground.

My gaze shifts and I find a trembling Coralo. Her face turns pale as I lock my eyes on her. Before I can send a blade for her, she flies back and lands a few feet from the spot she had stood.

"I told you to stay out of my way," Helenier hisses at her own daughter.

Hooves click against the ground behind me, and I want to sag in relief. Blaise is alive, but I can feel that she's weakened. I want to turn to her and wrap her in my arms.

Instead, I turn my attention back to Helenier as she floats into the air. Her lips are moving as she chants. Sparks of light start to surround her.

She makes her next attack. I throw up a shield and a force field of fire surrounds it. I give a grin. My little warrior is protecting me as she did that night in the forest.

We both lower our shields, but much to my annoyance, Blaise has to engage the warriors who have surrounded the castle. I stay focused on Helenier. I have every confidence in Blaise even if my spirit reflection weren't there to help her.

"You're in over your head," I warn Helenier.

"I will not be defeated."

Bringing my hands together, joining my blades as one, I release the weapon as it glows brighter and hotter. Helenier doesn't move fast enough. Her right arm is severed from her body.

"Mother," Coralo screams.

Everything from this very moment moves so fast, I don't know what has happened until the smoke settles and everything blurs before me as my throat turns raw with the anguish that leaves my lips.

Blaise

I bring my sword across the body of my last enemy, panting with the exertion. I need to heal from that blow I took, but there's no time.

The warrior I've just slashed falls to the ground as the magic fueling her leaves her body. This Helenier woman has been feeding these warriors with dark magic. It's taking more energy than I'd like to spare to get through them.

Argon's dragon moves from shielding me as I turn to help Argon. The dragon places his head to my back as if to lend me its strength. "Good boy," I coo and reach behind me to pet his head. It's then that I allow the truth to sink in.

Argon is fighting with me, for me. He didn't betray me as I thought he did. My heart swells. We will finish this together and I will tell him how I feel.

"Mother," the woman who comes from hiding in the woods cries out as Argon cuts off the floating woman's arm.

The woman from the woods pales. Her hands spark with magic. I know what she plans to do before she does it. Argon's focus isn't on her, it's on the woman she called mother. I move as fast as I can to cover Argon. I'm too weak to throw up another force field.

Instead, I throw my body in front of his. The bolt of magic she has sent toward Argon transforms as it builds power. It becomes an arrow, a glowing yellow arrowhead, sparking with white light at the fletching.

I have to make a choice. Mother or daughter? As I make the split decision, my memory clicks. *Helenier*. She's the one who called me from the party to meet the enchantress who cursed me and sent me here.

Decision made, with my last bit of energy, I hurl my sword and it ignites with a flame. My body is in motion, moving through the air to block Argon from the arrow still headed for him.

"No," Helenier cries out a moment before my blade pierces right through her chest.

I turn my gaze to the tip of the arrow headed for me. It's so close and I can't turn it to ashes. I try, I truly do. I close my eyes as it enters my chest and pierces my back.

I have no regrets. I feel the last petal fall just as I do. It's too late for me anyway. The least I can do is save the man I love.

Argon

I silence the screams of Coralo with my blade without turning to look at her. Dropping to my knees, I draw Blaise's body into my arms. My voice is hoarse as I cry her name.

"Blaise, wake up for me." I reach beneath her to snap the end of the arrow. I pull it out of her chest even as it sears my palm.

I'm numb. I feel nothing. "Come on, please wake up. I want to see those eyes."

She remains lifeless in my arms. I tug her into my chest and bury her face into my neck. I try to send my spirit into her to bring her back. Nothing is working.

"My Blaise, don't leave me. Please don't leave me. I just found you," I sob as I rock with her in my embrace.

My spirit reflection wraps around us both as it whines as if wounded. I understand the feeling. I hurt within my soul. He throws his head back and releases a cry that pierces the air and shakes the ground.

It's too much. My spirit reflection retreats within me. The ache inside growing as we become one.

"Blaise," I roar as more tears flow. "I gave you the rose, remember? You said if I gave it to someone I cared for, it would give them eternal life. I gave it to you."

Still nothing as her blood spills out on the ground beneath us. I'm losing my mate. I don't much care what this means for me. I finally understand my father and why he made that blood decree.

I will go with my soul match happily because I know I don't want this life without her. Images of her smile and the sound of her laugh float through my mind. I've failed. With all the power I have, I don't have enough to bring her back.

Something occurs to me deep within. I care for Blaise deeper than our spirit link could ever reach. This is more than her being my soul match. I fell in love with her. Her smile, her eyes, her laughter. The core of her, not the beast everyone sees.

I'm in love with Blaise.

"I love you," I whisper into her hair.

Suddenly, her body starts to rise from out of my arms. I release her as she floats above my head. Blue-yellow-and-orange light surrounds her and the bloodstain on her back begins to disappear.

She slowly starts to spin as she lifts upright and the light dances around her. The wound in her chest disappears. Her hair is the first thing that I notice transform. From there, her face becomes just as I saw in the hologram in my realm.

Her smooth, silky legs are next to change, all ending with her hooves turning to cute little stiletto-covered feet. When she lands, standing before me, the smile on her face is breathtaking. I stand to my feet. She stares up at me with shining amber-colored eyes.

I rush forward and cup her face. Crushing my lips to hers, I show all the feelings I have inside. She smiles against my lips. I break the kiss and place my forehead to hers.

"I love you," I breathe.

"I love you too. What took you so long?" she says with that gorgeous smile.

"Now that is a long story, princess. Let's get you back home first."

CHAPTER THIRTY

Welcome Princess

Argon

We stand outside the throne room's closed doors. Blaise is filled with nervous energy. I thought it best to give her and the others a few days to get acclimated before introducing them to my kingdom and Father.

I give Blaise's hand a little squeeze. "Relax, he's going to love you," I say.

"The last time we met, I was a beast who locked him in a cell. He probably already hates me."

I turn to her and wrap my arms around her waist, pulling her into me. Placing my forehead to hers, I breathe her in. "My father understands you were cursed, and he knows what you mean to me. He's not going to hate you. He's just ready to meet my soul match."

"Okay," she breathes.

I laugh when for the millionth time since we've been standing here, she changes her hair and clothing. I give her waist a squeeze and peck her lips. Reaching for her hand, I twirl her in front of me.

This time her hair is flowing and sweeps across her eye. She's dressed like the main character in the movie we watched last night. The flared skirt and corset are a mix of her personality.

The red heels bring a smile to my face. I haven't been able to keep my hands off her silky legs. There isn't a night since we've been back here when I haven't had her toes in my mouth as I plow deep inside her.

"You look perfect. I wouldn't change a single thing."

She smiles. "Okay, I think I'm ready."

I wink at her. "Good, the king is waiting."

I lace my fingers with hers and turn to face the throne room once again. I give a nod for them to open the doors. A huge grin comes to my lips as I see Father has added a throne chair for Blaise to join us. When we stop before him, my father stands.

"Father, my king, I'd like to present to you Princess Blaise."

"Finally, I've wanted to welcome you to Kunglig and thank you for saving my life," my father says.

"You are welcome, King Arkyn. Thank you so much for having me while I settle back into this world."

"It is a pleasure. We plan to do all we can to help in the transition. Although, I believe Argon has plans for your future."

Blaise turns to me and I'm ready on one knee. Her eyes widen. I smile and hold up the ring my father gave me. It was my mother's.

"You're already linked to me, my love. Will you marry me before my people and my king? Make me the happiest man in existence. Say you'll be mine, Blaise."

"Yes," she chokes out.

Father claps his hands. "Very well then, a royal wedding it is. I present to you all Princess Blaise of Puissance, the true soul match of Prince Argon of Kunglig."

Everyone applauds and cheers. I stand and pull Blaise in to kiss her soundly. "I love you," she whispers.

"I love you more. Welcome home."

Blaise

I stand before this mirror in Argon's bedroom in my panties and bra, staring at my reflection. It's been so long since I've been in this form I keep thinking it will change if I look away. None of this seems real.

I reach to touch my chin and my ring comes into view. Tears well in my eyes. He asked me to marry him. I cradle my hand to my breasts as the tears start to fall.

"I'm loved," I whisper.

"Yes, you are," Argon says as he appears behind me.

I look up at him in the mirror's reflection. He makes me feel so loved and protected. I didn't know I wanted this so much.

Placing a hand on my side, he slowly brushes his fingertips across my skin until he stops just below my bra. Goose bumps rise and I shiver from his touch.

He gathers my hair and moves it aside to dip his head and kiss my neck. He finds my gaze in the mirror and watches me. Releasing my hair, he reaches to cup my breast.

I rub my thighs together as more tears fall. This isn't a dream. For the first time since we've been back here, I allow myself to accept this is real, it's not going to burst like a bubble and vanish.

"Breathe, Blaise. I'm not going anywhere. I love you and I want to make you happy. We have the rest of our lives to be together."

I turn in his embrace and grasp the sides of his face. He looks me in the eyes with so much intensity. Music starts to play through the room. I smile.

"Dinesh has great timing," Argon murmurs.

"Dinesh, mind your business. Stop spying on me," I growl.

"Only listening in, princess," his voice floats through the room. "Need to make sure you're safe."

"That's my job now, Dinesh. Explore the castle. I've got Princess Blaise from here."

"Oh, all right," he huffs like a chastened child.

Everyone has been restored to their natural state, but they're still finding their purpose after so many years. I laugh and snuggle against Argon as he sways me to the music. I could get used to this.

Argon lifts my face with his fingers under my chin. I look up into his eyes and smile. He takes my lips, kissing me deeply.

Yes, this I can certainly get used to.

Family Magic

Blaise

"Again, Mama," Ayrilesse cries out as I pop the bubble I placed her in.

She floats down to her pink-covered bed, giggling. My daughter is adorable with her reddish-brown-and-blonde locks and her father's and grandfather's eyes. She has dimples in each of her cheeks that charm the treats out of Ms. Posh's kitchen every day and gets her out of music lessons with Dinesh anytime she wants to run the castle instead.

Everyone in the castle is wrapped around her little finger. Her grandfather's home isn't any better. She's brought new life to the king.

"Okay, one more time," I relent, shaking my head.

Argon growls at me, placing an arm around my waist. He has been trying to get me to put our daughter to bed so that we can go to our own. I tip my head back against his chest and look into his lust-filled eyes.

I purse my lips to keep from laughing at him. He narrows his eyes at me, causing me to lift to my toes to kiss him. Meanwhile, I place Ayrilesse into a bubble and lift her in the air as her father is distracted. Or at least, I think he's distracted until Ayrilesse starts to squeal.

"Pretty! Again, Daddy, again."

I turn to see Argon has been changing the bubble's color. Our daughter's eyes are huge as she watches the orb turn from blue to pink to purple to yellow. I sag into Argon's warmth and watch our baby play happily.

"I wish we could keep her safe inside one of those forever," I say.

Argon wraps both arms around me and tightens his embrace. He kisses the top of my head. I will never grow tired of this.

"She will always be protected. I will put my life on that," he murmurs to me. He then says to our daughter. "Time for bed, little princess."

"Aww, Daddy, no." She pouts. Her brown cheeks are so freaking adorable.

"Yes, sweetheart. We will play tomorrow. Tonight, we sleep."

"Okay," she whines as I burst the bubble and gently float her down to her bed.

"Sweet dreams, little one," I say and kiss her forehead.

"Sweet dreams," she repeats. "Night night, Daddy."

"Night night."

I hesitate to turn and leave, but Argon has lost his patience. He lifts me and tosses me over his shoulder. Ayrilesse giggles and snuggles into her bed.

"Put me down," I say when we get outside her bedroom and he pulls the door shut.

"Why? So you can find something else to keep me from my wife? You have been busy all day. You've felt our spirit link. I need you," he replies.

"Our reflections have been together all day. We can hold out a little longer."

His answer is a rumbling growl as he kicks our bedroom door closed. I laugh as my husband takes me to the bed and drops me onto it gently. Both of our clothes are gone before I hit the mattress.

He places a knee on the bed and looks at me lovingly. "I love your laugh," he says with a smile.

"I love you," I say as I look at him through my lashes.

"Gods, you know I adore you, woman. My Blaise, my soul match, my beautiful queen."

"My Argon, my soul match, my handsome king," I purr back.

Our spirit dragons roar in the distance somewhere and I laugh again. We both can feel what they're up to. Argon gives me a heated look.

"It seems we need to play catch-up."

I bite my lip and squeeze my breasts. "Maybe you're right."

"I'm always right," he says proudly.

"Ha, whatever," I laugh some more.

His eyes sparkle as he cups the back of my neck to draw me to him for a heated kiss. I moan into his mouth. I whimper and pout when he breaks the kiss and backs away.

"Blaise."

"Yes?"

"You're pregnant with my son. I can't keep it to myself anymore," he says with a wicked grin.

I sit up and wrap my hand around his hard length. I lock eyes with him as I look up into his face. I take a long lick under his shaft as a warning of what's to come before I return his naughty smile.

"Tell me something I don't know, love."

He drops his head back and roars with laughter. My mouth opens in awe. This is my husband. He's so gorgeous. That laugh is damn wicked. Priceless, in fact.

Although I want to bask in the sight, I know a look that he has that's even more beautiful. I cover his length with my mouth and silence his laugh. He looks at me with heated eyes.

Yes, I love that look. Priceless indeed. You can't put a price on happily ever after. I sure couldn't ask for a better ending.

His Cinder

BLUE SAFFIRE

Perceptive Illusions Publishing, Inc.
Bay Shore, New York

Blue Saffire/Perceptive Illusions Publishing, Inc.
PO BOX 5253
Bay Shore, New York 11706
www.BlueSaffire.com

Publisher's Note: This is a work of fiction. Names, characters, places, and incidents are a product of the author's imagination. Locales and public names are sometimes used for atmospheric purposes. Any resemblance to actual people, living or dead, or to businesses, companies, events, institutions, or locales is completely coincidental.

Ordering Information:
Quantity sales. Special discounts are available on quantity purchases by corporations, associations, and others. For details, contact the "Special Sales Department" at the address above.

His Cinder/ Blue Saffire. – 2nd ed.

You can get lost in what-ifs. Remember to stay grounded in what is.

−BlueSaffire

In The Moment

Princeton

I stand in my New York City apartment feeling hollow as always. Something is missing that I've yet to find. Story of my life.

"Your mother called. Your eight a.m. has been moved up," Williams, my adviser, says into the phone at my ear.

I groan. I want to go to that meeting like I want a hole in my head. I've avoided this long enough. I bare my teeth as I look out my apartment window at the view of the city.

"Tell me why the fuck I'm doing this again?"

All civilities went out the window years ago. I'm the damaged, rogue prince in the eyes of my people. We've all learned to accept it.

"Your Highness, you have to find a bride," he replies. He pauses. "Can I be frank?"

I blow out a breath and shrug as if he can see me. "You can be whoever you want."

"Ah, yes, funny," he says dryly. We've had this relationship for as long as I can remember. Williams is like an uncle to me. He knows me well. I trust his words.

"You've searched long enough. I think it's time you try to move on. You've become bitter over something that's out of your control."

"You're allowed to move past this. Some things are allowed to be out of your control. There's no law that says you have to find her," he says. "Besides, you never know what you might find."

"They owe me an explanation. This isn't about her. It's about why. I want to know why."

I clench my teeth. This has been a sore topic for me for longer than I'd like to admit. I unclench my jaw and the fist at my side.

"If that were the case you wouldn't have an objection to finding a bride, now would you?"

I clench my teeth again. I don't want to look at what he's suggesting. My reluctance has nothing to do with the past. I don't like being forced into anything and that's what my parents are doing.

That's why I'm against this ball and all it represents. However, I know my duties and I know that it's time to find a bride. This will also quiet the rumors and flapping lips.

I turn and walk to the full-length mirror propped against the wall. I stop in front of it and stare at the nude man before me.

I'm bare to myself and can ask the hard questions as I look into my own eyes.

"I'll call you back."

I toss the phone onto the side table and give myself a quick once-over. Have I grown to be a bitter man? Perhaps.

Women fall at my feet, but none of them add up enough to soothe the hit to my ego. A hit that was dealt before I grew my first pubic hair.

"There's too much pussy out there for you to be hung up on this," I say to myself.

Although, I know this has nothing to do with pussy. It's rooted deeper than some ass. All of this has shaped me.

America has become as much a home to me as my true home because of the past. A past that has been out of my hands.

Yet I wish to understand that past and quest to do so. I lock eyes with my reflection. Wise men say you don't return to the past and you don't pant for the future. You live in the present and relish in the moment.

"It's time to live in the moment, Princeton."

CHAPTER ONE

Not So Charming

Princeton

Something is fishy around here. I can be an asshole, but these people are making me look like a saint. I have no idea why my mother insisted on going with this event planning company. Apparently, they're all the rave.

Having this ball is ridiculous to begin with. Now, I have to sit here with these unprepared snobs. I'm getting more pissed by the second.

It's as if they never looked at the details of our event and not one of them had a hand in putting together this half-assed proposal. I narrow my eyes on the two sisters who run the company as they lock heads together and hiss at each other.

"Ow!" The one with the blonde, fake hair and tight pink sheath dress whines, drawing my attention solely to her.

She reaches under the table to rub at her leg, a pout on her pink-painted lips. I roll my eyes, my impatience rising. This is all a waste of my valuable time.

"Princeton, I can assure you that we have this event under control. Our assistant will be in shortly with the right file so we can resolve all of your questions," Bianca Estevez, the owner of Beauty for Ashes Event Planning and mother of the two sitting at her side, informs me as if we're old friends.

I've had to hear a dozen times how she's the owner along with these two. I grind my teeth at her use of my name. I don't have the patience to correct her.

Her light-brown eyes sparkle as she addresses me. I'm sure she's dreaming of the commission I'm about to pull from her and this shit show. I pick up my phone and get ready to turn to my mother to tell her I'm done with this crap.

At thirty, I'm just plain tired of playing the good son who keeps a smile on his face while I'm dying on the inside. Total lies and we know it, but public appearances are what I've been working on the last few years.

"I'm so sorry. I had to put out three back-to-back fires," says a curvy, dark-skinned woman who rushes into the room.

"Just leave the files," the Estevez sister in the green dress with the short red hair snarls.

For the life of me, I can't remember these two sisters' names. That's become irrelevant to me anyhow. My focus is on the new addition to the room.

Damn!

I haven't seen a woman as gorgeous as her in… yeah, never. Even in her frenzied state, she's stunning. That flawless skin and those lips. I'd feast on those all night.

She places a file in front of each of the three women sitting before me before she turns to leave the room. I'm almost too caught up in watching her ass walk away to stop her.

"Wait a minute," I call, freezing her in her tracks. I narrow my eyes again. "Who is this?"

"That's nobody important. You have the best of my team right here," Bianca says.

I don't miss the stiffening of my chocolate-brown goddess. She goes completely rigid, yet she doesn't turn back around to face me.

"Something tells me that's bullshit," I reply.

That causes the beauty I have my gaze on to turn around and look me in the eyes. Her brows are pinched as she locks those big brown orbs on me. There's something in her depths that calls to me.

I tilt my head to the side and study her. There's a sharp wit that dances in her eyes as if her thoughts are quite amusing. Still, I get the sense that she's used to hiding. Too bad for her; when I find something I want, there's no hiding it from me.

"You three can leave," I say without taking my eyes off the dove standing before me. "Mother, I need to go. See to it that *Nobody* over there is at my apartment this evening by seven to pitch the proper event proposal. The one *she* just finished putting together for them."

With that, I stand and bend to kiss my mother's cheek. I turn to leave the room, but not before one last comment to the concerned-looking vixen I have every intention of getting to know better. Her eyes widen as I get closer and lean into her.

"Don't worry. I'll be gentle. I'll make this all easy on you," I whisper.

Cinder

He smells delicious. The kind of lingering scent that makes you want to drop to your knees and see if he smells as good down there. The man is pure gorgeousness.

I don't usually like blonds, but he's my exception, with his light-blond hair, crystal-blue eyes, strong jaw, and straight nose… good God. I just want to lie on his chest. That body is fine as hell too. I love a tall man. He has to be at least six-three. Not lean, but not bulky either.

Ooh wee, he's so right for my fantasies at night. Yes, ma'am, I'll be imagining those big hands under my sheets tonight. Phew, what did he just say to me? I stare after him, drooling as he leaves out of the door.

"What your son is requesting isn't going to be possible," my stepmother sputters, bringing me back to the room.

Her voice is like nails on a chalkboard. I can't stand this woman or her daughters. I clench my fists at my sides. They'll be the death of my family's legacy if I allow it.

"And why is that?" Mrs. Blake asks.

"Well… because… she doesn't do house calls. I'd rather be able to supervise her. You know how hard it can be to find good help."

"She looks like a capable young woman to me. This ball is important to me. I want my son to be happy with the outcome. If this young lady is the key to that, I think it would be best if you make this happen," Mrs. Blake says, lifting her chin.

"I will be happy to help in any way I can. However, she's right. I can't this evening. I'm already in charge of the Whitman event. I'll be attending their masquerade ball," I say softly.

Mrs. Blake claps her hands together. "I was invited to that event." She pauses for a moment. "Perhaps I can persuade Princeton to come along. His father had to suddenly leave on business and I was going to bow out, but my gown is so divine. Yes, I'll have Princeton come along."

"I'll be working. I don't know if I'll have much time to discuss your event with him," I say and start to chew my lip.

I have to save this account. Bianca and her idiot daughters are on the verge of ruining one of the biggest events we've had so far this year. I can't afford for this event to fall apart. If word gets out that we botched the Blake gala, the company will be ruined.

These three don't even know who these people truly are. They would if they did their homework. Bianca saw the budget for the event and suddenly became so invested in our new clients. If only she knew.

"We'll make it work, dear. Princeton has a way of making things work." She winks at me. "Ladies, thank you."

Mrs. Blake stands to leave. I'm dumbfounded as she starts for the door. I furrow my brows.

"But wait, everyone will be in costumes. Including the staff. How will he find me? The Whitmans have restricted cell phone use. All guests will have to turn in their phones."

She turns back to face me, her eyes rolling over me from head to toe. She gives a sly grin. "This just got more interesting. If he finds you, it was meant to be, dear. It will all work out."

I stare after her with my mouth hanging open as she leaves. I don't know what just happened. I've been swamped with all the work Bianca has been taking on.

I should've had the Blake proposal ready before this morning's meeting, but I had three parties almost blow up in my face and the meeting had been moved up from its original time. I had to scramble to get the proposal finished and rush it into the boardroom.

"What the hell was that?" My stepmother snarls after Mrs. Blake is out of earshot.

"I told you not to move the meeting up. I would have been ready had they come at their scheduled time," I say.

"We have a spa appointment this morning to get ready for the ball tonight. We needed to move them up," Glenda says, flipping her blonde weave over her shoulder.

As much as she spends on those damn hairstyles, you'd think they'd be able to make them look real. I fight not to roll my eyes at her. On top of everything else, the three of them are selfish.

"I'll take care of it." *Like I always do*, I think to myself. "I'll work out the details of the party with Mr. Blake and secure the account."

Bianca narrows her glaring eyes at me. I count backward in my head. Only a few more months and I can buy this witch and her spawns out of my father's business before they ruin it.

"I will talk to Princeton myself this evening. Leave the proposals with us. I'll make sure he sees the great ideas we've come up with," she says.

We, as in her and her twit daughters. *Bullshit*. These three wouldn't even know where to start. I sigh. It's no use fighting with them. They'll just find a way to make my life worse.

"As you wish." I turn to head back to my office.

"By the way, *your* rental for this evening must be returned by midnight. There was a slight mix-up. I suggest you make sure to get all your tasks done before then. The cars are the only way off the island, and you won't fit with us."

Sure, I won't fit into the twenty-passenger vehicle I booked for me and my staff that Bianca and her nitwits decided to take over. My poor staff will now have to stuff into an eight-passenger vehicle when there are ten of us. Good thing most of them will be finished at the event by twelve. I'll have to find the others a ride.

"Thanks," I say, but it's dripping with sarcasm. I can't wait to get them out of my life. Eighty-one days and counting.

CHAPTER TWO

Haters

Cinder

It's been a long day and it's nowhere near over. I shut down my laptop and get up from my desk to stretch. I need to get home to get ready for the ball this evening.

My neighbor, Ms. Randell, says she used to be a hair and makeup artist in Hollywood. She's been all too excited to get me glammed up for this event. I don't even know why I'm going all out. It's not like I'll be there to party.

I smile as I walk over to my dress hanging on the back of the closet door in my office. This is the reason I'm so excited. I finally slimmed down enough to wear my mother's wedding gown.

I worked hard to get my waist down, but thank God it flares at the hips. It fits like a glove now. I can't wait to pair it with the shoes I found. It's all going to be perfect.

I unzip the bag to peek at the dress one more time. I sent it out to be cleaned and had to pick it up on my lunch break. Pulling it out of the bag and fluffing it, I can't stop smiling.

"Cindy," Rosa snarls from behind me. I sigh and turn to face her. "You never gave me that vendor contact for the Anderson brunch. Are you trying to make me look stupid?"

Honey, you don't need me for that. You were born stupid.

"I printed the vendor list for you." *Again*, because she keeps asking instead of opening her damn computer to pull the information from the database. "It should be on your desk."

"Are you getting smart with me?" She points a finger at me over the wineglass in her hand. Who drinks wine at work in the middle of the damn day? "You do know I don't have to sell you shit. Even if you get the money, we don't have to sell you our shares."

I bite back my retort. I don't know what my father was thinking. He always promised this place was mine if anything ever happened to him. I couldn't believe my ears when his attorney announced that my father had divided the company among the four of us.

My mom has to be rolling in her grave. She and Daddy started this place together. They worked so hard to make something of their business and they had. After Mom died, my father threw himself into this place and made it an even bigger success.

I plan to do the same thing, but first, I have to play nice, so I can buy these creeps out. Eighty-one more days. I can do this.

"No, Rosa. I'm not getting smart." I move to my desk. "Here, I have another copy."

"Oops," she says.

A chill runs through me. Just from the sound of her voice, I know I'm going to kill this bitch when I turn around. I turn eerily slow to see what she has done.

I drop the paper in my hand and a whimper slips from my lips. My blood starts to boil. The front of my mother's gown is covered in red wine.

"You bitch," I snarl.

"What did you just call my daughter?" I look toward the door to find Bianca and Glenda standing there.

"She just ruined my mother's gown," I growl.

"Well, it looks like you won't be going to the ball after all. Hand me the file for tonight. I'll handle the event myself."

I don't know who I want to throttle more. Bianca or Rosa. I tighten my fists. I try to remind myself not to beat the shit out of them. I'm so close to buying them out. I can't allow them to push me over the edge now.

I snatch up the Whitman pack for tonight and my purse. As I storm out of my office, I nearly fling the file at Bianca. I don't even turn back to look at them as they snicker and whisper.

I hold my tears back as I punch the button for the elevator. I think of going back for the dress, but just the sight of it will make me change my mind and I will drag all three of them.

"Nope, you're not going to stoop to their level, Cindy. Keep moving. Payback is a bitch. It will happen soon enough," I mutter under my breath.

As soon as I step into the elevator and the doors close, hot tears start to fall down my cheeks. I've held on to that dress for sixteen years. Mom and I would play dress up and she'd always let me put it on and dance around, calling me her princess.

I was nine when she died. My father was devastated. I thought he'd never recover. Honestly, I don't think he ever did. Taking Beauty for Ashes Event Planning international was his way of running from it all.

It was also how he met Bianca. She started out as my nanny and somehow wiggled her way into my father's bed. I swear that woman was the death of my father. She did nothing but stress him out.

"Spoiled bitches," I fume.

Princeton

This is the shit I'm talking about. I asked Mother to do one thing. Get that chocolate beauty to my apartment. That wasn't asking too much. Now, I'm in a damn tux with a mask on my face.

"How do I get myself into this shit?" I mutter as I step out of my apartment building and climb into the waiting Wraith. The driver closes the door and I settle into the seat.

"You don't have to look so put out," my mother says from her seat beside me.

"I had no intention of going to this ball. This mask itches and I'd much rather be in my apartment nude. It's too hot for this nonsense," I mumble.

"Stop behaving like such a sourpuss," she chortles.

Puss, that's what has me in this predicament in the first place. I want to see that gorgeous goddess again. I haven't been able to get her off my mind.

Shit, I have to shift in my seat as my cock grows hard just thinking about her. This is going to be a long damn night. I can feel it.

"Now you will have to find her. She'll be working this evening, but if you can steal her away for a bit, you can get the details of what she has in mind for your event," Mother says.

"Yes, I'll be sure to get those details." I couldn't care less about planning that damn ball.

"She's a lovely-looking young lady, isn't she?"

I turn toward my mother to find her staring at me with an amused look on her face. Shit, I've given away too much. I'm sure she knows that I intend to pursue this woman.

"She is."

She narrows her gaze. "Just remember that it's time for you to find a bride. Whatever fun you're planning to have, don't let it get in the way of the purpose of your gala. You will find a nice girl and settle down."

I hear the warning in her voice. She and my father have had enough of my bachelor lifestyle. They have been after me to settle down for years, but this year it has become a demand. I must find a bride.

No one will mention my betrothed who disappeared. The one I was destined to marry even before her birth. The bride whose mother found our arrangement lacking and ran off with her child.

Nope, we all shy away from that topic, which is what this event we're planning is all about. I must find a replacement bride. Lucky me.

I bite my tongue to keep from saying anything cheeky. "I will have a bride before the year is over," I say dryly.

I'll hold up my end of the bargain. I'll find a wife. It will be difficult when the only woman to stir even an ounce of something inside me—in years—is the one who will be planning the event meant to find me a wife.

My mother clicks her tongue at my response. I guess I didn't keep my annoyance out of my voice as much as I thought. She shifts her body in her seat to look at me.

"You are a crowned prince, Princeton. Your father and I have been very lenient with you. This will not continue if you insist on defying us and shirking your duties," she says in warning.

"I have performed all of my duties and this gala you want to throw will allow me to do as you and Father ask."

"Just don't allow this young woman to be a distraction from all of that." She huffs and turns away.

I furrow my brows. She was the one to talk me into going to this event. She knew I would agree because of the beauty I'm after.

Why tear into me about it?

I remain silent for the rest of the ride. Mother is up to something. I can see it in the set of her lips. If I'm not careful, I'll end up in one of her traps. Good lord, if she tricks me into marrying one of the women she and Father choose, I'll jump from a cliff.

While all beautiful—well, mostly—they are lackluster. Too arrogant, too self-centered, too shallow. I can be all of those things; I don't need to have a wife that's a bigger asshole than I am.

I wonder if my little bird will check off all my boxes? Not that they'll allow me to marry a common woman. Although, my parents have bent a few rules for me.

I grin as I think of what I want to bend tonight.

"What's that little grin for?" Mother asks as we pull up to the castle on the private island the party is being held on.

"Nothing, Mother, nothing at all."

CHAPTER THREE

You Must Go

Cinder

"Cee-cee, what's wrong?" Ms. Randell asks as she sticks her head out of her apartment door.

"I won't need your help tonight after all. Thanks, Ms. Randell."

"What in the world have those monsters done now? You were so excited about this ball. You have to go."

I press my forehead to my front door and take a deep breath to keep from bursting into tears. "My dress was ruined. Rosa spilled wine on it."

"Oh honey, I'm so sorry."

I turn to face her. "I swear she did it on purpose. We had this client come in today and he insisted on working with me.

His mother said that they would find me at the ball to discuss their event.

"I… I just can't believe they would ruin my mother's dress over this. She could have had the account. I would have sent him right to her. I had planned to," I say and sniffle.

"I don't know why you're surprised," Ms. Randell deadpans. "If a man is involved, you have even less reason to question their actions."

"Bianca has been using your company to try to pawn off those terrible daughters of hers. Why do you think she tries to book all the socialite parties? It's not for the money. Well, not entirely," she says and purses her lips.

"Well, I have no intention of embarrassing myself thinking I have a chance with someone like Princeton Blake. He just wanted a competent party planner. Those two can throw themselves at him all they want," I grumble.

"Princeton Blake?" Ms. Randell stands up straighter. "He's the gentleman who requested your services?"

"Yes." I tilt my head. "Why?"

"You must go to the ball."

"What? Why?"

She waves a hand at me. "Princeton Blake doesn't make idle requests. No, you must go."

"How do you know about Princeton?"

Her cheeks turn pink. "It's a part of my job."

A part of her job. What job? I haven't seen her go to a job since I moved in here. I've always wondered how she can afford this place. She must come from money. Heck, I only live here because it was one of the properties my father left me.

The other place is a Château or something, someplace in Europe that I'd never heard of before receiving a letter after the reading of the will. I've considered selling the place, but something has always stopped me.

I've been too busy saving to buy back the company to go check the place out. It's on my list of things to do when I can finally take a vacation.

"I think I'll pass on this one," I mutter.

"You will do no such thing. Destiny is in the works, dear. We will meet up with it."

"Huh?"

"Trust me."

She looks down at her watch. Her brows draw together. I feel bone tired. I just want to go inside and go to sleep.

"I'll see you tomorrow. I'm going to forget this day ever happened."

"Nonsense. I'm going to make some calls and then we'll get started on your hair and makeup," she says.

"I don't have a dress."

"What do you think I'm making the calls for? Off with you. Go shower the day away and I'll be over in twenty."

I go to argue, but she gives me a firm look. I guess I'm going to the ball after all. I sigh and turn to push into my apartment.

"What a day."

***

"Wow," I whisper as I look at my reflection staring back at me.

I thought I was in awe when Ms. Randell arrived with four clothes racks pushed in after her as she made her way into my living room. Now I'm just floored. I can't believe it's me.

The strapless blue gown shimmers with silver and is beaded with crystals at the top. It's breathtaking. The wide skirts sway when I move. My hair and makeup are flawless.

Ms. Randell brushed all my natural curls into a ponytail and created the sleekest curly bun I've ever had. A far cry from the blowout I wear to work. I can't even believe she got my curls to spring back and behave for her.

I feel like a princess.

"I always knew this crown would fit you perfectly," she chokes out at my side.

I turn to her to find tears in her eyes. I lift a hand to lightly touch my collarbone. It's odd. I've never seen this crown before today. Yet Ms. Randell looks at me as if this is something she's longed to see.

"It's very pretty," I say. "Maybe I shouldn't wear it. I don't want to lose it or something. It looks expensive."

"I won't allow it. You will wear it to the ball. It's yours," she says firmly. "Now, where are those shoes you've been talking about?"

My cheeks hurt from the smile that comes to my face. The one thing that hasn't been ruined about tonight. My shoes. I lift my skirts and move to the shoebox.

"Oh, my. Those are breathtaking."

"Yes, they are. I had to have them," I reply as I hold a silver strappy sandal in my hand.

"Quick, let me help you get those on," she says.

I sit on the bed and she gets down on the floor to help put my shoes on. My phone vibrates on the bedside table. I pick it up to find a message that the car is downstairs waiting.

"Oh, I forgot all about the car coming. They're here. I'm the last pickup. I better go," I say as she finishes buckling the last strap.

I stand and she draws me into a tight hug. "You enjoy yourself. This is what your mother and father would have wanted for you," she whispers, her voice filled with emotion.

I pull away and get ready to ask her how she would know what my parents would want, but my phone buzzes again. It's one of my workers letting me know the driver is impatient and acting like a dick.

"I have to go. Thank you for everything."

"It was my pleasure. I hope this evening is all that you imagined and more. Make sure to enjoy yourself."

"I will as much as work will allow," I say.

"But you're off tonight. No one will know it's you. Since the evil ones wanted to handle this evening, let them. You go as a guest and enjoy time with a handsome prince, if you catch my drift."

I pause for a moment. She has a point. I could very well go through with being a guest this evening and no one would know. The staff riding with me wouldn't say a word if I asked them not to. They can let me know if there's an emergency or something.

This way I can find the Blakes and salvage their event before my stepsisters and stepmother lose the entire account. The idea starts to take root. I like it more and more by the second.

A handsome prince. She has no idea how right she is in that statement. Again, I think of what I found in my research.

"I might just do that."

CHAPTER FOUR

Arrival

Cinder

"Why me?" I huff and groan into my hands.

I had to send my staff ahead of me in two Ubers. Our car broke down, leaving me on the side of the road because even with the two Ubers there wasn't enough room for me, especially not with this big dress on.

"I'm so sorry, ma'am," the driver peeks his head into the back window to say. Funny how his tone has changed. "My boss said he's rushing a car here for you. It'll be the same; you'll have to leave the event by midnight. I'm sorry about that."

"At this point, I should just go home," I mutter.

I'm still stewing in the back seat thirty minutes later when the door opens. The driver gives me an awkward smile as he holds out his hand.

"Your ride is here. It's a beaut.'"

I sigh and take his hand to climb out. I stop in my tracks as the black-and-blue Wraith comes into view. It's not what I was expecting at all.

"I'll have you there in no time, ma'am," the new driver says.

"Thank you."

I melt into the seat as I sit inside the car. I truly feel like a princess. This day has continued to go from one extreme to the other. I'm liking the results.

I almost forgot how breathtaking the location is. As the car starts the drive over the bridge, I look down at the water crashing against the stone wall below. It gives such a majestic feel to the bridge and the castle-like structure on top of the cliff on the other side.

"This is one pretty place," the driver says before releasing a low whistle.

"Yes, it is."

When we roll up to the front of the castle, there aren't any cars ahead of us. It looks like I'm the last guest to arrive. The photographers and reporters are still milling around—I'm sure waiting for whatever scoop they can get once the guests are all drunk and reckless.

Everyone starts to come alive once the car comes to a stop. I inhale, trying to still my beating heart. I don't know what I was thinking. I shouldn't be here.

"Can you give me a few seconds?" I plead with the driver before he can get out.

"Sure, whatever you need. You look exquisite, by the way. They're sure to take some amazing photos of you."

That doesn't serve to help my nerves or my pounding heart. I get ready to tell him that we should leave, but something catches my eye as the doors open in wait for me.

Step One and Step Two are mingling with the guests and not handling the party as they should be. I know it's them because of those ugly, overpriced dresses they insisted on buying. I had to hear about them for weeks. As if seeing them wasn't enough to make me gag.

My blood is boiling. If they mess this party up, I'll kill them both. I need to get inside and make sure the clients are happy. This is still my family's business that I need to protect.

"I'm ready," I say as I fortify my nerves.

Princeton

I step out onto the balcony to fume all by myself. She's not here. I've stopped every worker with a clipboard to ask for their boss and they keep pointing me in the direction of those vile women.

When I asked for the one who gets shit done, I was told she has the night off. I'm so pissed. I could be in my apartment with her brown thighs around my neck if my mother would have followed my directive.

"Fuck," I mutter.

The flashing of lights gets my attention below. Looking down, my breath is stolen away. A beauty in a strapless blue-and-silver dress climbs from the back of a Wraith. She's stunning, even with her face covered.

I squint. Could this be her? I would think so if it weren't for the regal air of this woman and the confidence that oozes off her. The little beauty in that office this morning had a shy air about her, none of this self-confidence.

The woman walks to enter the castle, cameras still flashing to capture her beauty. As if knowing my eyes are on her, she stops and looks up over her shoulder. I feel this pull to get to know her. Narrowing my gaze, it occurs to me that I just might already know who she is.

Yet, I still don't know her name, which occurred to me only an hour ago. My mother hasn't a clue either. I'm growing more intrigued with my little vixen.

Even from this distance, she has a pull on me. When she drops her head and turns for the castle entrance again, I know it's her. For the briefest moment, that shyness appears.

I turn and head back inside. I need to get down to the lower level and find her. However, once inside, I run into my mother and Bianca. I've been avoiding this woman and her daughters like the plague.

I don't want to hear a word from her mouth. She smiles and it grates on my nerves. She doesn't need to wear a mask because that phony persona does enough to cover her face.

"Princeton, is that you? You look dapper."

"No, you're looking for someone else," I reply and keep moving.

My mother gives a low chuckle as I go, but she doesn't call me on my shit. I jog down to the first floor and move through the crowd toward the doors. They've closed once again.

"Fuck."

I push through the thick crowd, but I'm losing time. I have no way of finding her in this throng of people. Or so I thought.

Right as I think my luck has run out, the crowd opens as if hearing my frustration. There she is. Everyone stands and marvels at the gorgeous woman who walks through the opening.

The crown on her head catches the light. She looks like a true queen. Her head is held high as she moves forward. As if having a mind of their own, my feet lead me toward her.

She's more breathtaking up close. Her breasts are so inviting in her gown. There's a glow to her dark skin.

The music seems to get louder as we draw nearer to one another. Our eyes connect through the masks. The silver and blue of hers frame her gorgeous face perfectly.

"You're stunning," I say as we stand before each other.

"Thank you."

"I don't believe I've had the pleasure of knowing your name."

She tilts her head to the side. Her lips turn up into a mischievous smile. I suck my bottom lip into my mouth, thinking about how delicious her plush pillows will taste.

"It's a masquerade ball. Isn't the point to be anonymous."

I grasp hold of her waist and pull her into me. "Have it your way. I'll have it before the end of the night."

"So much confidence."

"I always get what I want."

"Hmm, okay," she murmurs with a smile on her lips.

I twirl her around the dance floor, feeling the eyes of everyone on us. I couldn't care less about their gazes. I'm entranced by the creature before me.

She fits in my arms perfectly. Her soft breasts have molded to my front. Her scent has my mouth watering. I've yet to pinpoint what she smells of, but it's as enticing as she looks.

"Do you often outshine your clients at their own parties?" I tease.

"I am a guest, just as you are. I haven't come to outshine anyone. I've come to enjoy an enchanted evening."

"Okay, if that's the way you want to play it. You are a guest, just as I am. Therefore, you can come with me for a stroll in the gardens. I hear they have truly enchanted them for this evening," I reply.

A moment's hesitation crosses her face before she looks around the ball. She releases a heavy breath before turning back to me with a nod. I give her a crooked grin.

I offer my elbow to lead her to a set of doors lining the back wall. They're all open to lead out into the lighted grounds. Once we step out, a gasp leaves her lips.

I'll admit, I'm impressed myself. The back of the castle has been transformed into something magical. Lights are strung everywhere, twinkling with a sort of pulse of their own. The thought of fairies and magical beings pops into my head like I'm a small boy who believes in those things again.

"Wow."

"You can say that again. Beauty for Ashes does amazing work," I say with a hint of humor.

"Yes, they do. You can tell this was done with love."

I smile at her words. She moves to straighten a string of lights before she catches herself and tugs her hands back. It's interesting to see her marvel at something of her own creation. I have no doubt she had a hand in this. It's like watching parents view their child for the first time.

We walk deeper into the backyard, entering the garden of mazes. The path narrows, creating a more intimate surrounding. Lights continue to lead the way and create a majestic ambience.

"It's awe-inspiring, isn't it?" I say.

"It's beyond my wildest dreams," she whispers.

"Makes you want to make a wish for the impossible or to believe in it."

She turns her face up to peer at me through her mask. "That sounds a bit deep."

"Does it? Are you telling me that you don't have a wish you want to come true?"

She shrugs her delicate shoulders. "I don't have time for wishing. I've had to make things happen in my life. Wishing is for those not willing to do."

I frown. "Are you calling me privileged?"

"I wasn't." She chuckles. "But if the shoe fits."

I catch her around the waist as we step through to an opening with a water fountain in the center. Music floats through from unseen speakers, causing me to sway her body with mine.

"I'll have you know I'm willing to work for what's mine."

"Are you?"

I draw her closer and drop my gaze to her lips. I lean in to kiss her, but she raises a gloved finger to press against my mouth, halting my movement. I look into her eyes questioningly. I know she has to feel this charge between us.

"Showing that entitlement, are we?"

I chuckle. "Maybe. Or maybe I just know a beautiful woman when I see one. I'm not one to play games. If I see someone I'm interested in, I make it known."

"Noted," she says and goes to remove her finger.

I nip it before she can pull the digit back. The way her breasts heave causes me to hold it for a moment. Her tongue darts out to wet her lips and I have to suppress a groan.

I release her finger and place my forehead to hers. "What's your favorite color?"

"My favorite color?"

"Yes, I'm working for what I want," I reply with a grin.

Her musical laugh fills the air. She runs her hands up my back as I tighten my hold on her, still swaying us to the music. I back away to watch how her face lights up.

"You're breathtaking. Has anyone ever told you that?"

Her laugh sobers. "No, not really. Not in a long time."

"You're gorgeous."

"And you can tell that through a mask?"

"Are we forgetting I've seen you without it?"

She gives that sweet, mischievous smile again. "Are you truly sure about that?"

"Ah, yes, I almost forgot. We're playing along with the theme tonight. Actually, it's refreshing to be someone other than—other than who I am."

"Perfection is such a hard life," she teases.

I place my fingers under her chin. "You find me perfect?" I breathe the words as I brush my thumb across her lips.

"I didn't say that," she says softly.

"Why, yes, I think you did. You implied, at the very least. So, we're both in agreement that we make a perfect connection. Something worth exploring."

She laughs that beautiful laugh again. I can't help brushing my fingers across her exposed cheek. She's... wow. I feel like I have a goddess in my arms.

"My favorite color is blue. I love truffle and salted caramel ice cream, but it's a seasonal flavor, so like many things in my life, it's been snatched away too soon. I'm happy with the simple things in life, but I work hard to have the better things as well."

I grin, loving that she's opening up to me. I lift her hand to my lips and kiss her fabric-covered fingers before lacing our hands together. I get lost in her gaze for a moment.

I should be alarmed by this deep connection I feel with her. I blame it on the night. We are pretending, after all. Tonight I'm a simple, ordinary man. I allow myself to care for once as she sucks me into her world.

"Gray, I like the color gray. I love chocolate ice cream. However, I love to eat it with vanilla. There's something about watching the chocolate run and drip over the vanilla. It makes me enjoy eating it more."

The fire that ignites in her eyes is exactly what I'm looking for. Her body softens a little more and she sags into me. I begin to stroke the bare skin on her back. My fingers itch to release the strings of her gown.

"Are you a dog or cat person?" she asks.

"Allergic to both, but I'll pet a pussy if given the chance."

Her well-arched brow lifts over the mask. "In that case, I'm allergic to dogs as well."

I release a deep laugh. We continue to banter back and forth. I truly enjoy the time we spend together. I haven't had a woman hold my interest like this in so long, if ever.

Her wit and challenging personality keep me on my toes. I'm very much enjoying the chase as I get to know her. I want to know more with each minute that passes.

"You mentioned loss earlier. What's the story behind that?"

"Excuse me," she says, looking at me in confusion.

"Your words referenced ice cream, but I could tell there was more to it."

"Oh," she says as realization lights her eyes. "That's a long story."

I look at my watch. "I have nothing but time."

"Unfortunately, I don't," she says, looking at my watch. "Oh my God, I have to go."

"What? Wait." She turns, lifts her skirts and begins to take off. I grab her arm to stop her. "Wait, what's the rush?"

"I have to go. My ride. I had a great time, but I need to leave," she says in a rush and pulls from my grasp.

A clock chimes loudly somewhere in the castle. I take off after her. With all I've learned about her, I still don't know her name. We can't end the night like this.

CHAPTER FIVE

Mix-Up

Cinder

I rush as fast as the gravel path and my heels will allow. It was so foolish of me to lose track of time. I truly got caught up in the magic of the night.

When Princeton stood before me on the dance floor, something inside me shifted. I felt beautiful and powerful. Everyone's eyes were on me, but his stare did something to me.

It was in that moment that I made the decision to be someone else this evening. I wanted to forget Cinder. Forget the responsibilities that have dropped into my lap in the last year. For once, I didn't want to feel like I was trying to stay afloat.

"Wait, damn it. You're going to hurt yourself in those shoes."

He calls from behind me. I don't stop. I push my way into the ballroom and dart through the crowd.

"Shit," I mutter, half out of breath.

I have to retrieve my phone. Megan, my assistant, took it when I arrived and gave me a ticket. She pushed me to join the party, promising she had it all under control.

I change directions and rush to the check-in area. I pull out the ticket and thrust it out with a shaky hand. If I miss my ride, I don't know how I'll get off this island.

Every car had to be approved. I called ahead to get the two Ubers' clearances for my staff. The same drivers agreed to return for them since they already had clearance. I look around for Megan. She's in charge of security and clearance.

I groan, knowing she has gone home. Bianca refused to pay her the overtime. I'm sure to spite me when she thought I'd be running the event this evening.

Honestly, everyone who was meant to get off and on this island had approval weeks ago. She had no need to stick around after eleven thirty p.m. Security has their list. I would have been here to oversee the rest of the event.

I'll have to walk the bridge in these shoes if I miss my ride. The attendant hands over my phone in the custom bags the Whitmans wanted all of their guests to leave with. I clench it to my chest and turn for the doors.

"Wait," Princeton calls from behind me as he pushes through the crowd, patting his pockets.

I don't stop. Rushing out of the castle, I find the Wraith parked out front. I breathe a sigh of relief and pull the door open to slip inside. I fall back against the front seat and put my head back, only to jump when an unexpected voice greets my ears from the back seat.

"Well, hello, dear. Are we giving you a ride home?"

I turn to find Mrs. Blake sitting in the back of the car. I look toward the driver and realize it's not mine from earlier. I groan and cover my face with my hands.

"I'm so sorry. I thought this was my car."

"No worries, my dear. I'm sure Princeton wouldn't mind giving you a ride home."

"No, I have a ride. I think," I murmur.

"You mean the Wraith with the worried-looking driver that just left?"

"Seriously?"

"Yes, seriously. I have a splitting headache. I've been out here for some time. I figured Princeton would show up when he was ready. The no-phone policy has turned into a pain," she says.

"I do apologize. I'll find a ride."

I turn to open the door and step out. Princeton appears with a smile on his lips. I bite my lip, feeling my cheeks heat.

"So, you run away from me to jump in my car?" he says and lifts a brow.

"I thought it was my car in my rush," I reply.

He has removed his mask, revealing his handsome face. Those eyes are even more piercing without it. He places his hand on my waist.

"Where's your car? I'll walk you to it."

"Your mother says it left." I do my best not to pout.

"Princeton, dear, help the girl into the car. I have a headache. You can drop me at the apartment in the city and then see that she gets to her home," his mother says from inside the car.

"You heard my mother. We'll take her home and then I'll get you to bed," he says in that sexy deep voice of his. It seems like everything he has said tonight has had a double entendre.

"You don't have to do that. I'll be fine."

He places his fingers beneath my chin, lifting my head so I have to look up at him. "I will get you home safely. Get inside, *princess.*"

I shiver at the way he says the last word. I go to protest just as my stepmother and stepsisters come out of the castle calling Princeton's name. I bite back my response and slip into the back seat of the car. I don't want them to see me here.

I know it will only cause me more trouble if they know that not only have I come to the event, but I've been with Princeton all night. Once I'm inside, his mother reaches for my hand and squeezes it in hers.

I look over to her and she gives me a warm smile. Reminding me of her words from earlier in the office, I'm curious about this woman. Her kindness toward me gives me pause.

"No, I've told you that you will not handle my event. If you can't accommodate my request, I'll take my needs elsewhere," Princeton says outside of the car, grabbing my attention.

"I assure you we can handle your needs," Rosa purrs.

"I doubt that. Good night," Princeton says before climbing into the front seat.

The door closes and I slump down in my seat as Glenda narrows her eyes and stares into the window. Mrs. Blake pats my hand, causing me to turn to her. She gives me that smile again.

"The windows are tinted."

"Oh," I reply and straighten, feeling like a dummy.

The rest of the ride is silent, allowing me to get lost in my head. I should find a cab once at his mother's home. Something tells me that Princeton would like to continue this night. The spell has been broken. It's time for me to go back to my real life.

My stepmother and stepsisters are a reminder of that. Princeton Blake is no ordinary man. I'd be foolish to allow myself to get swept up in him. I know the Blake event file well. His party is for him to find a bride.

The guest list of potential brides is a mile long. I'm nowhere near the pedigree for his perfect match. I shake away all the dreams and ideas I'd had while we talked in the gardens by the fountain.

"It was so very nice to see you again, my dear," his mother says as the car comes to a stop.

I furrow my brows. "Wait. How did you know it was me?"

"You, my dear, are undeniably your mother's child. You carry her grace and beauty. I would know you in a crowd of a million others because you would shine the brightest. Have a good night, sweetheart," she says, giving me a knowing grin.

I sit stunned. I have several questions, but I don't get to ask them as she climbs from the car, leaving me speechless. I break from my shock once they disappear in the posh high-rise we've stopped in front of.

"Tell Mr. Blake I said thank you for the ride back into the city. I'll get home from here," I say quickly.

I try to reach for the door to open it. The driver gets out and comes around to open the door and helps me from the back seat. I murmur my thanks as I take in my surroundings and try to catch my bearings.

Once I figure out where I am, I head for the subway. I roll my eyes at my hurting feet, but I keep moving until there's enough distance between me and Princeton Blake. I don't get far before my feet scream for me to find a cab. Remembering the expensive-looking crown on my head as a couple walks by, eyeing me, I stop to flag a ride on the next block before I get myself mugged.

"Boy, what a night," I say as I climb into the back of a cab.

Princeton

"How is your head, Mother?" I ask as we enter the apartment my parents keep in the city.

"I've fared better. Don't you worry about me. Go, make sure that girl gets home."

I narrow my eyes on my mother. Once again, noting her odd behavior when it comes to the little dove waiting downstairs for me. This time I choose not to ignore it.

"Mother, what are you up to?"

"Whatever do you mean?"

I fold my arms over my chest and rock back on my heels. I'm no fool. I know my mother well.

"Who is she? What's this interest with her?"

"With who, dear? I'm getting on in age. Not as swift as I used to be. You'll have to clue me in a bit more."

"Really, Mother? You're as sharp as a tack. Furthermore, you were very insistent on using Beauty for Ashes for the event.

"Considering that the event isn't going to be in New York at all and Beauty for Ashes has an office in Europe, yet you were adamant about using the New York office. I still find that to be odd."

"Not to mention that meeting this morning was absurd. I know you. You wouldn't allow such behavior or sit through such bullshit unless you had a reason," I say.

"You watch your mouth."

"Mother," I growl.

She sighs, turning with a huff. I'm not here for the dramatics. I want answers. I'm missing something important here and I don't like the feeling of not knowing what.

"Have you asked the girl for her name as of yet?"

"No. Well, yes, but she refused. You know, the whole masquerade thing. She wanted to play along... why?"

"I think you should go downstairs and ask her for her name. It will all become clear to you when you have that answer."

"*Mother*. You know I hate riddles. Why don't you just tell me?" I demand.

"Because I'm going to bed. You're a grown man, as you so often like to remind me. You can handle this. Good night, love. My head is starting to truly ache something awful."

I know there's no point bothering to argue with her. I decide that I'll go to the source for the information I want. However, that doesn't stop me from watching my mother for a beat. She has a smile on her lips that sends a chill down my spine.

"Good night, Mother. Feel better."

With that, I turn, placing my guard up. This woman is up to something. I'm sure of it.

My mind is occupied with my mother's odd behavior as I make my way down to the car. When I reach the vehicle and go to climb inside, I notice right away—she's gone. I want to tear my hair from the roots.

Something on the back seat catches my attention. I reach into the back for it. It's one of the bags the cell phones were placed in. Reaching inside, I pull out the device.

Tapping at the screen, the logo for Beauty for Ashes lights up before me. I grin. She may have gotten away tonight, but not forever. I have a mystery to solve.

"Who are you?"

CHAPTER SIX

If It Fits

Cinder

I've been a frazzled mess all morning. I can't find my phone. My entire life is in that thing. I've been trying to remember the last time I saw it.

Okay, I've been trying to pray away the last place I remember seeing it. If I'm right, that means I need to contact the Blakes to see if one of them found my phone in their car.

Yeah, I know which one would have been most likely to find it and I'm not ready to admit to that. I shove my hand in my hair. I have tons of work to get to and I need to stop agonizing over this situation.

"Ms. Ellis, there's a Mr. Blake here to see you." Megan's voice comes through the intercom.

I groan and palm my face. Of course, he's here. This is officially going to be the day from hell. I jump up, realizing I need to get him out of here before those witches show up for work.

They will all drag their asses in late because of the party last night. Well, later than usual. It's sickening. The rest of the staff has come to work on time, even if some of us are existing off of coffee or sheer will. Not to mention, we had a two-hour delay in our clock-in time because of such a big event.

"I'll be right out," I say to Megan.

I rush to the mirror to check my hair and face. When I realize what I'm doing, I freeze. I shouldn't be primping for a client.

Smoothing my hands down the front of my suit jacket, I turn and head out to the front desk. The man is more gorgeous this morning than the last two times I saw him. I don't know how that's even possible.

Instead of the parted, combed-to-the-side style from yesterday, he has a blowout. It works so well with his strong features. His suit and tie complement his body and bring out his eyes.

"Good morning, Mr. Blake. How can I help you?" I say, and thank God my voice comes out even.

"Ms. Ellis, is it?"

"Yes."

He narrows his eyes at me. "I do believe we can move to first names—"

He cuts off, waiting for me to offer my first name. I don't know why, but I hesitate to offer it. Just as I go to tell him, the elevator opens, and to my horror, my stepfamily steps out.

"Princeton!" Bianca cheers. "So good to see you this morning. We can have a conference room all set up so we can discuss your event."

"Mr. Blake. We're not friends. Address me properly," he clips out.

Megan has to stifle a laugh. I turn a sharp look on her and her eyes are twinkling with mirth. I know she just heard him tell me to call him by his first name. My staff hates my stepfamily as much as I do.

Heck, I would laugh, too, if I wasn't gearing up for the shit show about to happen. Here we are on today's episode of "things like this only happen to Cinder."

"Excuse me, forgive my rudeness," my stepmother says and fidgets in indignation.

"I'm not here to see you. I've come to return this phone to Ms. Ellis."

"Phone?" Glenda says.

"Yes, she left it after the ball last night."

"Cindy wasn't at the ball last night," Rosa says dumbly.

Princeton snaps his head in my direction. His eyes light up, but a look of confusion also takes root. The questions in his eyes draw me in.

"Cindy," he repeats.

"Yes, Cindy wasn't at the ball last night. She couldn't have left the phone with you," Bianca says, failing terribly at hiding the venom in her voice.

Cindy. I hate that fucking name. My name is Cinder Ellis. For years my father shortened it to Cindy, which I didn't mind from him. It was a sweet endearment.

These three hurl it like a weapon. Especially after finding out how much I hate it. It's even on most of my documents.

My mother said she named me Cinder because even as a newborn, I was quiet but full of this energy that was just under the surface, waiting to combust at any moment.

I always loved the way she explained my name to me as a little girl. Cindy is a fucking insult to my mother's memory. It always pisses me off, but I've learned to ignore it. Today, however, I want to lunge at the witch. She knows how much I hate it.

Princeton takes my phone from his pocket and holds it up in front of me. He has a smile on his lips as he looks down at me. That panty-melting smile almost calms some of my anger.

"Is this not your phone, Cindy?"

Before I can correct him on my name or answer him about the phone, Glenda saunters over to pluck the phone from his hands. She plasters on a fake smile and bats her lashes up at him.

"Oh my God! This is my phone. I was so upset. I thought I had lost it.

"That phone check business was so annoying. I couldn't even call my stepsister to see if she was okay. I felt so bad that she fell ill and couldn't come to the ball last night," she says and puts on a fake pout.

My face has to say all the shit I'm thinking. First, Glenda and I aren't even the same damn complexion. I'm dark-to-medium brown, a chocolate sister, and she's light brown, caramel colored.

Princeton would have to be blind to confuse us. Not to mention her tacky blonde weave. That dry thing could never be mistaken for my dark curly waves, not even when I straighten it.

I go to speak, but Princeton holds up his hand. I jerk my head back and frown, but I clamp my mouth shut. Something in his eyes tells me to let him handle this one.

"So, you're telling me that you're the one I kissed last night?" he says and lifts a brow.

I school my face quickly as all eyes shoot to me. We never kissed. I stopped him the one time he tried.

"Yes, that was me," Glenda says and moves closer to him, shooting me an evil glare over her shoulder.

"That blue gown you wore was stunning," Princeton says with a wolfish smile. "Funny, under the ballroom lighting, your hair wasn't blonde."

"Oh, it was a wig. I wanted to do something different for the party," Glenda lies.

"Hmm. Did you enjoy our time on the balcony as much as I did?"

"Yes, I truly did. Especially the kiss."

I want to burst into laughter. This witch is such a liar and idiot. She's playing right into his hands.

I fold my arms over my chest as I fume. Bianca looks at me with a smug grin on her lips. Rosa, the idiot she is, looks completely confused. Bianca has to pinch her when she goes to say something.

I can't believe these three.

"Here, unlock your phone. I want to give you my number. I had such a great time with you last night. We have to go to dinner," he says smoothly.

"Oh, um... I," Glenda fumbles as she takes the phone. I can see her face blanch as she fails to open it the first two times. "I thought this phone was a loss. So, we stopped to get a new one. That's why we were late this morning."

"You should still be able to unlock this one, right?" Princeton says.

Glenda's entire face is covered in a blush. Dummy didn't think this one through. No surprise there.

"I… I can just place your number in my new phone," she stammers out, pulling *her* cell from her purse.

"No, I want to make sure I give *this* phone to its rightful owner. I'm still pissed at the way you left me last night. When I spank the ass of the owner of this phone, I want to make sure it's the right ass I'm spanking."

My mouth drops open. Glenda crosses her legs the same way I cross mine. The lust that fills her eyes is clear. With new determination, she tries to unlock my phone. Several tries and nothing.

I'm still staring at Princeton in shock. His eyes are on me as well as he shoots me heated promises. I don't know if I want to run or jump in his arms and beg for him to make good on his words.

"Glenda," Bianca says tightly. "It's your father's birthday, silly."

I look at Bianca and scoff. It was my father's birthday. Before I upgraded a few months ago. I changed the password on a gut feeling. I guess I now know why I had that feeling.

Glenda pouts. This dummy doesn't even remember my father's birthday. So much for the clue.

Princeton plucks the phone from her fingers. He holds it out to me, but not far enough for me to reach. I have to move closer. I sidestep Glenda, stopping before him to take my phone from his long fingers.

"Can you unlock *your* phone for me?"

"Yes," I reply and unlock the phone on the first try.

I look up just in time to see him lowering his face to mine. It's too fast for me to react. He cups the back of my neck and places his other hand on my waist.

I open my mouth in surprise and he groans as he proceeds to devour me. I wrap my arms around his neck and he deepens the kiss. My toes curl in my shoes.

Wow. He can kiss. His hand tightens on my waist as if he's trying to draw some restraint. Breaking the kiss, he places his forehead to mine.

"Now that was the perfect first kiss," he croons. "I truly enjoyed our walk in the garden last night."

"Wait, what the hell? I thought I recognized you last night. Before you rushed into his car," Glenda seethes.

"Yet you stood there and lied to my face?" Princeton says with so much venom, I go to take a step back.

He doesn't allow it. He tightens his hold and pulls me into his side. His grip is nothing less than possessive.

"This is unprofessional of you, Cinder. How dare you engage in such behavior with a client? You weren't supposed to be at the ball. You slacked on your responsibilities to lust after a client. I'm so disappointed in you."

I snap. I forget that I want to buy these three out and that I've been playing nice to do so. As I think of my mother's ruined dress in my office, it all comes out.

"Unprofessional? *Unprofessional?* I almost missed the ball because you three plotted to keep me from going. Spilling wine on my mother's gown?"

"Of all the evil things you could've done, that was the lowest of the low. You all know what that gown means to me. You ruined it. I don't know if I'll ever be able to have it restored."

"That was the last piece of her I have other than this business. You three have done your damnedest to cost me this place as well. Overbooking clients, making promises you don't know how to execute, leaving me to handle the messes that you make."

"None of you have a clue how to run an event planning business. Good thing my father closed that international office. I couldn't even imagine what you guys would have done with that much reach."

"I'm done. You guys can have this shit. I'll start over. It will kill me more to try to save this place from you than it will to let my family's legacy go," I bellow.

"Why did you call her Cinder?" Princeton asks, causing me to turn to look at him.

His face is white as a sheet. I don't have time for this shit. I turn and head to clean out my office. I'm done.

"Mr. Blake, Mr. Blake," Bianca calls after Princeton, but I keep moving for my office.

I storm inside and grab my purse. Tears of frustration have started to roll down my cheeks. When I look at my mother's gown, still stained and hanging, I break down.

The door to my office closes, but I don't look to see who closed it. I wrap my arms around my middle and bawl like a baby. Strong arms wrap around my waist.

"This is your mother's gown?"

"Yes," I whimper.

"We will fix it."

"It's ruined. I have nothing left of my mother or father. I can hardly remember her anymore. All I had was the memories of dressing up in this dress and even those are fading with time. I don't remember her face," I murmur.

"You don't have pictures?"

I shake my head. "No. After my father got remarried to Bianca, my mother's things started to disappear and then there was a so-called accidental fire that burned only things that had belonged to my mother, including photo albums."

He sighs and rests his chin on top of my head. "So, you don't know," he murmurs.

"Know what?"

"Nothing."

I turn to face him, swiping at my tears. "I don't know what?"

He searches my eyes. "You said that the international office is closed. Where'd you get that idea from?"

"The lawyer that read the will said Daddy sold off that office before he died. I was away on a tour of Greece just before he died. It was a birthday gift from him. I'd been gone for months. No one told me he was ill. When I would call, he would put on airs."

"Bianca fired anyone who would tell me. Staff who were like family to me, all gone. I arrived the day he passed away after our old butler was able to reach me with the news that I needed to rush home."

"The lawyer said my father made a few changes to the will during that time and sold the other company," I explain.

Princeton tilts his head at me. I have no idea what he's thinking and the look is starting to make me nervous. I wrap my middle again.

"What?" I whisper.

"I would like you to come to Europe with me. I think the trip would be quite revealing."

"I don't have time to run away with you. I need to figure out what I'm going to do without a job. I have savings, but I can't live off of that forever. I... I don't know what I plan to do now.

I wanted to buy them out, but their petty asses will never sell to me now."

He cups my face and tilts my head back. "Cinder, I need you to trust me. Come with me to Europe. Everything will work itself out."

With that, he crushes my lips with his. This kiss is a bit different from the one earlier. It's more like someone who has found something lost. Someone eager to claim something that belongs to them, or in this case, someone.

When he breaks the kiss, I'm dazed. I guess that's why I open my mouth and babble like a fool. "Okay, I trust you."

Princeton

Cinder.

It's not a common name at all. However, it's a name I know well. My mother has a lot of explaining to do. I don't know how to feel about this.

I have so many questions swimming in my head, but I pushed them back after watching her fall apart in her office. Something inside me wants to do nothing more than protect her and get to the bottom of what has caused her pain.

I don't like Bianca Estevez and her daughters. I get a feeling that they have lied about more than a phone. I plan to find proof of just that.

"Are you all set?" I ask as Cinder enters the living room of her apartment.

"Almost. I need to let my neighbor know I'll be gone for a while. She'll worry. She's always looking out for me," she says with a small smile.

I nod. "Mother has decided to travel with us."

"Oh, okay. I won't be long. Do you need to make a stop for your things?"

"No, I'll have all I need when we arrive."

She palms her forehead. "Right, it's your home." She pauses for a second. "I can recommend some great planners for your event."

"Why on earth would I need another planner? You will do just fine. I love your work," I say with a smile.

She beams back at me. The ball from last night truly was a gala to be remembered. I have no intention of finding someone else. Although, I question the need to have the event at all. However, I won't be telling her that yet.

I reclaim my seat as she heads for the door. She jumps a little when she opens it. I go to stand, but she releases a laugh.

"Hello, Ms. Randell. I was just coming to knock on your door."

"I heard noises coming from your apartment. I thought you were at work. Was the ball that amazing that you had to take the day off?" the woman says.

Her voice seems familiar, but I can't put a finger on it. I can't see her from here. The door and Cinder are blocking the view.

"Actually, I quit this morning. It's a long story. I'm heading to Europe for a while. That's what I was coming to tell you," Cinder replies.

"Europe?" Ms. Randell says, her voice peaking with interest and dare I say excitement.

"Yes, I… wait. I don't know where exactly I'm going. I just know it's Europe," Cinder says with apprehension in her voice.

"I'm sorry. I should've given you more details," I say and stand to walk over to the door.

"Oh, my. I left the water going for tea. I'll see you when you get back, dear. You call me if you need anything," Ms. Randell says in a rush.

By the time I get to the door, I only catch the back of a little woman with gray hair. I furrow my brows. When Cinder closes the door and looks up at me, her expression mirrors mine.

"What was that about?"

"I'm not sure. That's the fastest she's ever run off. Usually I have to hint that I'm exhausted before she leaves." She shrugs. "Well, I think I'm ready. I have all my things packed."

I wrap an arm around her waist and tug her into me. I've been dying to kiss her again. I search her eyes before lowering my head to capture her lips.

All else goes forgotten as I deepen the kiss. Her small moans wrap around me and draw me in. I have a mind to lift her and carry her to her bedroom.

However, when I take her to bed, I want time to savor her. We don't have time for that at the moment. We have a plane waiting for us.

Yet I don't rush to break the kiss. I take my fill of her as she shoves her fingers into my hair and tugs. I glide my hands down to her ass and palm her full curves.

She whimpers into my mouth. I swallow the sound, drawing her body into mine. I can't get her close enough and I can't kiss her deep enough. The more I take, the more I want.

I don't pull away from the connection until her small hands push at my chest. I press my forehead to hers and catch my breath. She clings to the lapels of my suit jacket.

"Princeton… I'm not sure what you think we're doing, but I'm not the type to just throw myself at anyone. I'm not going to jump in your bed. You're a crowned prince. I'm not a fool.

"You could never do more than sleep with me and move on. I have enough going on in my life. I'm not trying to complicate it any further," she says softly.

I'm amused by her words. I should have known she did her homework to find out who my family truly is. We go by Blake in the States, but we are the royal family of Verlez.

I lift her chin until her eyes meet mine. "You have no idea what you're talking about, so I'll excuse your words. You're mine. I dare anyone to tell me otherwise."

A gasp leaves her lips. I peck them, then her nose and smile. She has a lot to learn and I plan to teach her.

I spot the crown she wore to the ball on the coffee table. "You should bring that along," I say and nod at it.

"What?"

I peck her lips again. "Humor me. Bring it along."

CHAPTER SEVEN

Kingdom of Verlez

Cinder

I truly don't know what I was expecting. However, this isn't it. This place is beyond breathtaking. I thought the castle back in New York for the ball was something.

Princeton's palace is twice the size and three times as grand. This is what fairy tales talk about. It dawns on me that I'm in the presence of royalty. Not snobby socialites and entitled rich folks. Royalty.

"You know, when the file for your event landed on my desk and I did the research, it took a while for me to grasp the fact that you're a prince. It's only the second time I've gotten to plan a royal party," I say sheepishly.

"You do know I never meant to deceive you? We prefer not to use our titles when in the States."

"I respect my clients' privacy. Honestly, if I were royalty, I don't think I'd want to be made a fuss over either. It seems a little pretentious," I say the words and blush when I realize I said them out loud.

Princeton snickers. His mother grins at me. Her eyes dance with mirth, but in a regal fashion she holds the laughter in.

"It comes with its pros and cons, love. I'm sure you would make a fine queen. There's nothing pretentious about you," she says with amazement clear in her voice. "I'm off to my chambers. You two get some rest."

Princeton kisses her on the cheek. "We still have a conversation to have," he murmurs to her.

"Yes, dear. I know we do. You just take care of the gift you've been given," she says and pats his cheek.

I observe the two with curiosity. Something about the smile on her lips reads of mischief. Princeton looks frustrated, but he says nothing more.

Turning his attention to me, he searches my face without saying a word. I think back to that kiss and his words back in my apartment. My lips are still tingling and my brain is still trying to figure out how I became his.

"Our chambers are on this side of the palace." He holds out his arm toward the stairs to our right.

"Ours as in your room and my room, right?"

"Yes, your room and my room," he says with a crooked grin.

"Wait, I didn't say that right."

"You said it perfectly correct. Come, let me show you to your room."

I hesitate for a moment before walking ahead of him as he gestures for me to do. We move up the stairs as I marvel at my surroundings. Elegant sconces, gorgeous chandeliers, gold-and-red damask wallpaper and gleaming mahogany stair railings.

The story of regal wealth lines every inch. Halfway up to the next level, Princeton places a hand on the small of my back. His palm scorches right through the fabric of my blazer and blouse.

I ignore how comforting his touch feels. It warms me from the inside out. I want to lean into him and his warmth.

When we reach the top of the stairs, we turn left and move down the long, wide hallway. More beautiful sconces line the walls along with paintings and ornate furniture and real-life knights' armor.

"This is all so beautiful."

"Not as beautiful as watching you take it all in." He stops in front of double doors at the end of the hall. "How rude of me. Welcome to Verlez, Cinder. My kingdom is your kingdom and my bedroom is your bedroom."

I don't miss the heat in his words. It causes my cheeks to warm. I fold my arms over my chest.

"Princeton, I have a hard time believing that there isn't a room I can call my own in this place," I say firmly.

"You can call this room whatever you like." That wolfish grin is on his lips once again.

"Would it be possible to have a room I can sleep alone in?"

He crowds me until my back hits the doors. His blue eyes light with something I can't quite place. Something between lust and possession, but there's something else.

"I spent years thinking I wouldn't find you. I won't be letting you out of my sight. When I take you, it will be because you beg me to. So we won't have a problem sleeping in the same bed," he says huskily.

Yup, speechless. Did this guy go to school for the art of melting panties? I fidget, sternly informing my body that I will not be begging this man for a damn thing.

I can't even think straight to comprehend what he has said. When he brushes his hand along my hairline, I get the feeling that's his intention. He intends to rob me of all thought.

"It's been a long flight. You look tired. Come, there are his-and-her baths. You can freshen up in peace. Your things have been brought up for you," he says before softly kissing my lips.

Like a lamb to slaughter, I follow him into the room. It's huge, with one of the biggest beds I've ever seen. Princeton leads me to the bathroom on the right side and flicks on the lights.

My gaze falls on the huge soaker tub and that's all she wrote. I move to it and start the water. Princeton releases a low chuckle.

"You're very easy to please, princess," he says.

"You shouldn't call me that here. Someone may get the wrong idea," I say and frown.

He snorts. "I have a few things to attend to before bed. Enjoy your bath, princess."

With that, he turns to leave. I stare after him for a few minutes before I shake off the feeling I'm missing something. I start to strip from my clothes and step into the tub to sink down into its warmth.

"What in the world have you gotten yourself into, Cinder? This is so not like you," I mutter to myself.

With a heavy sigh, I close my eyes. He promised to help me. I'm trusting a guy I don't know to fix my crazy life.

Opening my eyes, I look around this luxurious bathroom. I'm no stranger to living well, but this is a new level. Yet I don't feel as out of place as I thought I would. It feels more like coming home.

Just enjoy it. You're living like a queen.

Princeton

"Yes, Your Highness, Beauty for Ashes Event Planning International still has offices in London and Milan. Ms. Ellis is listed as the owner, although there is a law firm in Edinburgh that's managing the assets and interests of Ms. Ellis," Williams says as he reports the information I asked for.

I sit at the desk in my study, eager to learn more about Cinder. She hasn't a clue about so many things and I need answers. Answers I won't be getting from her.

"How long will it take you to get me more information on her interests in the States?"

"I'm working on getting that to you as soon as possible. There are some layers to be pulled back."

To be honest, he has turned over this information more quickly than I expected. I had mentally prepared myself for the wait.

"Very good, Williams. And the Heathworth Manor?"

"It is in her name. The staff has been keeping the grounds and caring for the manor. You are right, Your Highness. Something seems to be untoward. I will continue to look into it all."

"Thank you."

Williams looks me in the eyes, watching me silently. I lift a brow at him. He stands a bit straighter.

"I was wondering how it feels, Your Highness. You have found her."

"My mother has found her. I'm not sure how I feel. She's not what I expected. Although I never expected to find her at all."

Williams clears his throat. "She is quite lovely. She looks just like her mother. She was an enchanting young woman."

"Yes, so I've heard."

Williams reaches into his pocket and pulls out a photograph. He hands me the photo across my desk. I take it and stare at the image before me in awe.

The woman in the photo looks just like Cinder. The only reason I can tell the difference between the two is the out-of-date clothing. I've heard how beautiful the princess was, but I don't remember her.

"Magnificent, are they not?"

"The American never stood a chance. *Cinder*. I think I'm in shock, Williams. I was drawn to her from the moment I laid eyes on her. I had no idea she was Princess Cinder Marie Heathworth-Ellis, my missing betrothed."

Williams gives a rare smile. "Yes, that she is. I'm sure the young ladies who have been preparing for their invitations to the ball will be very disappointed to hear that there will be no grand gala."

"We're not calling off the ball. Not until I understand what's going on. She hasn't a clue who she is. This has to be for a reason. I want to get to the bottom of what has happened. Her identity is to remain a secret until I have this sorted," I say firmly.

"Your Highness, I beg your pardon, but you just agreed that she looks just like her mother. Anyone who knew of the princess will know who she is immediately," Williams says.

He's right. I sit back in my seat and steeple my fingers in front of my lips. I want Cinder to get to know Verlez, the kingdom and its people, but that could be a bit tricky if I want to keep her a secret until I have a handle on what's going on.

"You have a point. We'll have to be careful."

Williams gives me a cautious look. "As you wish. I will have a talk with the staff as well. They do love to gossip."

"Thank you."

CHAPTER EIGHT

Event Planning

Cinder

"These are the invitations I thought would suit you and the event best. Strong but elegant," I say as I pull the sample from my folder.

That's right, I took my files with me when I left. Those three can figure out how to plan the events they booked on their own. My email is loaded with clients wanting to know what happened to me.

It's a dumpster fire back in New York. It's burning me up not to reply. I want to fix it all, but those three need to learn a lesson. If I jump in, they will just take the credit like they always do.

Nope, I'm not having it.

"I like this one," Princeton says, taking the invitation from my hand. "Can we get it in navy blue?"

"Hold on. I believe we can." I pull up a catalog on my tablet and flip through to the invitation. "Yes, we sure can. Would you like to go with the gold lettering or the silver?"

"What do you think?" he asks, placing a hand on the center of my back.

My brain short-circuits. I've been trying to grow back brain cells all morning. I'm surprised I'm functioning.

The. Man. Sleeps. Naked.

That body is so much nicer in the buff. His body heat is so delicious. It's the only reason I got any sleep.

When I turned onto my side to give him my back last night, he took that as an invitation to wrap an arm around me and spoon my body. Talk about stunned. The erection that stabbed me in the butt all night was more than impressive.

"Cinder?" he says, rubbing his hand up and down my back.

"Um, yes. I think both will look amazing. Perhaps gold would be best. Yes, gold."

"Perfect. We'll go with that."

"Okay, let's move on to the decor."

"Good afternoon, lovelies," Mrs. Blake, or should I say, Queen Joy, sings as she joins us on the veranda.

Princeton stands and places a kiss on her cheek. "Good morning, Mother."

"Oh, these look divine. Is this the invitation we're going with?"

"Yes, ma'am—Your Highness."

"Oh please. We were introduced as the Blakes to you. You are welcome to call me Mrs. Blake, or better yet, if it's just us, Joy is fine," she says with a smile.

"Okay," I say nervously. In my mind, someone will jump out of the bushes wielding a sword if I dare to call her anything other than Your Highness or Queen Joy.

"What else have you decided so far?"

"We were about to get into the decor. Now that I'm here at the site, I have a few changes I'd like to make. I was able to take a look at the grand ballroom this morning. I think we can do some amazing things with the space," I say, almost gushing like a schoolgirl.

I love this part of my job. It's always fun to imagine a space when I have pictures as my only reference. I get to stretch my imagination in new ways. However, getting to step on-site and see it firsthand is inspiring as well. I get to step into the pulse of the space.

"I've been looking forward to seeing what you have planned," Queen Joy says and places on her glasses.

For the next thirty minutes, I lay out the plan I have for the ball. I won't lie and say I don't have conflicting feelings, as Princeton keeps a hand on my back or thigh as we go. We're planning a party for him to find a wife, yet this man has claimed that I belong to him.

Honestly, by the time we're done, I'm quite annoyed with him and my body's reaction to him. I nearly flinch when he places a kiss on my forehead at the end. He looks at me with those piercing eyes.

"Are you all right?"

"Yes," I reply.

"Maybe you two should go out for dinner this evening. Princeton, you can show Cinder a bit of Verlez," Queen Joy says.

"That's not necessary. I need to place these orders and set up a few new accounts with vendors. I'll also need to make some contacts here for a couple of things."

"Nonsense. You can take tonight to explore and have a good time. Work can wait for tomorrow."

"She's right. This can all wait until tomorrow. You will be happy with the surprise I have for you then. Perhaps we can take a ride to London. I'll be happy to have dinner with you there and we'll be in place for our meeting in the morning," Princeton adds.

"Meeting?"

My interest is piqued. I've been wondering how he plans to fix my mess. I've been thinking of a plan of my own, but I want to see what he has up his sleeve.

"Yes, there's something you need to hear."

I chew on the inside of my mouth. I'm not opposed to the meeting. However, I'm not sure about this date.

Princeton searches my face. He finds something that brings a smile to his lips. He pinches my chin between his fingertips.

"Pack a small bag and a dress for dinner. I'll have a car out front within the hour."

With that, he stands. "Mother, let's take a walk."

"Phew, I think I need a nap," she says.

"Nice try. Let's go."

She rolls her eyes and stands. "You would think you were king. Wait until your father arrives."

"Does he know what you've been up to?"

"Humph."

"I wonder what he would think of what I've learned," Princeton says.

I can't help my own curiosity as the queen narrows her eyes and huffs. They both leave me behind to gather my things and thoughts. This royal family has secrets.

Princeton

We walk the halls of the East wing as my mother loops her arm through mine. The halls are empty and we can speak freely here. It's time for her to fess up.

"How long have you known where she was?"

"I found out a few months ago. A parcel arrived with her location. I believe her father might have insured I would receive it," Mother replies.

"I don't understand. Why now?"

"That I have not figured out yet, but I would make a guess that he knew his latest wife was no Princess Beverly."

I snort. "Not in the slightest. That woman and her daughters are vile."

"Yes, the poor girl has had a go of it with those three," she says and frowns.

"Do you know she thinks the European locations of Beauty for Ashes are closed?"

"What? Why would she think that?"

"One guess. I plan to get to the bottom of it all. She loves that business. It was left to her and meant to be hers."

Mother smiles up at me. She stops in the middle of the hall and cups my cheek. "You are taken with her. I can see it in the way you can't keep your hands off her."

"Yes, well, I was very curious as to why you would help me get to her at the ball, then warn me off," I grumble. "You knew that would make me pursue her more, didn't you?"

"Princeton, from the time you could walk and talk, if your father or I told you not to do something, you did it," she replies and chortles.

"Yes, well, I was onto you this time."

"Yes, you were, but that's not going to stop you, is it?"

"No, it's not. She was always meant to be mine," I reply and lean to kiss her cheek before I turn to leave.

She laughs as I walk away. Yes, my mother knows me well. Now, it's time for Cinder to learn a few things about me.

CHAPTER NINE

Charming Talk

Cinder

"You look gorgeous," he whispers in my ear as we walk from dinner back to the car.

I hold off the shiver that wants to run through me. I look up into those blue eyes and have to bite my lip. He looks like he didn't eat his meal.

"Thank you," I whisper.

His gaze drops to my cleavage. The black bandage dress puts my breasts, cinched waist, and wide hips on display. I'm not sure what made me wear this dress.

Okay, maybe I do know what made me wear it. After the helicopter ride to London, we arrived at the hotel. Princeton made sure to keep a possessive hand on my waist the entire time we checked in.

Some of the looks other women shot his way made me a little possessive myself. I know I have no right, but it pissed me off. The stink looks they gave me made me feel the same way.

A big part of me wanted to show them all. Especially the woman behind the desk. Now, I'm not sure this dress was such a good idea.

"You know how to drive a man crazy," he says.

"That wasn't my intention."

He chuckles. "Are you sure? Those heels would look amazing around my neck. All you have to do is ask."

I stumble a little, but he catches me. His fingers dig into my side and he draws me into his body. He gives me a grin.

I want to palm my face. Leave it to me to become clumsy. I'm grateful for the safety of the car. I dart into the back seat as the driver opens the door.

Princeton folds his big body in beside me smoothly. He draws me close to him. When I turn to him, he's watching me intently.

"Speak your mind, Cinder. You've been in a mood since this afternoon. What's going on in your head?"

"I'm fine."

He strokes my cheek. "Never lie to me."

I blink and lean into his heat. I don't know why the command causes such a reaction. He kisses my lips lightly.

"Tell me."

"I'm planning a party for you to find a wife. What's the point of all of this? Why wine and dine me?"

Instead of answering, he takes my lips in a searing kiss. His kisses make my head spin. I cling to his neck with one hand.

"I don't think you heard me clearly yesterday. You. Are. Mine."

"I heard you. I also know we spent this afternoon planning a ball for potential wives for you. How does that work?"

"Cinder—"

"Wait, you know what? I'm going to be honest. I find you attractive, but you have been a bit assuming. What if I had a boyfriend? You haven't asked once."

He lifts a brow. "If he hasn't come up by now, he isn't much of a boyfriend. Then there's the fuck that I don't give about him. His loss. He should have kept a better eye on what he thought was his."

I scoff. "Seriously?"

He shrugs and gives me a bland look as if the topic is beneath him. I burst into laughter. A slow smile comes to his lips.

"I like it when you laugh. Your face lights up. I'll try to amuse you more often."

"Okay, humor me. I have questions."

"Ask away. I want you to get to know me."

"You're nothing like what I expected. You're... I don't know. You have this New Yorker vibe at times, but at others, I can see the royal European prince slip through," I say, tilting my head to study him.

"Ah, yes, I've gotten that a lot. I've spent a lot of time in the States. New York is one of my favorite places."

"I've always believed that in order to understand a culture, you have to become a part of it. When in the States, I become as much of a civilian as I can."

"I leave Prince Princeton in Verlez. Drives my father crazy, but it works for me," he explains.

"That makes sense." I nod my head.

He brushes his thumb across my lip. "What else would you like to know? I'm an open book for you."

"Why?"

He leans in to kiss my lips. I get the feeling he only meant a brief brush of our mouths. However, once the small gasp leaves my lips, he deepens the kiss.

He cups my breast and leans into me until I fall back beneath him. My back meets the seat and he slides me underneath his body. Moving to torture my neck, he groans around the flesh he sucks into his mouth.

"I've never wanted anyone the way I want you. I want you to know everything. I want this to be your choice. You're the one with the power this time," he murmurs against my throat.

His words come off odd. He's answering my question, but there's a note of something deeper that's not said. I cup his face and bring it into view.

I stare into his eyes, looking for answers. He turns his head slightly and sucks my thumb into his mouth. The smoldering look in his eyes causes me to suck in a breath.

He circles the finger with his tongue. My pussy clenches. Slowly, he drags a hand up my thigh, reaching beneath my dress.

"Your skin is so soft," he breathes.

"Princeton," I moan when he slips two fingers into my panties.

"God, you have to say my name just like that when I'm inside you. You're so wet. You're going to beg for me tonight, baby. I demand it."

Shit. The sexy way he says it has me considering the option. I reach for the thick erection pressing against his slacks. When I say thick, I mean *thick*.

He groans and dips his head to take my lips as he thrusts his fingers into me. I whimper into his mouth. He makes a growling sound as I gush for him.

"Come for me," he whispers in my ear.

I lift my leg back to open to him more. As soon as I offer the room, he finds my spot and sends me right over. I arch my back and cry out.

"Fucking gorgeous," he says through clenched teeth. "My Cinder."

I look into his eyes and I don't know if I can deny his words. I think he just broke me. I've never come like that or that fast.

He lifts his fingers to his mouth and sucks on them. His eyes fill with awe and delight. He pulls them from his mouth and reaches to drag his thumb through my folds before placing it to my lips.

"Taste," he commands. I wrap my lips around his finger. "Yes, you belong to me and we will consummate that tonight. Too bad I'm going to spank your ass for not waiting for me to break you open."

He kisses me hard before I can respond to him. I think this man is a little crazy. Too bad I'm not all there either. I think I gush from his words.

Princeton

Cinder has been quiet since I fixed her panties and let her sit up. I can still taste her on my tongue. I can't wait to get between her legs and truly feast on her.

She walks before me, stepping into the lift. I can't take my eyes off her in that tight dress. As if having a mind of its own, my hand glides across her ass.

She looks over her shoulder, biting her lip. The lust in her eyes has me aching to be inside her. I hold up my hand to my security guards.

"Take the next one," I say sharply.

I press the button for the doors to close before they can protest. I quickly pin her against the wall before she can turn fully, pressing my cock into her ass.

"Do you feel what you do to me? I've been like this all night. When are you going to beg me, Cin?"

She moans and throws her ass back into me. I clench my teeth and reach to splay my hand against her belly. I glide my palm down her center slowly, pulling her back into me at the same time.

"Princeton. I don't think we should," she says in weak protest.

"You don't believe that." I chuckle in her ear.

I drag my hand back up to cup her breast. With my other hand, I brush her hair to the side to get to her neck. Flicking my tongue out to lick her skin, I thrust into her at the same time.

Fuck.

I love women and I love sex but never have I ached to claim anyone the way I ache to claim her. When I allow myself to analyze that, I know one of the reasons. For years, I've resented the idea of Cinder.

The shame and embarrassment. The feeling of being inadequate. The prince, who was so unworthy his intended's parents whisked her away to America.

Everyone knows of my disgrace. I've blamed her parents and her. It's been a cloud over my head for years. When I was a boy, it made no difference to me. As I began to grow into manhood, it caused resentment and bitterness.

The trips to the States to find them, the whispers at home about my disappearing bride, it all fueled an anger I've barely kept under wraps. Now here she is before me.

My need to punish her for her parents' transgressions rises. It's a strange feeling. I want to protect, please, and punish her at the same time. I bite down on her neck and her whimper soothes the rage and turmoil within.

"You like that, baby? You want more, don't you? All you have to do is ask for more."

I lift her arms and pin them to the wall as I grind into her. Damn, I might come right here in this lift. The ding of the arriving floor is the only thing that stops me from lifting her dress and taking her.

Grasping one of her hands in mine, I tug her from the car and start for our suite. She stumbles a little in her heels, but my impatience has me crazed. I stop to lift her over my shoulder and head for the room with no further disruption.

Her yelp of surprise is cute. As is the gasp that follows. I get the door open and step inside. I slap her ass as a warning. Her cry mixes with a moan. I'm so turned on, I growl.

Women want to date me until they learn my preferences in the bedroom. Cinder's moans and submission have all indicated she's going to make the perfect bedmate. I slap her backside once more as I step into the bedroom.

Tossing her onto the bed with a bounce, I stare down at her as I take my suit jacket off. She goes to kick those sexy heels off, but I pin her with a stern look, halting her. I lick my lips.

"They stay." She nods. "You still haven't begged me yet, baby."

I see the wheels turning. She still doesn't get that she's mine. I'm not concerned with the ball or its guests. It's for show until I have all the information I need and she is settled into her title.

I haven't told her this because I don't want to overwhelm her with the unknown. Finding out that she's a princess will be shocking enough. Then there's the matter of her family I believe she knows nothing of and the assets that have been hidden from her.

Yes, I have my reasons for not making it clear to her why that party will be anything but a wife hunt. However, tonight she will know that she's mine by the time I'm done with her.

"Princeton," she breathes as she squirms on the bed.

I continue to strip as she calls out to me. It's on her lips. She's going to beg. I grin right as she gets ready to do so.

"Please."

That's my girl.

Cinder

The word slips free before I can stop it. It's only one night. It's been so long since I've had sex. My vibrator hasn't satisfied me in far too long.

I bite my lip as a fire ignites in his gaze. He's completely naked. The man is glorious.

"That will do, beautiful," he says before he pounces.

He moves to me swiftly. Reaching for my zipper, he finds it and tugs it down. Meanwhile, his lips are on mine. He devours me in a way that has my toes curling in my shoes.

My body coils in anticipation. I get this feeling that Princeton is amazing in bed. I want him so bad. I claw my nails down his back. He groans and bites down on my lip.

A tiny voice in the back of my head tells me to stop this. I'm not about to be some royal side chick. He says I'm his, but not once has he said that he's not still going to look for a wife at his ball.

Stupidly, I silence the voice and open to him. He gets me naked and steps back to look down at me. I reach for my aching clit and start to rub it. I've always been impatient. Guys learn fast that I'm not afraid to help get myself there.

Princeton drops to his knees and pulls me to the edge of the bed. As I massage my nub, he starts his own feast. I rock my hips into his face, loving his aggressive attention to my all too willing body.

"Damn," I cry out.

I love that he works with me. Most guys I've been with take it as a hit to their ego when I help—not that I've had a lot to compare. Instead of growing frustrated with me, he actually covers my fingers and increases the pressure as he guides my pace.

My eyes cross and I lock my thighs around his head. The stimulation is perfect, exactly what I need. He sticks two long fingers inside me and I come all over the place.

"Fucking fantastic." His words come out so huskily I quake from the sound.

He lifts and settles between my legs as I come down from the second most powerful orgasm of my life. I get ready to ask him about a condom right as he thrusts into me. I cry out and buck off the bed.

"*Princeton.*"

"Yes," he grinds out. "Keep coming for me. Say my name again."

I can't believe I'm coming again as he swivels his hips and plunges deep. I dig my heels into his ass as he plows into me. He's so damn rough, but I'm right there with him.

He angles his body to hover over me as he thrusts down. Sort of like he's doing pushups off the side of the bed. The play of his muscles and the feel of him have me suspended in air as if I've left my body and have become a spectator.

I open my mouth to speak but he robs me of speech as he rolls his hips. Okay, this man has some demons he's chasing down inside my pussy. The look on his face throws me.

It's a mix of anger, pleasure, and determination. He clenches his jaw and glares into my eyes. For a moment, I feel as if I've wronged him in some way.

"Princeton?"

"This is what they took and tried to keep from me? You're fucking perfect. Was I not good enough?"

I crease my brows in confusion. Is he talking about my stepmother and stepsisters? Not good enough? He's a freaking prince.

"Princeton—"

"Why?" he demands.

However, he doesn't give me a chance to reply to that confusing inquiry. He pulls out and flips my over. My feet land on the floor and he lifts my hips into the air.

I cry out when he drives home once again. He locks one hand under my arm and over my shoulder. With the other hand, he grasps my waist. With this new hold he guides my body back into his forcefully.

"Oh my God," I cry out.

"You feel so fucking good. Open that pussy for me," he hisses before slapping my ass.

It stings like hell. I yelp seconds before his heavy hand comes down again. Another slap has me gushing all over him.

"Ah." Tears come to my eyes and I'm not sure if they're from pleasure or pain.

Princeton begins to knead my stinging cheek. "My little goddess likes that. Look how wet your pussy is for me."

My lids grow heavy. I think I'm going to pass out. However, he's not done.

He flips me onto my back and lifts my legs to his shoulders. My limbs feel like jelly and my belly is sore from his thick dick digging me out. However, I grab the sheet and take all he's giving in this position.

Eventually I do black out from his expert lovemaking, but not before drooling on myself and him. The man's sex truly is droolworthy. This one night was more than worth it.

CHAPTER TEN

Beauty for Ashes

Princeton

I try not to grin as I watch Cinder sit down gingerly. I was none too gentle with her last night. That sweet pussy drove me to the edge of sanity.

Once she passed out, I spent a few hours staring at her in her sleep. I have so many questions. Not for her, but about her.

"Your Highness, it's an honor to have you here." A short man with a balding head rushes into the conference room and greets me with his hand out.

I take his offered palm and shake it. His face beams and he puffs his chest out. He turns to Cinder and his face turns white.

"Oh my, she looks—"

"This is Cinder Ellis. I brought her in to discuss the ownership of Beauty for Ashes Event Planning International."

He clamps his mouth shut, catching his near blunder. I informed Williams to make sure this office knows not to address Cinder by her title or reveal to her who she is. I'm not ready for that to happen.

"Ms. Ellis. It's so good to finally meet you. Your father spoke so highly of you. I've been keeping things in order as he requested. Those Americans have been pushy, but I had my instructions," he says and tugs at his suit jacket.

I lift a brow at his words. Interesting. I'd like to hear more about these pushy Americans, but I'll save that for later.

"I'm sorry, I'm confused," Cinder says.

"Oh, how rude of me. I'm Larry Beasley. I've worked for your family for years. Your father hired me some time ago. Right before his nuptials to his second bride."

"Oh, nice to meet you," Cinder says, taking his offered hand. "However, I'm still a little confused."

"Right, it's my understanding that you've been sorely misinformed and it's apparent you haven't been receiving my correspondence. I've been sending reports quarterly."

"Wait, reports for what?" She turns to me. "What do you mean Beauty for Ashes Event Planning International? My father sold off the overseas offices."

"Oh, dear. Your father did no such thing. He didn't have the right to. When your mother passed, she left you the business. Your father was only authorized to look after the interests of your inheritance, he couldn't make decisions for them," Beasley says with a frown on his face.

"How could that be possible? My father started the international company after my mother died," Cinder says with wrinkled brows. "You just said my father hired you?"

"Yes, yes, I am your mother's family attorney. Your father came to me when he felt your interests needed management. He didn't want the assets your mother left to you to be associated with his."

"It was quite the delicate situation with your mother's—" He pauses to clear his throat. "He wanted to secure your future. Your mother started Beauty for Ashes Event Planning International in London before leaving for the States. After her passing—I'm so sorry for your loss—after, he returned here and picked up where she left off."

"My head is spinning. So you're saying that I have a company here in London?"

"That I am. I've been managing things here for the business and the estate your mother left in your name. Again, I've sent word of your inheritance numerous times."

"All I've ever received were some papers for a Château. I just haven't had the time to look into it. The papers said it's being looked after," Cinder says and rubs her forehead.

I reach to rub her back. A stress line forms between her brows. I bite back all the things I want to say. It's clear someone has been interfering with her getting information.

"And I must make a correction, my dear. You're the owner of Beauty for Ashes Event Planning in London and Milan. Your company is quite successful here," Beasley says proudly.

Cinder sits quietly as the wheels turn. She frowns and alarm fills her eyes. She wipes her palms on her thighs.

"So what does this mean? Can my stepmother and her daughters make a claim on the companies here? I don't know what my father was thinking when he gave them shares of the US company," she says and starts to chew on her bottom lip.

Beasley's brows furrow. He looks between Cinder and me. I don't like the look I'm seeing. I know he's going to reveal something that will make me furious.

"This is the second time I'm hearing this. I don't understand it. Your father asked me to draw up his will. He planned to take it to the States to file it, but I personally drew up the documents for him. Unless he changed them once he returned to the States, you were the sole beneficiary," Beasley says.

"I was told he changed it sometime before his death," Cinder murmurs.

"That's odd."

"How so?" I ask.

Beasley scratches his bald head. "I remember asking him if he was sure he didn't want to add his new bride to the original documents. He was adamant that everything was to go to Cinder and Cinder alone."

I begin to grit my teeth. I can make heads of what has happened to Cinder's inheritance from her father. Or I should say, who happened to it.

"Do you mind providing those reports for her to have a look at now?"

"Not at all. You will be very pleased, I'm sure."

Beasley hands over a file for Cinder to look through. I rub her back as she begins to shake a little. Her mouth falls open. She looks over to me with tears in her eyes.

"I can buy them out," she whispers. "Thank you."

"There's no need to thank me. And we'll wait on you buying anyone out. First, we need to find out if they have any rights to *your* company in the first place."

"Thank you all the same, Princeton. I never would have known if it weren't for you," she chokes out.

Cinder

I'm still in awe. I have more than enough money to buy those trolls out. All this time I've had a company waiting for me.

My head is still spinning as we head back to the hotel. I don't know where to settle my thoughts. I'm so overwhelmed.

"Are you all right?" Princeton murmurs against my temple.

I turn to face him as we ride in the back of the car. I wanted to go to the office of Beauty for Ashes, but Princeton said we have time for that tomorrow.

I agreed as I looked at the time. We spent quite a bit of time in Beasley's office. I can't wait to see this Château I've inherited. He made it sound so enchanted. Although I got the feeling there was something he was avoiding.

"Yes, I'm fine. It's a lot to process all at once. A whole lot to think about," I reply.

"It will be good for you to get this all sorted out so you can move on with your life."

I give a short laugh. "Move on with my life. I can move to London or Milan and run my company myself. I have so many options. Do you know, I've never been to the London or Milan offices. My father never stayed put. We traveled to the clients to plan their parties."

"It's how he met my stepmother. She was one of my nannies. A few years later, Bianca crossed our path again and out of the blue, my father announced they were getting married," I say and frown.

"You weren't too fond of that idea?"

"Hell no. My father was trying to outrun his memories of my mother. All the traveling… I think he felt guilty. He wanted me to have a mother figure, but I didn't need her.

"This last year, it's been rough. Bianca and her demon spawns haven't made it any easier. I've felt like the world has been on my shoulders. I'm only twenty-five."

"Twenty-four. Your birthday hasn't come yet," Princeton corrects.

I give him a smile and tilt my head as I stare into his deep blues. I study him for a moment. He's a man of many facets. This is yet another side of him I'm getting to see.

"You keep surprising me. I truly can't thank you enough for all of this. I should be upset that you've pried into my life, but I can't say that I am."

He brushes his fingers against my cheek. "I care for what's mine and hold what's mine close. It comes with once losing what was promised to you."

"That sounds like that entitlement coming through again," I tease. I reach to mirror his gesture, relishing in the stubble just starting to grow in. "Who hurt you, Princeton? How did they reach a prince?"

His jaw works as he stares into my eyes. The car comes to a stop before he can answer the question. Disappointment hits as I see him shut down.

"We'll continue this talk over dinner," he says tightly.

He steps from the car and rounds it. I'm lost in thought as I sit. Princeton opens my door and offers his hand. I take it and step from the car.

Placing a hand on my waist, he lifts the hand he's holding and turns our palms toward each other, locking our fingers together. Lifting my chin with our joined hands, he looks down into my eyes. His features have softened again.

He's like a swinging pendulum. However, I get the sense that there's so much more to his mood swings than lies on the surface. I believe I hit it on the head. He's been hurt and caution has become his shield.

Or maybe that's the Captain Save A Man in me. I want to see the best in everyone and sometimes, I'll project. Although, the look in Princeton's eyes says I could be right this time.

He dips his head to press a soft kiss on my lips. It's tender and sweet. A contradiction to the man before me in so many ways.

"You have much to celebrate. Perhaps we should go somewhere special to mark the occasion. I'm sure your parents would want that for you," he says.

"I'd like that."

He goes to peck my lips once more, holding me a little tighter this time. It's in the middle of the searing but sweet kiss that cameras begin to flash all around us. I'm stunned at first.

I genuinely think the kiss is the source of the flashes behind my lids, I'm so intoxicated by it. When I open my eyes to the flashing lights and voices calling out to Princeton, I snap out of my daze.

Princeton turns my body into his as he shields me. He covers my face with his hand as he rushes us into the hotel. We don't stop moving until we're on the elevator and his security is crammed inside with us.

My heart is racing. The reality that I was right outside kissing a prince sets in. My heart sinks a little as I realize he probably doesn't want to be seen with me. Why else would he cover my face?

"Are you all right?" Princeton asks as we step off the elevator and he looks me over.

"I'm fine," I murmur.

"We're returning to Verlez, now," he barks at his staff.

I stumble to a stop inside the suite. "But I thought... I wanted to go to the office."

"Things have changed. For your safety we will return home. I'll schedule a return trip once things are settled," he says firmly and taps one of his men to follow him, leaving me to stare after him.

I guess I have been dismissed.

Princeton

"You're more enchanting than I dreamed," I murmur and brush a lock of hair behind Cinder's ear.

I look down into her sleeping face. She looks like a work of art in her sleep. So peaceful and serene.

My men feel it would be better to allow some of the reporters to tire and leave before we make our move. Frustrated and feeling like a caged lion, I agreed. Cinder's safety comes first.

After drawing her a bath and feeding her, I ravished her body for a few hours to keep her distracted. At first, she was hesitant to open to me after I confirmed our plans with my team, but I was able to soften her up. Cinder is much like a little kitten.

Once I stroked her a few times and whispered sweetly in her ear she melted into me. It was easy to get her to talk to me and pull that witty banter from her cheeky lips.

I think my anger is growing because she's so perfect. If she were foul and self-centered, I'd count her parents' actions as a blessing. However, she's anything but, and that causes me to feel robbed.

So much time has passed and so much has been lost. I look down at her body and marvel at the pleasure it has brought me in the last twenty-four hours. She's a siren even in her sleep.

"You're staring at me," she murmurs but doesn't open her eyes.

"Yes, we will need to get up soon."

She stretches, causing the sheet to slip from her breasts. I can't help growing hard. However, we do need to go. Those pictures will be in every paper in London. I need to get Cinder back to Verlez before she sees the headlines.

I'm not a fool to think that someone won't put two and two together. London will know that the princess has returned. The Heathworth crown has been surrounded by generations of controversy. It didn't start with Cinder.

Having something new to talk about concerning the royal family is like catnip. I won't allow them to place that pressure on her. Her life has been hard enough as it is.

"Hey, where did you go?" she asks, pulling me from my thoughts. She reaches to touch my jaw.

The simple gesture tugs at something within. I look into her eyes and more questions surface. Whether I found Cinder or another bride, I never once thought that I would have love in my marriage.

Yet as I look at her, I wonder if I could have more. A marriage of more than duty. I wrap an arm around her and drag her closer to me.

"I want to show you more of Verlez when we get back. I think you will be surprised by what you find there. It's not all hills and valleys. I've done my best to push my parents to modernize," I reply.

Her eyes light up with a glow that's so alluring. "I think I would like that."

"Good."

"But first, I would like it if you would answer my question from earlier. I get the feeling you've been hurt before. What happened?"

I search her face as the question chafes as much as it did the first time. Yes, I want her to get to know me, but it seems she keeps going for the jugular. I don't want to lie to her. To tell the truth, is to tell her story.

I brush a lock of hair from her face. "The ball to find me a bride is sort of my mother and father's last resort. I was once engaged." I pause and rub the back of my neck.

"What happened? Did you run off to New York to be an entitled playboy?" she teases.

I scoff. Someone ran off, but it wasn't me. I push back those angry thoughts.

"In my world, you don't have to be born to be promised to wed. My fiancée was chosen when I was five and she was still in the womb."

"Oh," Cinder says and furrows her brows.

"Story has it her mother decided to take her and run off to America."

"Really? I'm so sorry."

"As a boy, I didn't understand what was going on. I remember there being a stir in the castle and upset voices. One minute I was at my betrothed's christening, and the next, she, her mother and father were nowhere to be found."

"It wasn't until I was older and I started to hear the whispers and understood the trips to the States that I grasped what had happened and the shame that came with it—"

"But you were a boy. She was a baby. Why should you be ashamed?"

I look into her searching eyes. What she says is logical. I know it is, but I've never been able to accept that reasoning.

"I'm a prince, next in line for the throne. Why would a mother not want her daughter to marry me? What was so wrong with me?"

The words come out angrier than I mean for them to. Cinder leans in to kiss my lips. When her eyes meet mine again there's an understanding in her gaze.

"I think I get it. I was upset with my dad when he first remarried. I felt like I wasn't enough. As I got older I realized he did it for me. So I'd have a mother. Maybe this family had a reason. Something that had nothing to do with you," she says softly.

As I get lost in her gaze I allow her words to sink in. For as long as I can remember, I've blamed Princess Beverly. I've always felt robbed by the princess and whatever scandal she had going on.

"I guess I am a bit entitled when you put it that way," I murmur. "I always thought it was about me. I never thought the real reason could've been about something or someone else."

I sound like a chastised child to my own ears. Honestly, it's my father who has held the most resentment of this. I only follow in his ire. This union meant a lot to him.

"I've found that people always have reasons for their actions. We make assumptions according to our feelings. However, it's not always about us, or sometimes it is and the other party is only trying to protect us," Cinder says.

I crush my lips to hers and kiss her deeply. Shifting our bodies, I settle between her legs. Sliding into her warmth slowly, I relish in the feel of her around me.

I break the kiss and look into her eyes. "I don't know if any of that matters to me anymore. I've found what I've been searching most of my life for."

With that, I kiss her again and for the first time I truly make love to her. Slowly and gently, as my princess deserves.

CHAPTER ELEVEN

If You Ask

Cinder

"Where are we going?" I ask as I stumble forward with Princeton leading me.

Dinner was amazing. I laughed and ate well. Now we are heading for the surprise he has for me. I can't imagine what it will be.

I have a blindfold on and my belly is tight with anticipation. We haven't gotten into a car or anything, so I know we're still at the palace, which makes me more curious. As I think of it, he's made sure to keep me in the west wing all day.

"We're almost there," he says in my ear.

Music starts to play, and I smile harder. I mentioned to him how much I love this band. However, when he releases the blindfold, I'm not expecting to see the band on stage with a Ferris wheel behind them and lights shining all over.

I also mentioned wanting to ride one of these. I gasp and cover my mouth. Looking around, I'm in even more awe. They did all of this in the backyard of the palace. It had to all be done today. I was back here yesterday evening.

"But how? When?" I stammer.

"Since this morning. I wanted to do something special for you."

"This is crazy. I love it."

He turns me to face him and pulls me into his chest. I wrap my arms around his neck as he kisses me. I'm still stunned that he did this for me. I know the permits and hoops he must have had to jump through to do this.

"This must have cost so much to do last minute. We just had that conversation the other day."

"I think you're forgetting who I am." He chuckles.

"No, this is reminding me of just that."

"Come, we have a ride to ride."

He takes my hand and leads me around the stage to the Ferris wheel. The attendant helps us on. I look to Princeton with a goofy grin. He leans in to peck my lips.

I'm so excited as the ride starts. We get to the top and it stops. I can still hear the band playing from up here. Princeton places his hand on my knee and slowly moves it up to my thigh.

"I may have had selfish reasons for this," he murmurs as he leans into my ear.

"Is that right?" I pant.

Reaching into my blouse, he cups my breast. Kissing my neck, he begins to pinch my nipple. With his other hand on my thigh, he creeps his fingers higher until he's able to move my panties aside and play with my folds.

"Princeton," I moan.

"How many times do you think I can make you come before the ride ends?" he groans out.

"I don't know, but I'm willing to find out."

"Look at you, already panting for me."

He sucks the flesh of my neck into his mouth as he pushes two fingers into me. The sounds of my pants and my wet pussy singing for him fill the air.

I throw my head back and cry out. The adrenaline flowing through me intensifies the feeling. My first orgasm hits and I whimper as he takes my mouth.

He doesn't stop, he continues to finger fuck me and devour my mouth. I lose count of how many times I come by the time we reach the bottom for the second time. I barely realize we've made two passes.

The ride stops and Princeton places his fingers into his mouth while staring into my eyes.

"Delicious," he croons.

"Oh, my God, that was amazing," I breathe.

He kisses my nose. "I'm not done. Do you want to take another turnabout or are you ready to go inside for a different ride?"

"Will the wheel still be here later?"

"If you ask for it to be so, it will."

"Yes, please," I say with a smile that shows all my teeth.

"You've got it, love." He grasps hold of my neck and gives it a little squeeze. "Now let's go. I can't wait to fuck you."

CHAPTER TWELVE

Simplicity

Princeton

Her laughter rings out and my heart swells. I want to make her laugh like this for the rest of my life. The sparkle in her eyes warms my heart.

"You are such a sore loser," she giggles musically.

I wrap an arm around her and tug her close to me. Mini golf. She has me playing miniature golf. It's been a month and I have done more things on this island than I've done in my thirty years of life.

Cinder has made Verlez feel like home again. I've tried to make it feel like home for her as well. Whenever she mentions something she loves or something from home that she misses, I make it happen or find places like it here in Verlez to make her wishes come true.

"I wouldn't be a sore loser if you didn't insist on rubbing it in my face every time you win," I mumble.

"What fun would it be if I couldn't rub it in your face?" she purrs.

I squeeze her ass, then slap it. I've grown fonder of this woman in so many ways. Her teasing has become something I look forward to.

Pecking her lips, I relish in her presence. I search her eyes, not for the first time, in a quest to find what it is about her that makes me so crazy about her. I release a sigh and kiss her again.

"What's wrong? You've been moody all day?"

I release her and rub my forehead. I've been avoiding this for a few days now. I have so much I need to tell her. I finally have most of the answers to many of my questions.

I won't be able to keep her in this bubble I've created for much longer. She's been asking to take a trip back to London. I've distracted her every time. Cinder is too smart for me to continue this.

At this point, I think she may be angry with me when she finds out all I've been keeping from her. I've fallen in love with the woman before me. I can't bear the thought of losing her.

"I'd like you to accompany me somewhere this afternoon," I say.

"Okay, but what's up with the mood?"

I chuckle. "I don't know. I might be nervous."

She gives me that little teasing smile. Moving closer, she looks at me through her lashes. She places her arms around my neck and lifts onto her toes.

"Is my prince turning shy on me?"

"Your prince, aye?"

Her smile faults a little. I want to kick myself. I drop the club I've been holding to wrap my arms around her.

"I didn't mean to—"

I kiss her before she can finish her words. I am hers. I've been hers from the moment I saw her in that office. She captured me in one glance.

"Come, I've waited long enough. I want you to see this," I say against her lips.

I kiss her forehead and a ghost of a smile returns to her lips. If I could wrap her in my arms and steal her away from the world, I would. I'm starting to understand her parents more.

"Now I'm excited," she says.

Cinder

He keeps peeking at me out of the corner of his eye. He's starting to make me nervous. I already feel like I completely embarrassed myself earlier.

I didn't mean to call him *my* prince. Over the last month I've been planning every detail of his ball by day and sleeping in his bed at night. I've told myself that I can enjoy him until the time comes for me to leave.

However, I've forgotten to tell my stupid heart not to fall for him. Boy, have I fallen for this man. He doesn't make it easy for me not to. The dates and time he spends with me have only made it that much harder not to fall.

"This is it," he breathes as we pull up to a stunning castle.

And this is what I'm talking about. First, mini golf on the most beautiful course ever. The grounds were so peaceful and charming. Such a romantic setting for a miniature golf course. Now this.

The castle is simply breathtaking. I can't stop my mouth from dropping open. I thought his family's castle was a stunner. This place is so gorgeous I start to imagine my wedding being somewhere like this. No, scratch that. I can totally see planning my wedding here.

"Where are we?"

"Château Heathworth. The Heathworth Manor," he says.

I turn to find him staring at me intently. I crease my brows in confusion. I shake my head, not understanding.

"But... that's the name of my Château. It's in Fru Fru Palms."

"Verlez and Fru Fru Palms are connected by the bridge we crossed. They are neighboring islands. The two kingdoms have been on friendly terms to keep others from invading them for centuries."

"So you knew where this place was all this time?"

"Yes, I had Williams ensure they got it ready for your arrival. There were a few repairs I didn't want you to have to deal with. She's ready for you now," he says.

His pink cheeks still my frustration, along with the boyish smile. I can't get angry when I know he's only looking out for me. I lower my lashes and nod.

"Thank you."

He leans in to kiss my forehead. "Anything for you."

When I look up into his eyes, I see something I've only gotten glimpses of a few times over the last few days. I thought I was tripping the first few times. There's no way he has feelings for me, but that look in his eyes says differently.

I clear my throat. Yup, I know I have a way of projecting so I shake the stupid thought away and turn to get out of the car. The driver opens my door and I climb out.

Looking up at the castle before me, I suck in a breath. It's larger from outside the car. I still can't believe this is the Château I inherited. In my head, this place was going to be some little house with a quaint kitchen and living room with a fireplace.

"It is a beauty, isn't it?" Princeton says from beside me.

"Yes, I'm almost afraid to move. This has to be a dream."

"No, it's not. Come, let me show you around."

I turn to look up at him. "Have you been here before?" I palm my forehead. "You said you handled the repairs."

"I didn't have to come here for that." He chuckles. "Remember? Entitled prince at your service. Williams has been making the trips to ensure all is well. I received reports on the progress.

"But to answer your question. I've only been here once as a young boy."

"Oh, okay. Right. You have staff that takes care of things. I will need one of those for this place," I say absently. "We had house staff, but I've never had to hire my own."

I'm totally overwhelmed. This, the offices in London and Milan, the money from the business. My life has done a three-sixty in the last month.

"Actually, you have staff already. They have been keeping the place up. The repairs were something they didn't have the resources to fix," he says.

"Are they not being paid?" I say in concern.

"It's a bit more complicated than that. Yes, they are paid. That's taken care of by Beasley. However, the grounds are a different source of funding."

I'm even more confused. I rub my forehead and frown. I feel like I'm missing so much.

"Listen, we'll get to all of those details. Allow me to walk you through."

I nod and take his hand. He laces our fingers together and it feels so natural. Like we've been together for years.

When we enter the castle there's an entire staff lined up. I feel so out of my depth. A tall, thin man steps forward.

"Ms. Trueman is the manager of the estate. However, she has been away on business. My name is Arthur Darcy. I'm your butler and I'll be at your service whenever you need me, Your Highness."

"Thank you," Princeton says tightly. "You can call me Princeton and Ms. Ellis is fine with Cinder."

Arthur turns beet red. He clears his throat. "Yes, sir. Cinder, it's very nice to meet you."

It feels like forever since I've had staff working in my home and never this many. I'm at a loss for what to say. I chew my lip nervously until I find my voice.

"Yes, it's nice to meet you all," I say shyly. I turn to lean into Princeton. "Um, is there something I should say or do? Like, dismiss them?"

Princeton bursts into laughter. I pout and glare at him. He pulls me into his chest and kisses my forehead.

"You're fine, darling," he says, looking down at me adoringly. "Thank you, everyone. We're going to take the tour of the grounds on our own. You're welcome to go about your day."

When I turn back to the staff a few of the women have amused and admiring looks on their faces. Princeton can do that to you. I figure they're crushing on him and shake it off.

When they start to file out of the foyer, they begin to whisper and giggle. Yeah, they must be fans of Princeton's. I don't get as jealous as I did in London. These women truly look innocent.

One of the younger ones turns to look over her shoulder and waves at me. I wave back and she beams from ear to ear. See, they're totally sweet.

"Shall we?" Princeton says, kissing my temple and placing a hand on my back.

We proceed through the castle in a leisurely stroll. If I thought I was impressed with the outside, I'm completely floored by the inside. This place is nothing short of true opulence.

The more we walk through, the more I question returning to the States. I don't even know if I can call New York my home. Without my father, I have nothing keeping me there.

"Well, that's it. What do you think?" Princeton asks as we return to the veranda in the backyard.

"It's gorgeous. I may never leave," I gush like a schoolgirl.

"Really? I was sort of hoping you would say that."

My heart sinks. I can't help wondering if he fixed this place up for me so that he could have his sidepiece close. I'm not that woman. When the ball happens, we end. I'm not taking this any further than that.

"It's a beautiful place. It tugs something inside. Like I've been here before," I whisper, glossing over his words.

"Perhaps you were." He looks at me silently for a moment. Several thoughts and emotions cross his face. I can't nail any of them down, but I can tell his feelings are at war. "Cinder, there's something I need to tell you."

"Okay," I say and inhale a sharp breath.

If he wants to end things here that's for the best. I'll call for my things at his palace and move in here until I figure things out.

"As you know, I've been—"

His phone rings, cutting him off. I release the breath I've been holding as he reaches for it. Wiping my sweaty hands on my thighs, I turn away from him so he can't see the expression on my face.

I don't know if I'm relieved or terrified. I know I've said I'll end this, but my heart isn't ready. It will never be. When this is over, I'm going to be completely heartbroken.

And living in this huge castle. I wonder how many cats I should get? Maybe Ms. Randell will come live with me.

"I'm on my way," Princeton says curtly into the phone.

I guess I'll have to wait for whatever he was going to say. Again, I'm not sure that's such a good thing.

CHAPTER THIRTEEN

The Whole Truth

Princeton

I had been on the verge of telling Cinder the truth about who she is and what it means for her to take over Heathworth Manor. However, the call from Williams requires my attention. It's what I've been waiting for.

"So this is the reason?" I say with my brows drawn.

I fall into my seat in my study. I can't believe this. I'm in too much shock to sort out my feelings. I flip through the docs once again. Hoping something will change on the second pass.

It all remains the same. Every detail outlining why my life was changed twenty-five years ago. Cinder was right. Princess Beverly had a reason. A reason that didn't have anything to do with me.

Well, at least not in the way I thought it did. Rage consumes me. They say it's the ones who claim to love you who will hurt you most.

"Have you shown this to Mother?"

"No, Your Highness. You were the first one I wanted to see it. This information has so many implications that are above my station. I thought it best to bring it straight to you," Williams says.

"Yes, yes, you're right." I lick my dry lips. I don't even know where to begin. If my anger could set a fire, all of Verlez would burn.

"He had no right to do this."

"I know, sir. Your mother will be furious."

"As she should be. This isn't who we are. It's disgusting."

"That it is. Forgive me for saying this, but it seems karma was swift."

I scoff. "But the damage was done. They were gone. No one could tell them it was safe to return. How could he take my future in his hands like this? He had no right. This is sickening."

"Indeed. However, I don't think this is something your parents will want to come out. You will have to handle this with care. Not like a bull in a china shop," Williams says while looking at me knowingly.

I run a hand through my hair. He's right. I want to destroy something or someone, but the someone in question isn't available for punishment. I feel more lost than I did in all the years I had questions.

"I want to know who else knew. If anyone else was involved, I want this dealt with before the ball. I will discuss my intentions with my mother. Enough time has been lost."

I stand to leave my office to find my mother. However, she walks in right at the same moment. I look at her and wonder, could she have known of this?

"What's wrong?" she asks with a concerned expression as she looks at my face.

I turn the file on my desk around and slide it in her direction. She moves farther into the office and takes a seat in front of my desk. I observe her intently to see her reaction as she flips through the pages.

She lifts a shaky hand to her lips as she turns a few more. Tears come to her eyes. I get the feeling she had no idea about this, which is a relief and then she speaks.

"I didn't know he went to this length. I—I can't believe he went this far. I just..." she trails off and shakes her head.

"Why? Can you explain this to me?"

She swallows thickly and nods her head. "My brother was what you call a purist. He believed that the bloodlines should remain *untainted*. It wasn't about color, if that's what you are thinking."

"Your uncle had affections for Queen Nia. Had she not been promised to King Alvin he would have been happy to suit her. It was Princess Beverly's choice to marry the American that he was against."

My mother pauses to take my handkerchief and wipe at her tears. I reclaim my seat and wait for her to continue. Taking a deep breath, she looks me in the eyes.

"When we chose Princess Cinder for you, he was furious. She wasn't a full-blooded princess. He saw her father as beneath us. I thought he let it go after your father told him our decision was final.

"Your father was furious at first, he wanted the merger of the two kingdoms. It was his hope to grow Verlez and Fru Fru Palms together. He saw a great opportunity with all of the connected land and potential," she says and gives me a warm smile.

"Your father was much like you in his younger years. He wanted to bring Verlez into the future. He was so discouraged when that young girl ran off. He felt as if our traditions may have been as antiquated as the lands and the kingdom had become."

"How so?"

"Why do you think your father is so lenient with you? Have you ever wondered why he agrees to the changes you suggest so easily? Your father is no weak king. Yet he bends so easily for you."

"It's because he sees himself in you. You reflect all of the changes he once dreamed of. Your father hasn't wanted to force your hand into marriage. He had hoped you would find love in your quest for the lost princess."

I take in my mother's words. It all adds up. I have so many gaps that are starting to fill in.

"This wasn't right," I murmur.

"No, it was not. If your uncle were alive, I would take him to task for this. My heart hurts for all the lives he changed with his menacing actions. However, we can only move forward from here," she replies.

"How?"

"It's time to tell her who she is. You can't continue to keep her in the dark about this. Her parents have done that enough.

"I understand you all have done this for her safety for one reason or another, but this will not go over well for you if you don't tell her soon," my mother says.

I rub the back of my neck. She hasn't told a lie. I have to tell Cinder soon. However, I don't know what that will mean for us.

"You love her," my mother says more as a statement, not a question, when I don't say a word. "I can see it in your eyes. You're in love."

"I believe I am."

My mother clasps her hands together. "I knew it. We'll change the plans for the ball. It will be your engagement party. You will make the official announcement of her return then."

"Slow down, Mother. I have to tell Cinder first."

"Yes, yes, you must tell her. I'm so pleased. You're going to make a handsome groom and what an exquisite bride your princess will make," she sings.

"One step at a time, Mother." I chuckle.

"Oh, I'm so excited. I've waited for years to be able to plan your wedding. Oh, and grandchildren. I'll finally have grandchildren!"

"Williams, I believe my mother has truly gotten beside herself. Please inform the families that I will not be looking for a bride. It's no use stringing anyone along any further."

"I will get right to it, Your Highness."

"Also, will you inform Cinder in the morning that I've taken a trip? I'd like to have dinner with her tomorrow evening," I say as my mind races.

"Travel? Tomorrow evening?" my mother questions.

"Yes, I'll be making a trip to find an engagement ring."

"Silly boy, I have the perfect ring for you. You will only need to size it," Mother says with a grin.

My chest swells with pride. My grandmother's ring. Yes, it will be perfect for Cinder. It was always meant to be hers.

"Then I'll be off to have it sized. It's imperative that I leave right away. There are a few other things I want to take care of in London before tomorrow evening," I say and stand. "Would you like to accompany me to London?"

"Oh, yes, let me get a few things and the ring," she says excitedly.

My own excitement burns through me. I want to make this trip quick so I can return to my future. I will tell Cinder everything and then I'll propose.

"Well then, shall we claim us a princess?"

"That we shall."

CHAPTER FOURTEEN

Foolish

Cinder

I swipe at my tears as I pack my things. I've been so stupid. He has found a bride. A princess at that.

I won't sit around for him to tell me that I'm not worthy and he has found a princess to marry. I sniffle and run a hand beneath my nose. I didn't mean to eavesdrop on Princeton's conversation.

I couldn't sleep and I'd been on my way to his office to inquire about some things for the ball. A ball that won't be happening because he already has someone in mind to marry. His mother's voice carried from the room as I approached.

'We'll change the plans for the ball. It will be your engagement party. You will make the official announcement of her return then.'

I stood there stunned. Princeton's words from earlier returned. *Cinder, there's something I need to tell you.*

He was going to tell me that he had found a bride, a princess. How stupid of me. I feel so foolish.

I have no idea why I'm so hurt. I knew this was coming. I try to hold in the sobs that want to burst free.

I need to get home. I go to check for the rest of my things and that's when I see it. The crown Princeton insisted I bring along.

I scoff at it. Was I always a joke to him? Some commoner to play with and make feel special.

I inherited a castle but that still doesn't put me in his world, on his level. I shake my head and wipe at fresh tears. Reaching for the crown, I take it and place it on the bed. It can stay here with all the lies I've told myself, as well as the hurt.

"So stupid," I mutter to myself.

I close my bag and pull it from the bed. Moving to the next bag, I go to do the same and a shoe from the ball in New York falls out.

I stare down at it. I've been pretending since that night. I don't belong here, just like I didn't belong there.

I close my bag, not bothering to pick up the shoe. It can stay here too.

I pull my phone out and call Mr. Darcy. He's the only person I know here that can help me. I chew on my lip as I wait for him to answer.

Looking at the clock on the wall, I see that it's pretty late. I heard Princeton tell Williams to give me a message that he and the queen were leaving for London.

I won't be here when they return. I'm saving him the trouble of having to dump me. I've humiliated myself enough.

"Your Highness?" Arthur answers the line.

"No, this is Cinder," I say into the phone.

"Yes, yes. My apologies, Ms. Cinder. How can I be of service?"

"I need to get out of here. Can you help me arrange transportation to the States?"

There's a pause on the other end. I have to check to see if the shit reception here has cut my call. It's still connected.

"Hello?"

"Yes, yes, I'm sorry. Does the prince know you are leaving?"

I stomp my feet in anger. "I don't need the prince to know that I want to go home. I'm a grown woman. I'd like to go home now," I say through my tears.

"Yes, okay. Very well. I'll send a car for you. I will make all of the arrangements for you to leave from here."

"Thank you." I sniffle.

"You are welcome." He doesn't sound too sure of himself. I think about trying something else, but he speaks again and I relax. "I'm at your service, Ms. Cinder. I will get you to your home."

Princeton

My hair is a tousled mess and my clothes are rumpled. I was in bed when Williams called to tell me Cinder was gone. He'd gotten up in the middle of the night and found the door to my bedroom open.

Sensing something was off, he entered and found the room empty. I woke Mother and we rushed back to find out what's going on. I've been on edge the entire time.

"Where is she?" I demand as I climb the stairs two at a time.

"A car came for her. She's returning to the States, Your Highness."

"What?" I bellow and move to my bedroom faster.

There has to be some clue as to what's going on. I storm the room and freeze. It feels cold and empty. I can feel it in my bones. She's truly gone.

Sitting on the bed is the crown she wore the night of the ball. I look to the floor at the foot of the bed and one of her shoes from that night rests on its side.

I move to the shoe and squat to pick it up. I've spent so many nights getting to know her body. Her little feet are something that I love.

I've kissed them and sucked her toes into my mouth. I close my eyes against the memories that flood my mind. She can't be gone.

I stand and reach for the crown on the bed. The diamonds twinkle at me, taunting me as my princess slips through my fingers once again. This time of her own volition.

"I'm leaving for the States. She won't get away from me this time," I say without turning to face Williams or my mother.

"I will come with you," Williams says, causing me to turn to him.

I narrow my eyes. He hasn't come with us to America since I was a little boy. However, I'm grateful for the offer.

"As will I," Mother says. "We will bring our princess home for good."

I lock my jaw and tighten my hold on the shoe in my hand. Yes, I will bring her home for good. Whatever sent her running this time will not keep her from me.

Cinder, you can run, but you will always be mine.

CHAPTER FIFTEEN

Miss Fire

Williams

"She has arrived," Coraline says.

"Is she okay? Has she told you why she has returned?"

"No, the poor thing has done nothing but sob since she arrived."

"I don't understand. She seemed to be so enamored with him. I was sure it was all going to work out. Finally." I sigh.

"It's only a small misfire. He's on his way, isn't he?"

"Yes. He's determined to bring her home. He has the ring and all. He's truly in love with her."

"Whatever has happened, there's still hope."

I rub my forehead. It's been two days since Cinder ran off. Prince Princeton is in a mood and the entire castle is on edge.

The only reason he hasn't left as of yet is the sizing of the ring and his visit to the King and Queen of Heathworth. This shall all be interesting.

"I believe there is." I sigh again. "I can't wait for this all to be over. All the secrets and deception. Princeton has taken this so hard for so long. He finally stopped blaming himself for her disappearance and here she has run off again."

"The poor boy. She's a lovely girl. It will work out."

"If the boy finds out that I knew where she was he'll strangle me."

"You didn't know for that long. Besides, you were following a royal request. I thank you for all of your help, Harrison. I appreciate it."

I rub my tired eyes. "Whatever you do, don't let her out of your sight. We will be there soon."

CHAPTER SIXTEEN

Greed

Cinder

I've been locked away in my apartment, licking my wounds. I can't believe I let this happen. I look around my small room and it's a reminder of how foolish I have been.

How did I think I belonged in those castles? This is my life. My Manhattan apartment is spacious enough for me and those cats I plan to get.

I pull my knees farther into my chest. I've been trying to figure my life out today. I have enough money to take a break, but I honestly think I'm ready to move forward with my life.

I've considered going to see Bianca and her brats to discuss buying them out. I look at the clock. It's Saturday. Those three are never in the office on Saturday.

I blow out a breath and make a final decision. It's my family's business. I want to make this right.

I drag my body out of bed and head into the shower. After washing my hair and getting the filth from the last three days from my body, I get dressed and braid my hair in two braids on each side of my head.

Yeah, not the most polished look, but I'm not in the mood to impress anyone. I look down at my jeans and T-shirt. My heels and blazer are the only things keeping my outfit from screaming my mood.

Bianca and her spawns can bite me, but I'm not going to let them see me completely slipping. I grab my oversized bag and start out of my apartment. I nearly run over Ms. Randell as I step out of the door.

"Love. It's so good to see you," she chirps as she pulls me into an embrace.

"Hello, Ms. Randell."

"You know. I think you should start calling me Coraline. We've become friends. Ms. Randell makes me feel so old," she says with a smile.

I give a small laugh. "Okay, Coraline it is. Listen, I'll stop by when I get back. You can tell me all about what's been going on around here since I've been gone," I say.

"Oh, where are you heading? Maybe I can come along. I can catch you up and you can tell me all about your trip."

I drop my head and look at my feet. The last thing I want to do is talk about that trip. All the wonderful things about it have been tainted by my last night there.

"Uh, I'm actually headed to see my stepmother. I'm going to buy those trolls out once and for all," I murmur.

"Oh," she says. I lift my head as her words come out odd. I search her face. Ms. Randell fidgets and looks around the hall. "I'll still take the ride with you. It's good for my bones to get out of here sometimes."

"Um. All right. Okay."

I don't know what else to say. She's been checking on me every day. I know I've been gone a long time. She probably missed having someone to talk to.

I shake it off and wait for her to grab her things from her apartment. When she returns she proves me right. The woman talks all the way to my stepmother's brownstone.

"Are you sure you want to do this, love," she says.

I look into her brown eyes and think long and hard about it. I want what's mine. Do I want to pay them for it? No, but it means something to me. I don't want my family's legacy in the hands of these ungrateful monsters.

"It's not good for the brand. Yes, I own Beauty for Ashes Event Planning International, but they have their hands on my US company, and I won't allow them to ruin that. This ends here," I say firmly.

Ms. Randell stares at me and a small smile comes to her lips. Her eyes sparkle with pride. I find myself standing straighter. She looks down at her phone and her smile grows. She sends a text faster than I think her fingers should be able to.

"Yes, it does," she says almost to herself before she rings the bell for me.

I furrow my brows at my neighbor. She reaches for my hand and gives it a firm squeeze. The gesture calms me. In this moment, I'm glad she's here. I've been feeling so alone the last few days.

"What the hell are you doing here?" Glenda snarls when she tugs the front door open.

I bite back my retort and force a smile to my lips. "I'd like to talk to you guys about buying you out."

"We don't need shit from you—"

"Move out of the way, moron," Bianca growls, pushing Glenda aside. She rolls her eyes at her daughter before turning her attention back to me. "Come in. We're busy so let's make this quick."

I clench my teeth against all the things I want to say. Ms. Randell places a hand on my back as support. Again, I'm grateful to her.

"Wait, who's this?" Bianca says when Ms. Randell enters with me.

"I'm her counsel," Ms. Randell replies before I get a chance to.

I turn to her and she gives me a little smile. Looking back at Bianca, she has her eyes narrowed at the both of us. I shrug my shoulders.

"I'd like to settle this as soon as possible. I thought it would be better to bring her along," I say.

"Yes, we'd like to get this all over with quickly as well," she says and turns to lead the way to the living area.

The sound of Glenda and Rosa hissing at each other like cats enters the hallway. A grin comes to my lips as I overhear their words. Bianca picks up her pace. I'm sure it's to shut them up.

"I still don't get it. Why is she here?"

"Because she wants to buy the company. Duh," Rosa says to Glenda like she's so much smarter than her.

"She doesn't know?" Glenda snickers. "She's so stupid."

"Well, we need the money before we're out on the street so shut up," Rosa snaps.

"If you two don't shut the hell up," Bianca seethes as she enters the room with her overgrown brats.

Ms. Randell has grabbed my hand to make sure we're right on her heels. The look on all of their faces is priceless. Glenda and Rosa look like two sulking toddlers and Bianca looks like she wants to throttle them both.

Interesting. I take note of the desperation in the air. I know Megan quit weeks ago.

After I calmed down and thought about it, I didn't want to leave my old clients hanging. So I had Megan flown out to the Milan office, where she could reach out and manage our New York clients without interference from these three.

"Have a seat, Cindy," Bianca says coldly.

I clench my fist. I know she knows how much I hate that name. I have to talk myself out of mopping these floors with her.

Instead, I move to take a seat across from them all. I make a mental note that the price I plan to offer has dropped three times since we've walked into this room.

"You said you would like to buy our shares," Bianca starts. "As we have worked so hard to grow the company after your father's passing, I think it's only fair that you pay us one million each."

I snort. Tilting my head to the side, I look at this woman as if she's crazy. She must be.

"Three million dollars?" I laugh. "Yeah, that's not happening. You three have lost it."

"Then you obviously don't want to buy us out. You're wasting our time. You can leave," she says, waving a hand at me.

"Okay, thanks for your time," I say and stand.

Bianca's face turns white as a sheet. I had a feeling that would be her reaction. You see, I noticed a few things while entering this brownstone. This was the home my father bought when Bianca talked him into moving back to the States.

While this place is no Château, my father allowed Bianca to furnish it with the best and most expensive things. Items are missing. Some of Bianca's prized possessions are no longer on display.

Glenda's weave looks more torn up than usual and they all look like it's been a month since they've had fill-ins. I've never known these three to go a week without getting their nails done. The Band-Aid around the nail of Rosa's index finger screams that something is off.

I don't think any of this is a coincidence. They're having money problems. They need me more than I need to buy the company.

"Just give us the money," Glenda stands and shouts. "You're rich. A fucking princess, for crying out loud. I hate you."

"It wasn't good enough that you stole a prince from my sister," Rosa joins in. "You go over there and find out you're a princess. Every damn paper in London has your face plastered all over it."

"What?" I stumble back and look at them in confusion.

I turn to Ms. Randell, but she's no longer sitting in the armchair she had taken when I sat. My confusion grows. I knew these two were spoiled and jealous, but damn. That shit has caused them to go insane as well.

Rosa stomps off. Bianca covers her face and shoves her hands in her hair as she vibrates with anger. Glenda glares at me like I'm some piece of shit.

"Don't try to play stupid with us," Glenda snarls. "We know you have money. That's why you're here. You found out about the money and companies in Europe. Then you found out you're a princess."

"You ruined our lives. Clients don't want to sign with us. Our reputation is shit because of you. All of our parties were canceled because you threw dirt on our names."

"Why are you here? To gloat. Big fancy princess with all that money and a prince pining after his long-lost princess. You made us look like fools. We're losing everything because of you," she hurls at me.

"Here, you want to lie to our faces now?" Rosa storms back in, tossing a tablet at me.

I look down at the screen. This time the blood drains from my face. Pictures of the day Princeton kissed me in front of the hotel are splashed on the screen. There are also a few pictures I had no idea anyone had taken during my time in Verlez.

However, it's the headline that's put a lump in my throat. *Lost Princess has Returned.* I start to skim the article and I freeze.

It has been confirmed. We've lost Princess Beverly. May she rest in peace. However, all is not lost. While we will keep our fond memories of the princess, we can also rejoice in the gift she has left us.

Prince Princeton Duke of Verlez looks elated to have Princess Cinder Duchess of Fru Fru back on this side of the pond. We all know the story of the prince who lost his bride before she was old enough to speak. We're hoping for a happily ever after for our beloved prince this time.

I stop reading as my brain begins to catch up. My mother was a princess. I'm the baby princess.

"Oh, wait," Glenda snorts. "I don't think she knew."

"She can't be that stupid," Rosa replies.

"Enough," Bianca bursts out and stands from the couch. "Give us your best offer for our shares and they're yours."

"She will do no such thing."

A chill runs through me. My heart skips a beat at the sound of his voice. I don't turn to face him. I can't.

I close my eyes and all the threads start to come together. Arthur wasn't talking to Princeton when he said Your Highness the day Princeton took me to the Château. He was talking to me. And the night I called to get help to return home, he had another slip of the tongue, which means Princeton knew.

My knees nearly buckle. I have no one I can trust. Once again, I've been played the fool.

"You knew," I choke out.

Princeton

"This is the address," Williams says from the front seat as the car comes to a stop. "She's inside."

"How do you know?" I suddenly have to question how Williams knew Cinder's exact location. He knew she wouldn't be at her apartment.

He turns to look me in the eyes. "Once King Edmond fell ill he commanded the princesses be found. Ms. Trueman was charged with coming to the States to find them. When she did, she found Cinder alone and grieving."

"That's when she came to me. Cinder's life was so tangled in deceit we knew she needed help sorting it. And dare I say, Your Highness. You were so angry and unhappy. We didn't think you would come for her if we told you her whereabouts."

"That's when we hatched the plan to send your mother the letter from Mr. Ellis. I'm sorry, but I'm not sorry. You two needed each other. I did what was best for my country and my prince," Williams says, drawing his shoulders back.

"Do you mean to tell us that you and Coraline Trueman have been working together?" My mother says beside me.

"Yes, Your Highness."

"Well, the both of you will be rewarded. I've always liked that Coraline."

"She will open the door for you," Williams says, a look of relief crossing his face.

For now, I let it go. I need to get inside to Cinder. I have to find out why she ran off.

I step from the car and jog up the front steps. Before I can ring the bell, the door opens. Familiar brown eyes greet me. Yes, I know this woman.

"Ms. Trueman?"

"Yes, Your Highness," she whispers and bows. "You can call me Coraline. Come, come. I believe she needs you."

Hearing those words, I enter the brownstone quickly. My heart races as I think of Cinder being in danger. All of London has been talking about her return. I should have protected her better. There are so many dangers that she could face now that people know who she is and what she looks like.

"Enough," The word is yelled as I approach the room Coraline leads me to. "Give us your best offer for our shares and they're yours."

My blood boils. This woman has a lot of fucking nerve. I had planned to handle her since finding out she had papers forged to claim shares of Cinder's company here in the States.

Mr. Ellis left her and her daughters nothing. Not a cent, not one thing. Cinder has put up with them long enough. This was one of the things I planned to tell her.

"She will do no such thing," I say, my voice booming into the room.

Cinder stands before me frozen. She doesn't turn toward me, causing great alarm. I still have no idea why she left.

"You knew." Her voice is full of hurt.

When she finally turns, tears are in her eyes and her lips are trembling. She looks so cute with the two plaits on each side of her head. Her jeans hug her lush hips and the T-shirt beneath her jacket fits snugly against her breasts.

Yet her teary eyes are my undoing. It feels like an eternity since the last time she was in my arms. However, caution tells me now isn't the time to draw her into my embrace.

"I only recently found out that she had false documents drawn up to place a claim on your company for her and her daughters," I reply.

Cinder's body jerks as if she's been hit. She wraps one arm around her middle. I take a step forward and she holds out the tablet in her hand as if to stop me with it.

"No, I wasn't talking about that. God, you people are out to destroy," she says on a sob.

"Cinder, baby, what—"

"You knew who I was. Who my mother was. You said nothing to me for a month. How could you? I don't understand... wait, no, I do. You were so angry at my mother you decided to take it out on me.

"Did you plan to hide this until you could humiliate me? 'The princess that planned her replacement' ball. The event of the season. The perfect prince truly screwed her over." She scoffs.

"Made her fall in love with him while he planned to dump her in front of his entire kingdom to validate his manhood. I was right, you're an entitled prick. Fuck all of you. You deserve each other," she shouts before tossing the tablet to the floor, where it smashes.

"You can't talk to him like that," the stepsister with the blonde hair snarls in my defense.

I don't think anyone sees it coming when Cinder slaps the shit out of her. I wince, peeking through one eye to see the stunned look on everyone's face.

"We're going to press charges and sue you. Let's see you spend that money from prison. I told your father you had a problem," Bianca seethes.

"*I* have a problem, *me?*" Cinder vibrates with rage. She points at me. "He has revealed that you and these two ragamuffins have been stealing from me since my father died, and you dare to threaten *me*? Yeah, good luck with that."

"You've always been jealous of us. You're selfish. It's why your father died of a broken heart," Bianca retorts.

It happens so quickly but in slow motion. Cinder hauls back and slaps Bianca harder than she slapped her daughter. Spit flies and her head snaps to the side.

"Yes," my mother and Coraline cheer in unison at my side.

Their reactions snap me out of my shock. I've been speechless since she started to tear into me. She has it all wrong.

"Cinder," I call. She turns her glare on me. "You have it all wrong."

"No, I have it very right. I heard you. You're planning an engagement party, not a ball to find a wife. Why are you here?"

"I did you a favor. You don't owe me an explanation. I left so you didn't have to look me in my eyes to crush my heart." She stops to suck in a breath.

Tears spill over as she continues. She shakes her head with her next words. "Oh, right, you want me to pay for my parents' sins. I knew I was being foolish to start things up with you when you had your duties to fulfill as a prince.

"But I lied to myself, thinking I could have my cake and eat it too. Unfortunately, the cake devoured me and my heart. Bravo, you found the missing princess and got your retribution," she says with a coldness so unlike her.

"We're going to bury you," the other sister says as she stands next to her mother and sister, who are cradling their bruised cheeks.

Cinder spins on her and feigns lunging at her as if she's going to slap her too. The stepsister flinches and hides behind the other two. "Try me. You ruined my mother's dress. I'll drag you through this house for that alone," she hisses.

I move to get closer to her, placing a hand on her back. She turns toward me, fire in her eyes. I look down at her and want to tug her into me.

"Will you let me explain?"

She looks past me. "Ms. Randell. Your accent, where are you from?"

I close my eyes, this is getting worse by the minute. I noted Ms. Trueman's accent as well. It's very distinct from Verlez and Fru Fru Palms. Something Cinder pointed out about my people while she was there.

"Fru Fru Palms. I—"

"Say no more," Cinder says sharply. "You can all go to hell."

With that, she storms from the room. My mother and Coraline call after her. I start after her, but I'm stopped in my tracks by the words that come from behind me.

"My daughters would never behave like that. She doesn't deserve a prince or anything else. I plan to take everything she has," Bianca vows.

I spin on her. "She deserves everything she has and so much more. You have taken enough from her. I plan to make it my personal business to see to it that the three of you rot in a jail cell."

"If you so much as breathe in her direction, I'm going to make hell a place you wish for to get away from me. I'm no fucking Prince Charming. The dark shit I'll dream up to torture you will make the devil blush and offer me his seat."

"Stay. Away. From. What's. Mine," I say in a calm that belies the rage within.

The three of them look back at me like kicked puppies. I couldn't care less. It's time I go after my princess.

CHAPTER SEVENTEEN

Alone

Cinder

My soul is crushed. Even my sweet neighbor, who I thought was a friend was in on all of this. Right when I was starting to trust and lean on her, she pulled the rug right from under me.

I need my key back from her. I'm selling this apartment as soon as I can. Like, God, how long have they been planning all of this? That woman has lived in that apartment since I moved in, or at least a week after when I first met her.

"Why am I so alone?" I cry into my pillow.

I came back home, not knowing what else to do. I guess I should be happy to know I don't have to buy those three ass warts out of my business. However, I can't find the triumph in this.

I feel broken, alone, and hollow. Not even slapping the taste out of Bianca and Glenda's thieving mouths can make this feeling go away. I have millions in my bank accounts, but that will never replace my father and mother or give me someone I can trust.

"Please leave," I call out, not lifting my head from my pillow. "Leave the key behind on your way out."

Heavy footfalls continue through my apartment into my bedroom.

"You haven't given me a key yet. Coraline let me in and went to pack her things to return home. She has an estate to run. Especially since the princess has been found," Princeton says from behind me.

I sit up and turn, pulling the sheet up over my body. These people are out of their minds. I know that woman didn't just let him into my home.

"You need to get out," I growl.

I level him with a glare of death. If looks could kill I would finish him like a game of *Mortal Kombat*. Yet what he does next is not at all what I asked him to.

Princeton

She will listen to me this time. I'm not leaving until she does. I loosen my tie, then shrug out of my coat, tossing it into the chair in the corner of her bedroom.

The glare on her face matches my own. She claims to love me, but she doesn't know me well enough to know I would never do anything to hurt her.

"Name one time that I've hurt you, Cinder. Just one," I say as I come out of my suit jacket and toss it with my other things. "Tell me when I haven't done all I can to take care of you and your needs."

She pokes her lip out and folds her arms over her chest. She still has those cute little braids in. If I weren't so pissed at her, I'd think she was adorable.

"Right now, if you continue to strip from your clothes in my home, I promise I'm going to hurt *you*," she says, her words dripping with venom.

"I like this side of you. Even though you're bullheaded and won't listen."

"Okay, I'll humor you. You have five minutes. Starting now."

"I had no idea Coraline lived across the hall from you. Your grandfather sent her in search of you. She's the one who tugged my mother's attention and pointed her in the right direction to find you."

"I was the last to know who you were. I figured it out when I first heard your name. While we were looking for you here, it seems your mother had already passed on and you were traveling the world."

"It should have been easy to find a girl named Cinder, but it wasn't," I say as I come out of my shoes.

"I didn't start using my real name until a few years ago. Cindy is on all of my paperwork," she murmurs.

"Figures. Your parents didn't want to be found because my mother's brother was a bastard and he threatened them and you behind everyone's back. My parents, nor your grandparents, had any clue of what really happened."

"Your parents clearly didn't know my uncle acted alone or the fact that he met with an unfortunate accident not long after they fled."

"I had no idea what the reason was for your family's actions which is why, until I figured it out, I didn't want to tell you any of this. I thought I could keep your presence a secret. It was stupid of me to take you out in London."

"It took them all of two days to figure out who you were. You are the spitting image of your mother. Which is the reason I rushed you back to Verlez and tried to keep you there while I got all the details."

"Details? What else don't I know?"

"Your mother left you Heathworth for your home. Your grandmother and grandfather wish to see you return home. They stay in a small manor not that far from Château Heathworth, hoping for your return."

"When they received word that you had arrived at Heathworth and were indeed in Europe, they made their way to Heathworth and are waiting there for you. You are to be crowned princess. Right before *our* engagement party," he says pointedly.

"Oh." Her mouth falls open. "So… you weren't going to dump me?" she says in a small voice.

"No," I say as I start to stalk my way up the bed toward her, nude. "I went to London with my mother to have my grandmother's ring sized for you. I planned to propose when I returned the following evening."

I get nose to nose with her and tilt my head to the side. Then I continue. "However, I was awakened in the middle of the night to be told that my woman, my princess, the woman I love was gone. You left me, Cinder. Now, how should I punish you?"

"Punish me?"

"Yes. You love it when I spank you, so that's out of the question." I lick my lips.

I'm going to devour her, and from the way her brown eyes dilate, she knows it.

Cinder

His blue eyes darken. He's so close his breath fans my lips and I can see every color and change in his orbs. As I lock gazes with him, I feel kind of stupid. I made a lot of assumptions and I was wrong about them all.

"There's no other princess?" I say sheepishly.

"No, baby." He shakes his head. "It has only been you. I didn't call the ball off sooner because I was putting the pieces together and I enjoyed watching you plan while I got to spend time with you."

"I had planned to turn it into our engagement party before my mother's suggestion. Yes, I should've told you sooner, but you should have come to me if you thought something was amiss."

"You were going to propose?" I look at him through my lashes.

"Yes, you cheeky little monster. I've fallen in love with you, Cinder. I want you to be my wife. When I said you were mine, I meant it," he says and crushes my lips.

I wrap my arms around his neck and open for him. He devours my mouth, deepening the kiss as he groans. He tugs the sheet away and tosses it aside.

I'm in my bra and panties. When I arrived home I stripped out of my clothes on autopilot and climbed into my bed. I wasn't expecting to have company.

However, now that Princeton is searing my lips with his kiss, I'm glad there's little between us. He cups one of my breasts in his hand as if in agreement. Breaking the kiss, he starts a trail of kisses across my jaw to my ear.

"You still haven't told me when I hurt you. Why would you run from me?"

"I thought... I'm sorry. You're right."

He clicks his tongue. "I don't want to be right, Cinder. I want you to see that I've always had your best interests at heart. Say it. I want to hear the words when you're not angry at me."

He looks in my eyes and waits expectantly. It takes me a moment to grasp what he's asking for. Realization hits and I smile shyly.

"I love you," I whisper.

"I love you too."

He captures my lips again. This time his kiss is tender. Although his hands aren't as gentle. He tears my panties right off my body. I reach to unfasten my bra before it meets the same fate.

"I've been trying to get you pregnant since the first time I entered you. You will stop your birth control as soon as we have the wedding."

"So entitled." I laugh.

However, my laugh is cut short as he lifts me to wrap around his body and stands. In the next motion, he drives into me and slams my back to the wall over my headboard. I cry out and cling to his back.

"You feel that? That's what you do to me. How could I not love you," he says into my ear as he rocks into me slowly.

I drop my head back against the wall. He presses a palm to the wall as his other arm wraps my back and his palm grasps my ass. When he bites down on my shoulder, I know this is going to be a slow, sweet torture. That will be my punishment.

"Princeton, please." I already know that plea is going to fall on deaf ears.

This man is nothing if not determined. He will see his plan through. I think that's one of the things that made me fall in love with him.

All of my neighbors must be on his payroll. Chris Brown's "To My Bed" comes on from the apartment over me. Princeton thrusts into me to the sensual rhythm. Memory foam is a great investment.

This man is tearing it up slowly while standing on my mattress. This is some hot shit. I can't help but drip down his shaft.

His tongue against my neck isn't helping. When he starts to drag his teeth against my collarbone, I'm done for. I claw my fingers through his hair.

"Babe." I gasp.

"I feel you coming." He chuckles and stops.

I whimper. I see where this is going. My orgasm was right within my reach. He pulls out to the tip and pecks my nose. The smile on his lips is almost sadistic.

I look at him with pleading eyes. "Please."

He groans and pushes inside me achingly slow. It's still not what I need, but it stokes the fire within. I dig my nails into his back, hoping to break his restraint.

It doesn't work. He continues the snail's pace that's likely to drive me crazy. At least, I think that's his plan. He takes a step back, angling my hips and lower body.

I scream so loud when he starts to pound into me I think I drown out the music. Sweat drops from his face onto my torso. He looks at me through his lashes and it's the sexiest thing I've ever seen.

"Don't come, Cinder," he commands.

"What? Why?"

"Because I said so," he growls and slaps my ass.

"Princeton," I cry, trying not to fall over the edge.

He slaps my ass again. "I said don't come."

I squeeze my eyes shut. I'm not going to be able to hold back if he keeps slapping my ass. His fat dick is already stretching me and hitting my spot.

My body starts to quiver. I curl my toes and reach for the wall behind me. It's all I can do to try to keep from coming.

He slams my back against the wall again, moving in closer to seal us tightly together. He wraps one of my braids around his hand and tugs my head back and to the side.

Licking from my shoulder to my ear, he doesn't miss a beat. Fuck it. I'll take my punishment because there's no way I'm not coming.

"Oh shit, babe," I call out as I gush around him, my walls tightening on his shaft.

"My hardheaded girl. Didn't I tell you not to come?"

He places my ass on the edge of the headboard and drops to his knees. I cling to his hair as he eats my pussy like his last meal. I wonder if royalty is born with a special talent for sex?

Maybe it's just my prince.

"I'm going to fuck you until you can't breathe. You'll never run from me again. Your legs won't work to carry you away from me," he hisses in my ear.

I come again from his words alone. If he thinks I'm complaining, he's crazy. I take my lumps like a big girl for the rest of the night, well into the morning.

Make-up sex is at the top of my list of all-time favorites. Fights and make-up sex are a monthly must. It will be my first law as princess. Wait, do I get those?

Princeton

The sun is rising and she's fast asleep. I've been reflecting on all the things that have happened over the last month. I could be angry with so many people, but I don't think I'd change a thing.

She was well worth the wait and all that came with it. I kiss her forehead and go to climb from the bed. I have something I need to do.

I pull on my pants and collect my phone. I move out to the living room. It's the perfect time to do this.

"Hello."

"Good morning, Your Highness."

"Princeton. Do you have her?"

"Yes, Queen Nia. She's safe and sound."

Cinder's grandmother releases a tired sigh. She is up there in age, as is her husband. Although Cinder has cousins, she's next in line for the throne. This has been a long time coming.

"Does she know?"

"Yes and no. She knows she's a princess. She doesn't know about the throne. I can leave that for you to tell her if you like," I say.

"It might be best coming from you. She doesn't know us," she says sadly.

"Actually, I was calling to get the king's permission to ask for her hand. I know she was meant to be my betrothed. However, with everything, I wanted to make sure—"

"You've waited to claim her as yours for a long time. I can hear in your voice that you care for her. We enjoyed the time we spent with you. You're a fine young man."

"My husband and I approve of your union. Go on, claim your princess. We'll be here waiting to meet her when you return for the engagement ball," she replies.

I chuckle. "Word travels fast."

"Indeed it does. See you soon."

I end the call and stare out the window at the street below. I can't help the smile that comes to my lips. We have so much planning to do. So much is about to change.

"What throne?"

I spin to face the direction her voice comes from. She looks sleepy and sexy in my shirt. I move across the room to her. When I reach her, I tug her into my arms.

"You are next in line to be queen. Just as I'm next in line to be king. Your grandparents are waiting back home to meet you."

Her eyes grow wide and her knees buckle. I'm right there to catch her. I hold her close.

"You're lying."

"Nope, looks like you're going to have to keep me from becoming even more entitled. Such titles can go to the head."

She straightens and shakes her head. "You know what? Come on. I need a dose of reality right about now."

"Where are we going?"

"Gray's, I need a hot dog. Doesn't get more New York than that. That will bring my ass back down to earth."

I roar with laughter. Yup, just what I needed. She'll keep me grounded.

CHAPTER EIGHTEEN

New Event

Cinder

I look up from my desk to find Princeton leaning in the doorway of my office. It's only been two months since all of that drama and returning to Fru Fru Palms to meet my grandparents and attend our engagement ball. It was all overwhelming and I needed to return to New York to regroup.

However, we've become closer after it all. I've learned to live in the moment more. It helps for transitioning through all the changes.

"What are you doing here?"

"I can't come to see my princess?" he asks with a grin and a lifted brow.

"I thought you had that meeting across town."

"Yes, I did, but I have someplace I'd rather be," he says and pushes off the door.

He closes the door and locks it. I eye him warily as he moves toward me and rounds my desk. He has a seductive smile on his lips.

"What are you up to?"

"I miss my fiancée. I need to give her a little reminder of all the things waiting for her in our future," he croons.

"Princeton, if you don't get your nasty ass out of my office." I giggle.

He plucks me from my chair and tugs me into his chest. The kiss he lays on me has my toes curling. I cling to his jacket as he deepens the kiss.

"You taste divine," he groans.

"Thank you for having the ice cream sent over. It was delicious."

"I wanted you to know I was thinking of you. Did you think about what we talked about this morning?"

He rubs the tip of his nose against mine. I groan internally. Yes, I've been thinking about our talk this morning. It's all I've been thinking about.

"I have. I still have so much to consider. I have this place here and I have employees who depend on me. I don't know," I reply.

"I never said you had to give this place up. You have a great staff. This place has proven it can run without you."

"Taking up your duties as a queen are not going to allow you the same time you have now. I wanted you to fall in love with Verlez in hopes we'd be able to make it our home," he says.

"But I thought you loved New York?" I tease, looking up at him through my lashes.

He grins at me and pins me with a look that causes me to pout. He pinches my chin and lifts my face for a kiss. It's a light peck of the lips, but it still stirs my belly.

"I do like it here, but I've been longing for home more. It's time for both of us to step up. Moving home will have so many benefits."

"Name a few," I say.

"How about I show you a few instead?"

Before I can reply he covers my mouth with his and turns our bodies so that I'm facing the desk. He lifts me to perch on the edge, all while keeping our connection. Our tongues dance and glide against each other.

Slowly, he peels my jacket from my shoulders and tosses it onto the desk beside me. He continues to devour my mouth as he unbuttons my blouse. Once my top is gaping open, he sticks a hand inside and cups my breast.

"Princeton," I moan as he moves his lips to my neck.

He uses his fingertips to trace the lace of my bra, hooking his fingers in to tug the cup down. Swiftly, he dips his head to suck my nipple into his mouth. I have to remind myself where we are.

I bite down on my lip to keep from crying out. My eyes roll and I close my lids. I draw in a breath as he moves a hand beneath my skirt and starts to slowly, but not too gently, drag his fingers up my thigh.

"Look who's wet for me. Should I eat this delicious pussy, or should I fuck you right here on this desk?"

"Whatever you like, Your Highness. Don't let me stop you," I purr as I arch into him.

He chuckles and moves to pull down my other cup and draw my hardened peak into his mouth. When he pushes two fingers into me, I lose my battle and cry out. He's driving me insane as he pushes his digits in and out as he rubs my nub over the silky fabric of my panties with his thumb.

I want the barrier completely gone, but at the same time the friction is perfect and I need it to stay. I shove my fingers in his blond locks and hold on tight. His hot mouth on my body has me ready to do anything he asks for.

"Babe, please," I plead, needing more.

He breaks the seal he has on my breast and it pops free. He looks into my eyes and the lust and love I see there make my stomach clench. He drops to his knees before me and begins to feast on me.

I bite my fist to keep from screaming. He only pushes his face farther in. I gasp and rock my hips against his face as I hold on to the edge of the desk with my free hand.

It's not like he didn't go down on me this morning before I showered for work. However, the man is that damn good at what he does. He makes me want to do this all day.

My heart pounds as I come all over his face. With blazing blue eyes, he rises to stand before me. He makes quick work of releasing his belt and shoving his pants down.

Princeton covers my mouth with his hand as he uses the other to guide his erection to enter me. I whimper into his palm and let my head fall back. He doesn't move, but his hard length pulses within my walls.

"You're so perfect," he says huskily.

I wrap one leg around his waist, needing him closer. Right when he goes to move, the phone on my desk beeps.

"Your Highness, um, Ms. Ellis, um, boss?" Megan says, sounding so confused.

I laugh into Princeton's shoulder. He chuckles into my hair. My poor staff has been having such a hard time with what to call me these days. I've tried to tell them nothing has changed.

"Yes," I say as I try to hold in my amusement at her and the fact that Princeton is still throbbing inside me.

"The queen is here to see you," she replies.

Princeton groans into my neck. Slowly, he pulls from my body. I shake my head at him. The queen will wait today. He's not leaving me like this.

"Megan, would you be so kind as to take her into a conference room and make her comfortable? We'll be there in about fifteen," I say, much to Princeton's amusement.

He pulls my panties from under my skirt lightning fast and plows back into me. I barely have time to stifle my cry. He works his hips into me even as Megan gives her reply.

"Yes, boss."

"You should start calling me boss. I think that would sound sexy." He chuckles in my ear.

"Dream on, pretty boy," I pant.

He lifts me from the desk and starts to bounce me on his rock-hard dick. Okay, maybe I could call him boss on the weekends. He latches his mouth onto my breast. Well, weekdays may be able to be added.

"Yes, boss."

"That's what I thought." He chuckles darkly.

Fifteen minutes later, my back is flat on my desk and I'm panting for the smallest gulp of air, but I'm thoroughly satisfied. Princeton grabs tissues from inside my desk drawer and starts to clean me up.

"Now, I think it's fair to say that's a great reason to move back home," he says with a smile in his voice.

I lift to my elbows and wait for the power to speak. "Maybe. I'll think some more about it. You may have to give me a few more reasons." I give him a seductive smile.

"As you wish, but for now let's get to Mother."

He fixes the rest of my clothes quickly. When I stand my legs are shaky. He looks down at me with a smug grin. I can only shake my head at him.

"Let's go," I murmur.

We enter the conference room to find Ms. Trueman and my soon-to-be-mother-in-law. Princeton lifts my hand to his lips and kisses the back. I observe him curiously.

I get the feeling that this isn't a random visit. I turn to look over my shoulder as Megan enters the room carrying a garment bag in her arms.

"I promise I haven't looked, but Mother has informed me that they have gotten the stain out completely. You will be able to wear the gown to our wedding," Princeton says sheepishly as he watches me for a reaction.

I start to tear up. "Oh my God, my mother's dress," I say as my chin wobbles and my lips tremble.

"Yes. I told you we'd get the stain out. Since your birthday is in a few days, I thought this would be a great birthday gift."

He catches me as I throw myself into his arms, holding me in a tight embrace. He kisses the top of my head. This man has only ever worked to make me happy. I can't believe this is my life.

"We thought you would need this. It was your mother's as well," Ms. Trueman takes the crown she gave me out of a black velvet bag. "It seems you misplaced it."

I love this woman. She's become so important to me in the last few months. I don't think I would've been able to navigate all of these changes without her. She's been invaluable to me and Princeton.

"Wait, that was my mom's?"

"Yes, dear. It was." She gives me a warm smile.

I turn to Princeton and tug him down to me by his ears to kiss him. I don't know what else to do with these overwhelming emotions. He smiles against my lips as he returns the kiss.

"So, does this mean we can set a date?" Queen Joy says.

I place my forehead to Princeton's and nod. "Yes, we can set a date."

"Are you saying you're ready to go home?"

I slide down Princeton's front and wrap my arms around his waist. I savor in the warmth and strength coming off of him. He looks as handsome as ever, even after a quickie in my office.

"If by home you mean that huge castle waiting for us in Fru Fru Palms, then yes. I'm ready to go home."

"What about this place?" Megan asks.

"Well, I was thinking about giving you a promotion. I trust you to keep things going here."

She gasps. "Seriously?"

"Yes, our clients trust you as much as they trust me. It's time you spread your wings. I think I've planned my last event for a while."

"Well, I'm actually here to see if you'd be willing to plan one more event," Queen Joy says.

"Oh, okay. What kind of event is it?"

She gives me a mischievous smile. "It's my son and daughter-in-law's wedding."

I burst into laughter and Princeton tugs me into his chest, squeezing me tight. He kisses my forehead as I look up at him. The joy in his eyes is contagious. I can't stop smiling.

"Beauty for Ashes. That's the perfect way to explain us. Yes, you will definitely have to be our planner."

"Proposal accepted. It would be an honor."

Ever After

Princeton

I've finally made Cinder my wife. The fire that used to be anger inside me has now turned to passion for her. My Cinder.

I burn for her every day and try to find new ways to bring a smile to her face. However, I don't think I've ever seen her look this happy.

The beaming smile on her gorgeous face is something I'll live the rest of my life trying to recreate. Her eyes are sparkling and her cheeks are glowing.

"I love you," I say without thinking.

"I love you too."

I flex my fingers on her waist as I dance her around the ballroom. Ray LaMontagne's "You Are The Best Thing" plays and I couldn't think of a better song to say the words I feel. Cinder is the best thing that has happened to me.

"What?" I say as I look at the little smile on her lips. I know that smile, she's thinking something cheeky.

"Nothing," she says.

"That isn't a nothing smile. Tell me."

"Well, if you insist. I was wondering which room we should make the nursery. I want to pick out new wallpaper and a crib when we get back from our honeymoon," she says.

"I like the room across... wait." I narrow my eyes at her as her eyes light up. "Are we in need of a nursery?"

"I was never on birth control. You never gave me a chance to tell you that," she says with a brilliant smile.

I cup her face and kiss her deeply. I love this woman. I could never have asked for a better princess.

The only reason I break the kiss is that our guests stop around us to applaud. I remember that we're in the middle of our wedding. I look around at all the smiling faces, but it's the smile before me that takes all my attention.

I look in those brown eyes and my world comes full circle. I exist to be hers. I've waited all my life to find my way back to her.

"I love the fuck out of you," I whisper against her lips as I put my forehead to hers.

"You're my happy ever after," she whispers back.

ACKNOWLEDGMENTS

I freaking loved writing these two! If I had it my way, I would write a lot more paranormal romance. I've been wanting to publish something PNR for a while and was bummed when I had to hold off on a project, but this!!!! This right here, I think they are so stinking adorable and funny and the fight scenes were so lit in my head. Love, Love, Loved these.

OMG! His Cinder was a cool idea in concept. I ended up challenging myself with this. ROTF. This was not easy to do because I didn't want to tell the same fairy tale we've read over and over, and I also didn't want to move away from the original completely. I had to strike a balance and I think I have. I love this book.

Thank you to everyone for your support. This project was a labor of love. Thank you to everyone for being patient with me. Thank you to my readers for taking a chance on me. Thank you in advance for the reviews, posts, comments, shares, and emails.

Once again! Thank you to my husband! Man, you the best. Thanks so much for the support and bobbing your head when I come up with crazy ideas. LOL Sometimes I need to laugh at myself, and you make sure I do. You are always there to listen to me figure things out. I always want to give my readers the best experience and sometimes that takes a lot of thought and you're always my sounding board. Love you to the moon and back for your support.

Let me stand up and give praise where it's due! The Lord is with me because life tried to eat my lunch and I wasn't having it. I had to dig into my faith and God reminded me who HE is and who I Am. To God be ALL the Glory. It's not what the darkness you create looks like, it's what you look like when you step from the darkness. I've been taken to task. However, God has continued to remind me HE is there and HE's got me, every single step of the way. ON GOD!

Next! Well that's all for this release. Let's get these A**holes done. Let's make more magic this year. Hold on, I'm coming.

ABOUT THE AUTHOR

Blue Saffire, award-winning, bestselling author of over thirty contemporary romance novels and novellas, writes with the intention to touch the heart and the mind. Blue hooks, weaves, and loops multiple series, keeping you engaged in her worlds. Blue is a hybrid author, writing for Sourcebooks as well as her own publishing company, Perceptive Illusions, as Blue Saffire and Royal Blue.

Blue and her husband live in a house filled with laughter and creativity in Long Island, NY. Both working hard to build the Blue brand and cultivate their love for the artists. Creative is their family affair.

Blue holds an MBA in Marketing and Project Management, as well as a MED in Instructional Technology and Curriculum Design. She is also an NLP Master Practitioner.

Wait, there is more to come! You can stay updated with my latest releases, learn more about me, the author, and be a part of contests by subscribing to my newsletter at www.BlueSaffire.com
If you enjoyed *Beautiful Beast* and *His Cinder*, I'd love to hear
your thoughts and please feel free to leave a review. And when you do, please let me know by emailing me TheBlueSaffire@gmail.com
or leave a comment on Facebook
https://www.facebook.com/BlueSaffireDiaries
or Twitter @TheBlueSaffire

Other books by Blue Saffire

Placed in Best Reading Order

Also available....

Legally Bound

Legally Bound 2: Against the Law

Legally Bound 3: His Law

Perfect for Me

Hush 1: Family Secrets

Ballers: His Game

Brothers Black 1: Wyatt the Heartbreaker

Legally Bound 4: Allegations of Love

Hush 2: Slow Burn

<u>*Legally Bound 5.0: Sam*</u>

<u>*Yours 1: Losing My Innocence*</u>

<u>*Yours 2: Experience Gained*</u>

<u>*Yours 3: Life Mastered*</u>

Ballers 2: His Final Play

<u>*Legally Bound 5.1: Tasha Illegal Dealings*</u>

Brothers Black 2: Noah

Legally Bound 5.2: Camille

Legally Bound 5.3 & 5.4 Special Edition

Where the Pieces Fall

Legally Bound 5.5: Legally Unbound

Brothers Black 4: Braxton the Charmer

My Funny Valentine

Broken Soldier

Remember Me

Brothers Black 5: Felix the Watcher

A Home for Christmas

Be My Valentine

Work Husband Series

Unexpected Lovers

My Best Friend's Wish

The Ones Left Behind

The Last Ones Standing

The Lost Souls MC Series

Forever

Never

Always

Check out Blue Saffire exclusives on the

BlueSaffire.com website

His Miracle Baby

The Fixer

Razor

Exclusives Coming Soon...

Dane

Trip

Other books from Evei Lattimore Collection Books by Blue Saffire

<u>*Black Bella 1*</u>

Destiny 1: Life Decisions

Destiny 2: Decisions of the Next Generation

Destiny 3 coming soon...

Star

Other books from Royal Blue Gay Romance Collection written by Blue Saffire

Kyle's Reveal

Beau's Redemption

www.ingramcontent.com/pod-product-compliance
Lightning Source LLC
Chambersburg PA
CBHW051059030726
47504CB00006B/1706